# THE VAMPIRE OF SIAM
# THE RECKONING

## JIM NEWPORT

Encyclopocalypse Publications
www.encyclopocalypse.com

# BOOKS BY JIM NEWPORT

**The Vampire of Siam**

**Ramonne: The Return of The Vampire of Siam**

**The Reckoning: A Tale of The Vampire of Siam**

**Chasing Jimi**

**Tinsel Town**

**The Siamese Connection**

**A Dark Christmas**

# PRAISE FOR JIM NEWPORT

## *THE VAMPIRE OF SIAM*

"Grand Guignol entertainment…good for nibbling on the beach."

*— JAMES ECKARDT, THE NATION.*

"Chilling and morbidly hilarious. Newport's intimate knowledge of the Far East makes this an ultra-realistic journey into terror."

*— PULITZER PRIZE NOMINATED AUTHOR CHRIS BUNCH.*

"Well-researched, engrossing, smart and sexy. A graveyard smash."

*— BOBBY 'BORIS' PICKETT, SINGER-SONGWRITER: THE MONSTER MASH.*

Rating: 5 stars

*— JOHN WALSH, MANGO SAUCE.*

## RAMONNE

"Newport retains, from his first novel, a sharp sense of place for modern Bangkok. This is the trendy Bangkok of the Emporium Suites, the skytrain, the Q Bar, the Bed Supperclub."

*— THE NATION.*

"Newport artfully adapts the vampire legend into a Mekong cocktail of surprises."

*— CHRISTOPHER G. MOORE.*

## THE RECKONING

"Newport's novels succeed in their purpose: they entertain."

*— THE NATION.*

"The books are rich in cinematic imagery...and fascinating details of Thai history."

*— THAILAND TATLER.*

## CHASING JIMI

"Did you miss the 1960s? This funny yet loving and respectful adventure mystery will take you back."

*— JERRY HOPKINS, AUTHOR OF THE DOORS: NO ONE HERE GETS OUT ALIVE.*

"Newport has gone from the vault of the dead to the electrifying life of Jimi Hendrix. If you can remember Woodstock, you will enjoy this book."

*— LANG REID, PATTAYA MAIL.*

## TINSEL TOWN

"It moves like a runaway asteroid."

*— TIM HALLINAN, BESTSELLING AUTHOR OF THE POKE RAFFERTY SERIES (SET IN BANGKOK).*

"Tinsel Town is the best introduction-to-Hollywood novel I've ever read."

*— DAVID GILER, PRODUCER/WRITER OF THE FILMS ALIEN, UNDISPUTED, MYRA BRECKINRIDGE AND MANY MORE.*

## THE SIAMESE CONNECTION

"Jim Newport is a writer with great skills. Non-stop, hold your breath action. A true thriller. "

*— LANG REID, PATTAYA MAIL*

"Newport clearly knows Bangkok…An easy read."

*— BERNARD TRINK, BANGKOK POST.*

# THE RECKONING

# INTRODUCTION

When I originally sat down to write a vampire tale, it was intended to be a movie script. I'd tried unsuccessfully to make my own film in Thailand: an eco-adventure that was continually rebuffed. I heard the phrase "genre film" over and over (as in 'your film does not fit in with our genre'), and enjoyed no further encouragement. Horror films seemed to be the favorite genre, and I was told to come back when I had a vampire script.

Once I began, I felt that a screenplay was too confining for the tale that started to pour forth. I realized, of course, that the vampire was a metaphor for the jetlagged 'thing' I'd become on my excursions to the land of dreams fulfilled.

The first tale, *The Vampire Of Siam*, flowed like red wine from my veins to the page. The protagonist, unannounced and unexpected, seemed to leap from my loins.

I was soon done with the tale; had taken it to its conclusion. And yet the *beast* wouldn't stay buried. I talked with friends in Hollywood about this urge to give life once again to my dead villain. I was assured that there were highly paid script 'doctors' who do nothing else but rebirth vampires.

And so *Ramonne* came about. It was a chance to revisit old friends; take them down new roads; kindle a fine romance and explore anew what had only been hinted at in the first book. But that was enough. *Fin.* On to other things.

And then one night, very late, there came a knock upon the door to my lair above the Hollywood Hills. An iron gate prevents unannounced visitors, but it seemed this nocturnal guest had overcome that mere obstacle. Stumbling to the great oak door, my faithful Labrador growling at my heels, I cracked open the inset panel and peered without.

"Yes?"

*Open this door*, was the unspoken reply.

I knew at once who it was. Nothing could have prevented my opening that door. My hands were not my own. My visitor bid me join him on the redwood deck. The night sky was clear and the city lights twinkled below.

*The tale is not complete.*

I tried to look into his eyes, but they were as smoked mirrors to me. *You want to tell it all. It is yours alone to tell.*

There were other things that transpired on that fateful eve, but they were fortunately lost to the great voids where such memories should disappear.

As a mere vessel, commanded to tell this tale I have done my best.

Jim Newport
Bangkok
March, 2006.

*Dedicated to Chris Bunch*

*Please listen to the children.*
*You are the ones who will rule the world.*

*Jim Morrison.*

*My apologies and gratitude to the heirs of Henri Mouhot. I have tried
to be true in spirit to the occurrences of his great exploration, but as
this is a work of fiction, I have taken liberties, often in altering the
timetable and location to better suit my narrative. (For example,
Mouhot did not forge into the interior of Africa.)*

*There are passages from his journal Travels In Siam, Cambodia, Laos
and Annan that I have attributed to my own Msr. Delacroix, but as
Msr. Delacroix purports to have been Mouhot's companion, his words
would have no doubt mirrored his master's on many occasions. My
apologies again, but perhaps this humble work will serve to cast a new
light on the great work and spirit of Msr. Henri Mouhot—for which
the world should be eternally grateful.*

**1**

---

*Orbs. Akin.*

The soft, pendulous orbs of the tawny-skinned maid in Gauguin's *"L'Amour Est Aveugle"* were very much 'akin' to the soft little melons that he had come to love in his adopted home of Thailand. Ramonne Delacroix breathed a heavy sigh, resonant with depth and meaning unfathomable to a human being.

It had taken over 150 years, but the transplanted Frenchman was finally back on native soil. And in the City of Lights, no less. Paris. The city he had so loved as a wild-eyed youth. He felt positively giddy.

*Orbs. Akin.* He repeated the mantra as he slowly wandered the narrow halls of the Jeu de Paume. After losing most of its permanent collection to the Musee d'Orsay, the museum had become a gallery for contemporary art. What remained of its collection of Impressionist masterpieces was unequalled and made the tiny museum a welcome breath of fresh air to anyone who had endured the madness and utter consumption of the Louvre.

It was dark outside, and though the museum stayed open this one evening a week, it was nearing closing time, and a polite young woman was gently shepherding the small group of visitors toward the door.

"Monsieur Ennomar?" An elderly man spoke the name in a tone that was just above a whisper. Ramonne turned to see a man so slight of stature that a stiff breeze would carry him away.

"Yes."

"I am Charles Serviette."

Ramonne nodded slightly. He took a cautious whiff and studied Monsieur Serviette. He detected no abnormal trepidation or malice.

"The museum is closing. Shall we have a coffee outside?"

"No. My time in Paris is limited to this one evening. I'm afraid I have a task that needs attending to before I can allow myself the luxury of a personal indulgence."

"Whatever you say, monsieur. I have arranged to make the archives available to you as requested. I am your humble servant."

"*Merci beaucoup.*"

"There is one more matter." Ramonne knew the little bookworm never ventured far from the no-doubt cluttered confines of his private collection of rare tomes.

"Yes?"

"Your letter mentioned a daguerreotype…A very *rare* daguerreotype."

Ramonne reached into the folds of his light black overcoat. He produced a flat leather pouch. As he slowly withdrew a sepia-toned metal plate, the little man gasped. The twelfth-century Khmer temple of the Bayon stood frozen in time, wrapped with huge, swollen vines. The roots of a giant banyan tree up-ended blocks of sandstone that weighed two or more tons. Graceful *apsaras* danced around the lintels, and the beatific smile of King Jayavarman VII crowned the ancient pagoda.

"*Mon dieu.* It's true. Mouhot photographed the ruins of Angkor. But how did you—"

"My time is precious. As I implied in my letter, this very rare treasure is yours. *After* you open your doors to me."

"I await your arrival, Monsieur Ennomar."

————

"Good night my sweet angel."

"*Sawatdee khrap, papa. Bon soir,*" the young boy replied, as he always did, in a mixture of three languages.

The man kissed his son's forehead and pulled the covers up.

"Papa?"

"Yes?"

"Are you mad at Maman?"

"*Mad*? No I'm not mad at Mommy. Why do you ask, my precious?"

"*Je ne c'est pas.* But...you don't kiss Mommy anymore."

"I don't?" He was taken aback. Walloped by a child's simple observation.

"Your eyes deceive you, angel. Of course I kiss your mommy. And in the morning I'll show you. I'll shower her with kisses. Now go to sleep."

He adjusted the blanket that had slipped off, flicked the Mickey Mouse light switch, and gently closed the door.

Hong 'Harry' Chalermphong walked slowly down the gilded hallway. *From the mouth of babes.* He mused. When exactly had the light gone out on the romance with Wannanee? As the old joke went: when they were first married they had sex everywhere—in the kitchen, in the car, in the bathroom—but now they only had 'hallway sex.' They'd pass each other in the hall and call out 'Fuck you.'

He smiled, but it was true. There was no more romance between them. Harry provided well. She wanted for nothing. She spent her days shopping on the Champs Élysées or sipping tea in the Ritz. She was on the opera's steering committee. Their son attended L'École Brantome with the other privileged foreign sons and daughters. They lived, out of necessity, in a seventeenth-century stone fortress. Known throughout Paris as La Maçonnerie due to its having been a stronghold for the Freemasons, it had been retro-fitted in the twentieth century by a Swiss banker, and Harry's own addition of a laser-based security system had rendered the castle 'impenetrable.'

His wife hated the 'bunker' as she called it, but Harry had enemies.

Harry left the mock-Versailles hallway with its gold mirrors that his wife had insisted upon. She had spent millions decorating the bunker. He crossed into the polished teak drawing room that was his own personal refuge. It was an exact duplicate of his father's study in the exclusive Tao Pun suburb of Bangkok.

He poured himself a brandy and settled onto the comfortable divan encased in Thai silk. Ever since he had been a little boy, his father had told him of his destiny. He was to be a member of parliament, the governing board of Thailand. All the Chalermphong men had held positions of power. For many generations. Through the generous 'contributions' of those whose interests they served, they lived like royalty. And when his father died, it was assumed that Harry would succeed him.

It was natural progression.

But Harry took more than his father's place. Once he was comfortably ensconced in the chamber, he became greedy. He realized that his father's sense of fair play had greatly limited his participation in the graft that was rife as Thailand suffered through one after another short-lived administration. He soon realized that his position as a member of parliament was likely to be usurped at any time by the whims and personal goals of whoever happened to be in charge. What became standard operating procedure as the twentieth century drew to a close was, for governors and ministers, to rake in as much booty as possible while the warring parties of Thailand's so-called 'democracy' circled each other like sharks.

Realizing that he had come in late on the 'legitimate' business fund—all the construction, telecom, and banking associations seemed to have already been corrupted—Harry pursued the 'dark' side. He offered sanctions and licensing probate to the mobs that controlled Thailand's lucrative gambling and drug trade. He soon had a cache of gold flown by Federal Express courier jet to Geneva. Harry purchased and learned to operate a laptop computer for the sole pleasure of accessing his numbered account on-line and reveling in its binary numerical display.

But Harry's newfound riches were over almost before he knew it. A new administration came in—one with incredible mass popularity—and soon this new prime minister made sweeping changes and Harry was forced to flee the scene. His departure was made possible by his nefarious relationship with Ping Narong, who provided his own son, Wang, as Harry's escort out of the country. However, young Wang was opportunistic as well, and tried his own hand at extortion. A struggle ensued and Joon, Harry's personal bodyguard, had killed the black-hearted offspring. They flew to Paris with a gun to the pilot's head. This had greatly cranked up the need for security, and it had been a terrible time of hiding in dark places before La Maçonnerie had been acquired.

Now Harry was lying low, waiting out Thailand's latest change of guard, hoping and assuming that the inevitable would take place. He assumed this was yet another in a succession of short-lived opportunistic leaders who would be history in a matter of months, if not weeks. But this one seemed to be cemented in, rather than simply 'appliquéd' like so many predecessors. Months stretched into years and Harry waited.

"*Nai than.*" Joon stood, shaved head bowed, at the entry to the study.

Harry smiled at his head of security and lifelong friend. "Go to bed, Joon. I'm fine."

"*Khrap.* Khun Roger is at the front entry and Jiap is outside your elevator." Joon waved a hand to the security monitors behind the bar. Views of the lobby and the elevator bank showed two dark-suited men standing guard.

"Good night, *mon amis*."

Joon bowed and backed out the door. Harry took another sip and briefly pondered the enigma that Joon presented. They had grown up together. Joon was the son of his mother's hand-maiden. Harry's father had appreciated the camaraderie and wisely sent Joon to a Shaolin school of martial arts. Upon his return, Joon had gladly accepted the role of Harry's personal bodyguard.

Though hardly more than five feet in height, the man's strength and agility were beyond belief. Virtues that had been drawn upon on more than one occasion to save Harry's life. Now that Harry was in exile, with a long list of enemies, Harry trusted the man to keep him and his family alive.

———

*Thwack. Whack. Clack clack*

That was the sound the loosened mortar and stone made as it descended and struck the cobblestone pavement.

Thwack. Whack. Clack clack.

Ramonne climbed. Straight up the stone parapet. He had been intrigued when Ping described it as impenetrable, and was enthralled by the tales of failed attempts to settle the score with Harry Chalermphong.

Ramonne liked a challenge.

He climbed effortlessly like a lizard stealthily approaching his prey.

Harry replaced the stopper in the crystal decanter and turned off the light. He padded quietly into the living room. The family and servants were all asleep. He'd dimmed the lights and opened the massive bay window. He breathed in the crisp fall air. This was Harry's favorite time of the day. Alone, gazing out at the magnificent city. He counted his blessings. He reached in his pocket and extracted a gold cigarette case. He lit a cheroot and exhaled a thin stream of smoke at the Tour Eiffel, which stood against the night sky a mere six blocks away.

He heard a sound.

*Odd.* He knew that this window, as were all the windows in La Maçonnerie, was protected by an invisible pattern of laser beams that would trigger the alarm system should there be any breach of their air space. He had been assured repeatedly by the broker that the building was impregnable and there was no need to go to such extreme. But Harry was erring on the side of caution.

He punched in a code on a small panel next to the window and the lasers were temporarily disarmed.

With both hands on the marble ledge, Harry leaned out into the night and peered down. He saw exactly what he expected. A sheer stone wall that dropped eight stories to the Avenue Bosquet below.

Satisfied, Harry retreated back into the room and finished his cheroot. Before turning the alarm back on, he flicked the glowing cancer stick out into the abyss. He re-set the code and a red criss-cross pattern of laser beams appeared for an instant and was then invisible.

Harry closed and latched the windows, admiring as always the lead fleur-de-lis patterns that encased the glass. He stretched like a contented cat, emitting a long loud yawn.

His mouth was still open as he turned to the room and froze. A man was facing him. A silver streak ran down the middle of his jet-black hair.

"Who are you? How did you get in here?"

Ramonne ignored Harry and instead took in the room. Harry unhinged his jaw and reached for the alarm button.

*"Don't."*

Harry stopped. He hadn't seen the man speak, but the

single-word command shot through his entire body like a cold electrical shock. His hand dropped to his side.

Ramonne picked up a gold-framed family portrait from a small gallery carefully arranged on a Louis XIV end table. He ran his fingers lightly across the smiling faces. Harry, his wife, and son in front of the pearly gates of Euro Disneyland.

"When was this taken?"

"Look, I don't know what you want—"

"*When* was it taken?" Ramonne walked slowly toward Harry, continuing to study the photograph. When he was inches from him, he looked up and Harry saw his fate set deep within his eyes.

"Please. I'll give you any—"

Ramonne placed a finger on Harry's lips.

"*When?*" Another cold shock went through him and he started to quiver.

"Last year. In the spring."

Ramonne smiled. "The boy is handsome. You must be proud."

"Y-yes," Harry stammered. "He's a good boy."

Ramonne put the photo down. "I'm sure he is. Children...all children are precious, but a *son* is special to a man, is he not?"

Harry nodded. He heard the man's words, but there was some other force holding him, riveting him to the floor. He could not move. He could not even cry out. He was immobile.

"A man sees the future in his son. *Propagation.* An heir to carry his name. To fulfill a legacy; run a family business. These are the hopes a man places on his son."

Ramonne now slowly circled the human statue.

"The loss of a son is devastating. Most men never recover and carry the remorse and loss to their own graves."

"*Ping.*" Suddenly, Harry knew why the man was here.

"Yes, Ping," Ramonne replied to Harry's unspoken thought. "You robbed him of his heritage. He sent me to rob you of yours."

*Dear Lord Buddha, no!*

Ramonne passed his hand in front of the man's eyes, allowing him to speak freely.

"Ping Narong has tried many times to have me killed. I have lived in fear of my life, and certainly that of my family, but if there was one thing that Ping had proved to be, it was *fair*. Certainly he wouldn't harm an innocent child."

Ramonne studied the man. His mind was sharp. Even when he had him under a spell of control, he was still plotting his escape. He had weapons secreted about the room. A 9-mm handgun in a secret drawer beneath the coffee table; a Glock 18 machine-pistol in a hollowed-out book; and an AK-47 in a large Edwardian vase next to the window.

One by one, Ramonne removed the guns and placed them on the table.

Rendered somnambulant again, Harry just stared at this continued breach of his 'impenetrable' fortress.

But Harry still had more than one trick up his sleeve. A timer had been installed in each of the rooms on this floor, the family living quarters. These were set to trigger a grid of 'intelligent' lasers—a technology supposedly known only to the CIA. These were programmable to recognize the identity of human heat auras and distinguish them as friend or foe. After 10:00 p.m., the lack of human presence in a room would cause these lasers to be automatically deployed. Only the immediate family and their bodyguards had been imprinted. Even servants would be barred from this floor between 10:00 p.m. and 7:00 a.m.

He watched the clock in the Fabergé egg: 9:57. Harry smiled. The tripping of the beams would automatically seal his wife and son in their rooms, and bring a response from Joon and his militia that would surely rid him of this morbid intruder.

Now though, his immediate hope lay in the arsenal the man had just put on display.

Ramonne smiled. "Sorry Harry. I'm afraid the discharge of any of these would disturb your family's slumber. However..."

He moved to the fireplace and a samurai sword resting in its ceremonial cradle. He picked up the elegant weapon. Unsheathing it, he admired the craftsmanship that went into its manufacture. He watched the light reflect and ripple across the glyphs delicately carved into the slightly curved blade.

Harry felt his full senses returning as the man replaced the sword in its scabbard and, to Harry's utter astonishment, handed the lethal weapon to him.

Immediately, Harry flung the sheath aside and swung the blade at Ramonne's neck.

His hand froze, spare inches from its target.

"Not the head, please." Ramonne opened his coat and unbuttoned his silk shirt. He laid bare his chest and guided the tip of the blade so that it rested against his skin.

"*Now.*"

With great relish, Harry plunged the blade deep into the man, feeling bone and cartilage snap before it struck the vital organs. He turned the blade sideways and wrenched it left and right.

Rather than writhing in agony, the man seemed merely annoyed, and grabbed the hilt of the weapon.

"Enough." He guided Harry's hand and the blade was withdrawn. Harry smiled at the spreading blood and visage that accompanied the sword's exit.

Then he gasped as, immediately, the gaping wound began to heal.

"My Lord Buddha."

Ramonne buttoned his shirt. "As you can see, there is no escape. Now...let's go see the boy."

Harry took an unsteady step forward. Shaken to his very core by what he had just witnessed, he was still certain that triggering the lasers would bring the help he so desperately needed. He passed through the open doorway and waited in the hall for the man to follow. Ramonne stopped at the opening and smiled.

"Harry. Have you no faith? Do you need further proof of my immortality?"

Harry waited silently. Ramonne sighed and stepped forward. The air was suddenly lit with the criss-cross pattern of red laser beams. They hit Ramonne...and passed right through him.

Harry waited for the alarm. It didn't come. The lasers disappeared and Ramonne walked on, unfazed.

"That...That's impossible."

"I'm invisible to your security system; impervious to your weapons."

Ramonne passed ahead of Harry. As his back was momentarily turned, Harry flicked up the crystal on his watch and jabbed at the center of the dial.

Suddenly the air was split by a piercing alarm.

Ramonne turned slowly, shaking his head. "Oh, Harry. Now look what you've done."

"I will defeat you, devil." Harry smiled as thick steel plates slid down to seal the bedroom doors. Simultaneous with this, two doors flew open. Joon appeared in one and another guard in the other. They both had machine-pistols, and instantly they leveled them at Ramonne.

"*Ka mun!*" Harry shouted. As he said the words, he fell to the floor. Joon and his partner opened fire. Caught in a crossfire, Ramonne merely held out his flattened palms and deflected bullet after bullet. Soon, both men had emptied their weapons and retreated to re-load.

Joon yelled out to Harry. "*Nai Than.* What sort of beast is this?"

Harry was crawling on his belly for the living room. Ramonne ignored Harry and started for Joon when he noticed the lights on the elevator. A cab was rapidly ascending. Joon saw it also and yelled out again.

"Don't worry, master. Help is on the way."

Ramonne went to the elevator doors. He wedged his hand in

between them and ripped them open, exposing the cable that was pulling the cab swiftly to their floor. He grabbed the cable and tightened his grip. Smoke flew through his hand as it ground to a halt with a hideous sound of tearing gears. The shaft shuddered and groaned as if in an earthquake, and then all was still.

Ramonne looked at Joon, who was watching in shock. "Help...? I don't think so." With one ferocious yank, he tore the cable free from its moorings. He held it for a moment and then let go. The cable slithered into the shaft as the cab plummeted downward. It scraped and tore against the sides with a tremendous noise until it crashed to the bottom.

"*Yed mae*," Joon cursed and opened fire on Ramonne again. Ramonne leaped across the hallway and knocked the weapon from his hand. He lifted the bodyguard by the throat.

"Die, bastard!" Harry had the AK-47 and sprayed vicious lead at Ramonne.

Ramonne spun around and used Joon's body to catch the fire. It did a macabre dance as the bullets tore it apart.

Harry realized what was happening and stopped firing. "Joon!" he cried out. He sank to his knees, devastated.

Ramonne flung the body into the elevator shaft. He turned to the other guard. The man was frozen with fear. His pistol was re-loaded and pointed at Ramonne, but he made no effort to fire. Ramonne looked at the man and he surrendered his body and mind. He started to let the gun drop when Ramonne nodded. The man calmly put the gun to his temple and fired one shot. His body crumpled to the floor like a bag of leaves.

Slowly, Ramonne walked to Harry.

Harry cradled the machine-gun in his arms and softly weeped. Ramonne gently removed the gun and put it aside. He helped Harry to his feet.

"Harry. Let's go see the boy."

---

The steel plate was Harry's last hope. His last wall of defense. Surely this *thing* couldn't penetrate ten-gauge steel. Surely his boy was safe.

*Wasn't he?*

There were still sounds coming from the elevator shaft. Mute cries of pain and agony. They were getting dimmer and Harry tried to ignore them. Harry tried not to show the *thing*— after what he had seen he could no longer think of him as a man —which was the door to his son, but it made no difference.

*He knew.* He stopped outside the boy's door.

*Dear Lord Buddha.* Harry prayed. *Don't let him take my son.* Harry thought the unthinkable. *Let him take me instead.*

Ramonne watched Harry in silence. Then he placed the palms of both hands against the cold metal. An eerie blue glow briefly emanated from where he touched the steel, and then the plate slowly recessed back into the ceiling, revealing a thick carved wooden door.

*Merde* was the only word that came to Harry's mind.

Ramonne put his hand on the handle that Harry knew he had latched himself, and turned it with ease. He pushed and the door slowly opened.

Amazingly, Harry's son was asleep. Harry knew that the steel plate would be an effective sound muffler, but he had no idea *how* effective.

Ramonne softly approached. Harry started to plead, but Ramonne raised a hand and he was immediately silenced. He studied the slumbering child. He placed a hand close to the boy's hair, but did not touch him.

Ramonne was overwhelmed. The aura the child projected was so pure and innocent that Ramonne could barely breathe. A normal person loses his childhood memories in the blush of adolescence. By middle-age we have become so jaded that it's practically impossible to remember ever facing the world with wide-eyed wonder. Imagine what 180 years can do to that loss of innocence and you have a tiny grasp of what Ramonne was experiencing.

The light was blinding to Ramonne. There wasn't a scene in the amalgamated images he was channeling that didn't take place in the sun. *The sun.* Except in pictures, he had not seen the sun in 145 years.

The boy was dreaming. Anything was possible to this boy. This vision of life was, Ramonne concluded...*magical.*

*Powerful magic.* Nothing seemed beyond the boy's imagination. Ramonne controlled adults by crawling into the crevices of their minds and manipulating their deepest fears. But here, there was no fear. No trepidation. No hesitation. He could detect only one chink in the boy's perfect world.

He sensed the rift between his mother and father.

It was inconceivable to the childish mind that anything would ever change. *Mommy and Daddy will keep you safe.* He believed in this with all his heart, but nonetheless the seed was there. The first seed of doubt.

Ramonne backed away from the boy. "He's a beautiful child, Harry."

He made a decision.

"I will not harm him."

"Thank Buddha." Harry wept openly.

"But you said something, Harry. Before. I'm afraid I will have to take you up on your offer."

Harry looked puzzled.

"You weren't speaking to me...Actually you weren't speaking at all. You were praying."

"You *heard* me?"

"Yes, Harry. I heard you. You said 'Take me instead.'"

Ramonne put a hand on Harry's shoulder. "Harry. Your child is magical. I assume *all* children are. I actually had no idea. But then I guess we're never too old to learn."

He led Harry to the boy's bedside. "He loves you very much, Harry. Let me show you."

Ramonne took Harry's hand, while he placed the other inches away from the sleeping child. Instantly Harry was jolted by a bright light. And then he saw himself—strong, handsome, larger than life. They were on the Côte d'Azur. It was last summer and he had given the boy a snorkeling lesson. The boy didn't swim, but strong handsome Harry said that doesn't matter. 'Just hold my hand. I will never let you go.' They floated in shallow water and large, friendly fish surrounded them. Another figure swam into view. She had no snorkel or mask. She too was movie-star beautiful. It was the boy's mother. Harry's wife.

Harry began to sob.

Ramonne allowed this to go on for much longer than he should. He was on a schedule—a tight one. On top of that, he would now have to explain to Ping why he had changed the plan. Why he had not killed the boy.

*To hell with Ping.* Ramonne could not kill the boy. Pure and simple.

Just like the boy, the answer too, was pure and simple.

After twenty minutes, Ramonne led Harry from the room. Harry was content. Resolved to his fate. Moreover, he had received a great gift. He had insight into his child that no parent ever had. He had seen into his mind.

His beautiful mind.

Ramonne took Harry into the gilded gold and marble bathroom.

He made Harry lie in the claw-footed tub.

Then, in one swift motion, he ripped out his heart and deposited it in a silver freezer bag. He closed Harry's eyes and descended the building as he had arrived.

**2**
___

L'É*COLE* F*RANÇAISE* D'E*XTRÊME* O*RIENT* read the sign in the curved art nouveau frame. A black limousine pulled up in front of the entry. The street was virtually deserted at this late hour.

The driver of the limousine was accompanied by a young Thai man in a tight black suit. The silver freezer bag had been deposited in a medical cooler which rested in his lap. He looked at his watch.

"One hour. That is all, *Jao Nai.*"

"It will be enough." Ramonne exited the vehicle. He carried a soft leather satchel. A doorbell dimly glowed under a carved lion's head. He pressed it. A moment passed and then there was the sharp crack of an electric lock being opened.

"*Bon soir, monsieur.*" Serviette was holding the door for him. "*Entrez vous, s'il vous plait.*"

"*Merci.*" Ramonne nodded. He entered.

He stood in an eighteenth-century *château.* Its arched halls led off to both sides. In front was a pair of leaded glass doors.

"Monsieur Serviette, my time is almost gone. We must make haste."

"Of course. I think all is ready for you." He opened the doors and led Ramonne into a study. A long table dominated the room. On it were piled stacks of ancient notebooks, bound journals, and portfolios.

"Please, *asseyez-vous*. I think I have provided what you seek."

Rather than sitting, Ramonne moved among the piles of documents, flipping quickly through them.

"Excellent."

"May I offer you some refreshment?"

Ramonne thought for a moment. There was *something* he desired, but that would have to wait. "*Vin rouge?*"

"*Certainement. Un moment.*"

Serviette was back in a moment with a bottle and a glass. "*Le Beaujolais nouveau est arrive.*"

Ramonne was already absorbed in the documents before him. Serviette poured the wine and bowed. "Monsieur. The hour is late. I will leave you to your study. There is a Xerox machine behind you for any copies you need to make. Some of these are original documents…I shouldn't even be letting you see them. Please handle them with care."

Ramonne nodded and drank a glass of the young wine without looking up from the book.

"Monsieur Ennomar…? The photograph?"

Ramonne was momentarily annoyed at the interruption, but then he remembered what the old man desired. He handed him the daguerreotype.

"*Merci beaucoup.* This will be a much treasured addition to our collection."

The old man bowed slightly and backed out of the room, tightly clutching his prize. "Please close both doors behind you when you leave. The alarm will automatically be set. *Bon soir, monsieur.*"

Finally alone, Ramonne was able to assess what lay before him. In the folders were copies of hand-drawn maps of nine-teenth-century trade routes. One map was identified as MAP OF CAMBODGE, THE LAO COUNTRY, ETC. ROUTE AND NOTES OF M.

*Henri Mouhot 1859-61*. The route traveled by the explorer was inscribed in red. Starting at Bangkok, it encompassed a circle to the east and south through Cambodia and another went singularly north from Bangkok to Louang Prabang where it abruptly stopped.

Ramonne's finger traced the route east of Bangkok to the great Tonle Sap Lake. He slowly went north of the lake and rested on what was labeled *Ongcor*.

Angkor. The great temple ruins of Angkor Wat. Ramonne knew this route well. *He should.* He had been there. He was with the legendary explorer in 1860. He had been by his side when the first temple ruin was recognized in the ever-encroaching jungle. Upon his first sighting of the great temple of Angkor Wat, the world's largest religious building, Mouhot had turned to Ramonne and, in his excitement, proclaimed the ruins grander than anything left by the Greeks or Romans.

Next were copies of Mouhot's precise observations of the vast temple complex. It was here, where Ramonne's right index finger now rested, in the temple of the Bayon, that his destiny had been shaped. There, under a flickering torch, an eager young French explorer, Ramonne Delacroix, came face to face with a 1,000-year-old Chinese vampire.

There were many more maps, some original and encased in thick plastic laminate. Ramonne put these aside. There were drawings, some original. These he took particular interest in. All of Mouhot's were copies. Each inscribed with the initials "H.M." on the bottom. Ramonne smiled. He remembered the images. Riverside villages. Siamese women. Children at play. Apes. Tigers. Crocodiles. Elephants. He remembered them all. The drawings of Angkor were similar to the photographic plate he had given to Serviette.

He put Mouhot's drawings aside and picked up the portfolio of original sketches. His heart leapt when he untied the black strings and opened it. Water buffaloes wallowed in a great bog. The surrounding hillside was dotted with thatchroofed huts and graceful palms. At the bottom of the idyllic landscape were the initials, "R.D."

Ramonne was delighted to see his sketches preserved. He lingered over each until he suddenly became aware of the passing of time. He carefully replaced them in the portfolio.

Next he went to the books: ledgers, ships' logs, bills of lading, and a bound book of transactions for the years 1850-1870 for the Far East Trading Company. A cracked leather case contained Father Bouillevaux's own journal of his years as a missionary in the jungles around Angkor.

A thick bound copy of Mouhot's own journals was hard for Ramonne to resist. He could get lost in their pages. He had to force himself to put it down. He turned to the rest.

Once again his heart nearly stopped beating. Four leather-bound diaries, simply engraved with the initials "R.D."

The covers had been encased in clear plastic, but the pages were untouched. He had to will himself to breathe so as to steady his hand as he picked up the first book. Immediately, as he touched the cover, he felt a wave of memories rushing toward him. As if it was made of red-hot lava. He gently put it down. He realized the danger of allowing himself to succumb to the seductive force before him.

He must wait. To indulge now would mean catastrophe. He knew that once he began, he would be unable to put the journals down. He would wallow in their tales...revel in the past... his long forgotten youth...

*Enough. It's time.* He opened the satchel and carefully placed the books within. Next he inserted the portfolio of his drawings.

He turned out the light and shut both set of doors. The alarm blinked to life.

*Impenetrable.*

--------

They arrived at the small private runway at the eastern end of Orly Airport just before 5:00 a.m. Approximately an hour before dawn.

Ramonne smiled at Lek, the Thai in the front passenger seat.

"*Jao Nai.* You have time for a quick meal before the plane boards."

Ramonne nodded. This had been pre-arranged. The driver opened the door for Ramonne. Instead of getting out, he grabbed the driver's wrist in an iron grasp and pulled him into the rear of the limo.

Lek shut the screen between them as Ramonne devoured the helpless driver.

———————

Ramonne sat in a thick leather armchair in the Lear Jet and watched through the window as Lek wrapped the driver's corpse in plastic sheets and placed him in the trunk of the limousine. It was still the dark of night, but dawn would soon be upon them. Ramonne contentedly sipped a glass of burgundy.

Lek boarded the plane and sealed the cockpit door. "Are you ready for departure, *Jao Nai?*"

Ramonne finished his wine and placed his glass in a rack. "Yes." He stood and walked to the rear of the cabin. He drew open a curtain revealing an ebony coffin. He removed his shoes, raised the lid, and climbed in. As he had demanded, the coffin was constructed with a latch that locked and released only from the inside. He trusted Lek with his life, but there were others beyond his control. A pilot and co-pilot, and ground crews in both Paris and Bangkok. Though Ping had assured him of his complete security, it was certainly better to be safe than sorry.

The whine of the twin engines was barely perceptible as the jet taxied down the runway, but to Ramonne's finely tuned ear, it was deafening. The sensation at this point was akin to traveling in a fast moving car. Nothing more. But when it lifted off the ground—that was something new. And yet it was not so new to Ramonne. After all, he was able to levitate. But the most he had been able to attain had been a few meters—and this was somewhat out of his control. It occurred in situations of heightened stimulation. The moment of draining the very life from a victim, to be exact.

But when the plane had lifted off the ground in Bangkok, Ramonne felt as if he was going to be sick. That was new.

And now here it came again. He held his breath as the plane climbed. He felt the wheels being drawn in below him. He felt as if a great weight was bearing down on him. He knew this would last but a short time as the plane climbed to what they called 'cruising altitude.' Then it would level off and the weight would be removed.

As for the landing, he assumed that, as had occurred yesterday, he would be asleep. As at Orly, the plane would roll into a private hangar and be under guard until night fell.

When Ping Narong told him of his plan, Ramonne thought he was crazy. The vampire had been in his employ as a hired assassin for over two years. His unique skills had allowed the Chinese gangster to vanquish many of his enemies. *Fly to Paris?* For one hit? Ridiculous. He had laughed out loud at the proposal. But when Ping explained it in detail, it sounded less absurd. And Ping had offered a small fortune for this service. More than triple what Ramonne had become accustomed to. It was obvious that there was a strong sense of betrayal here. And Ramonne had been moved by Ping's continued grief at the loss of his son.

So he had agreed to the great adventure. Initially he had thought he would spend a week in Paris.

*A week in Paris, would ease the bite of it.*

He loved that line in "Lush Life," the great Billy Strayhorn song. See the sights, do the town. He remembered the city from his youth. He and some other art school chums had stayed at a hostel for boys in Pigalle, climbing over the iron-spiked gates to return after curfew. He'd never returned as an adult, but he'd lusted and yearned for it. He'd read many books either about the city or with the city as its focus—*The Phantom Of The Opera* being his favorite—and from what he could surmise, it was perhaps the only metropolis in the Western world to retain its old world charm. Montmartre, the opera, the cave bars where *le jazz hot* was played all night long. He would revel in it all.

Ping was quick to point out that there must be no notice taken of his presence in the City of Lights. He needed to be invisible for this to work. He needed to be in and out in the blink of an eye. The success of the mission depended on it. This was not a holiday. It was a mission and, as such, it needed to be accomplished with military precision. If Ramonne was to spend a week in Paris, he'd leave a pile of corpses. And the *gendarmes* would, perhaps, be more thorough than their Thai counterparts, whose more unscrupulous members were attached to Ping's payroll.

Ramonne had to admit that he was a creature of habit and that he might make dangerous mistakes on foreign soil. He agreed that it was best to restrict it to a simple overnighter.

*Baby steps.*

However, he wasted no time in contacting Monsieur Serviette and arranging for a visit to where he suspected his past might be stored. This was imperative. He told Ping nothing of this plan. Some things were best left unsaid. But he manipulated their arrival to coincide with the one evening a week when the Jeu de Paume was open, so that he could begin his foray with a reverential trip to view a painting that he had longed to see.

Lek had been most accommodating and discreet. Ramonne liked the boy. He had mettle.

Ramone also realized that he admired Harry Chalermphong

in an odd way. The insight he'd gained into Harry and his side of the tale had caused Ramonne to see it differently. Harry, after all, had been there. Ping had not. And what Harry told the vampire was the truth. This he knew without doubt. Ping's son had actually been the one to betray the trust. Harry had been innocent, Not 'innocent' like his young son, but justified in defending himself against Wang's threats.

In a way, he regretted killing Harry, but the mayhem caused with the signaling of the alarm warranted the elimination of any eyewitnesses.

Nonetheless, Ramonne had a contract with Ping. He had never failed to honor a contract with Ping. This would be no exception. With one very real difference. The heart that was now on ice and being returned to Bangkok would pass the DNA test that Ping would no doubt have performed. But it was the heart of an adult male...not a child.

For that, Ramonne would be called to task.

He was prepared to deal with it. He had made the right decision. That he knew.

The plane leveled off and the weight was lifted from his chest. He reached for the handle and closed the lid.

In the darkness he wondered if he could survive a plane crash. He supposed he could, but the regeneration would be painful. Comparatively, he thought, the bomb blast that he'd survived in the Patpong terrorist attack would seem like a mild concussion.

**3**

---

*The voyage on the good ship Christienne has been much as expected. Apart from a five-week Safari at Kenya, we have spent 168 endless days and nights at sea. Accommodations are average and the pitiful food and general discomfort are offset on occasion by replenishment of stocks offered by the myriad network of trading ports that have been established in but the last half-century. The weather holds true to the stalwart Captain's predictions…*

    *We were standing proud until the seas then took a turn…*

*Took a turn?* Ramonne recollected it as rather like riding a roller-coaster; he'd never been on one, but he could imagine. His journal had been kept mainly as a factual research manual, and not as poetic musings. It omitted any emotional stand or romantic flights of fancy. Also omitted were all but the most mundane personal references to the hardships endured in removing oneself so succinctly from hearth and home.

Specifically, there was no mention of *her*. His beloved Giselle. No mention of the heartbreak that he could never forget enduring within just the first hour at sea. The last sight he'd seen as the ship had sailed from Marseilles on that winter's day in 1858 had been her figure standing at the very tip of the bay and waving her kerchief.

He put the journal down for a moment and picked up the drawing that had been included amongst his sketches. Drawn from memory, it showed a fair-skinned girl of 25, soft auburn curls framing her angelic face.

*To live is to love.* Lord, how he loved that woman.

He'd been a student at the Académie d'Lyons when they'd met. She was fourteen, a child. Ramonne's taste for café au lait and fresh croissants led him to her mother's *boulangerie* each morning. Each time she re-filled his cup, Giselle eyed the young man's drawings. By his senior year, she shared his one-room studio overlooking the harbor, and was the sole subject of most of his paintings. He would give a fortune for them today.

They were wed shortly after he graduated.

His parents had been against Ramonne's desire to pursue his talent, preferring the more respected and certain paths of the business world, and true to their predictions, he struggled. Too proud to ask his father for money, they existed on her paltry income for years. In an attempt to find a patron, Ramonne undertook architectural studies and landscapes. These he followed with a series of local portraits. But the few sales he made were but a pittance. Life was bittersweet. Ramonne wanted so much more for his love. She never once complained, but the longing was there.

Then a miracle occurred. A young man with a large moustache and an even larger fire in his heart, wandered into the girl's café. Clearly a man of means, Giselle was immediately impressed by his *joie de vivre*, something she now found sorely lacking in Ramonne. Henri Mouhot inquired about the artist whose work adorned the walls. Giselle calmly removed her apron and asked *monsieur* to wait five minutes. Then she raced to Ramonne's side.

Having fallen into a deep depression of late, and taking to drink, he was suffering the effects of alcohol-abuse and begged to be left alone. But she was not to be dissuaded. She literally dragged him out of bed, shod his bare feet, and pushed him down the stairs and up the street to the café.

Surly and hung-over, Ramonne demanded a carafe of wine be bought by the young dilettante before he would join him. Recognizing a kindred spirit and having suffered the same sense of self-doubt and insecurity himself, Mouhot ordered, instead, a single glass of absinthe, referring to it by the English term, 'a tail of the dog,' and proclaimed it medicinal to the exasperated Giselle.

With the liqueur's arrival, Ramonne reluctantly sat down.

The two men soon discovered their backgrounds to be similar. Both were born under the astrological sign of Taurus the bull. Mouhot was born May 15, 1826; Ramonne on the 10th a year earlier; both to parents not rich but respectable. Henri's father devoted himself to the education of his two sons. Henri first studied philosophy, intending to become a teacher, but he was unable to remain in pursuit of any one field of endeavor for very long, and soon set out on the path of exploration that was to be his destiny. Using his professorial degree as a meal ticket, he traveled to Russia. Here he began as a teacher but soon became an artist. He devoted his hours of leisure to the cultivation of the arts and sciences. He was admitted into the Academy of Voronege. He studied photography and drawing, soon compiling a collection illustrating different parts of the country, portraits of distinguished men, museum specimens, and buildings in the semi-Byzantine style.

With the imminent arrival of war from the east, he was forced to leave Russia and return to his native land. However, before his departure he was introduced to Louis Daguerre in person, and his process of photographic etching on tin plates that was being heralded as imbuing the formidable 'land camera' with the compactness and portability desired to take it out of the studio and into the bush. He mastered its mechanics and left Russia determined to carry the new invention into foreign lands.

Sober and with his spirit re-awakened by Mouhot's energy and drive, Ramonne invited him to his studio. Here a lasting bond was formed, as Mouhot marveled at piece after piece. When Giselle returned in the evening, the two greeted her with the news that Ramonne was now employed as Mouhot's *chargé d'affaires*. When she asked what that meant, they laughed in unison and professed that they hadn't the slightest idea. Suspecting them both of being drunk, she was about to leave them to their cups when Mouhot unscrolled a document from the French consul that authorized the granting of a considerable sum to M. Henri Mouhot for the "Exploration and documentation by photographic and traditional means of the territories of Germany, Belgium, and northern Italy." He had acquired the commission that very afternoon and had made Ramonne his first employee. In essence, Ramonne had been hired to be a kindred spirit, for Mouhot was about to embark on a series of expeditions of a scientific and artistic nature that would require physical stamina and endurance equal to his own—Mouhot was a gymnast and a hunter and in excellent physical condition —as well as artistic talent and, above all, the desire to explore for the pure pleasure of knowledge gained.

Ramonne was up to the task, and the two left by train the next day for Mouhot's family home in Montbeliard where his portfolio and equipment was stored. Within a fortnight they embarked upon their first expedition, through the Black Forest of Germany.

Mouhot proved as gifted in the skill of marketing as he was at exploring, and soon their drawings and etchings were regular features of the syndicated newspapers in France, England, and America. All bore the by-line "M. Mouhot" which meant that Ramonne was contributing anonymously to Mouhot's fame, but he was delighted at the simple pleasure of seeing his work appreciated, credited or not. And Mouhot was more than fair in distributing the income.

Ramonne and Giselle relished their time in between his journeys. Their love grew stronger than ever, as he gained the self-confidence he'd been lacking. Soon, Ramonne was able to give Giselle a taste of the life he desired for her. Nights at the opera, weekends in Avignon, jewelry…things she'd never known.

Within two years, Mouhot had gained a worldwide reputation and began to seek a wider field of research—one less explored by modern travelers. Upon their return from a successful sojourn through Holland, he came into possession of an English book on Siam, and soon an expedition to that country became the sole object of his aspirations.

And so it was on that chill February morning in 1858 that Ramonne and Giselle said goodbye at the dock, Mouhot watching from aboard the ship. This journey would last a year or more. Sweet Giselle would wait. She would be there upon his return. She slipped from his embrace and handed him a packet. He unfolded the tissue wrapping and discovered an ornate silver pocket watch. Inside was her portrait. She wound it for him and he put it into his breast pocket.

He held and kissed her…for the last time. Then climbed the gangplank and watched her beautiful figure become reduced to a speck.

She was gone. *Forever*.

*It had perturbed the Captain greatly when Mouhot had announced his intention to dock at Kenya and embark upon Safari into the bush. Henri the botanist wanted to study the flora and fauna, while Henri the hunter wanted to add a leopard to his trophy wall. Of course, he has been successful in both ventures.*

*The Safari, planned and foretold at the beginning of the journey's preparations was resisted to no end by the Captain, who had wanted to round the Cape well ahead of the onset of the Monsoons, which we did. Due no doubt to our dalliance in Africa, we have sailed directly into the rains. The good ship weathers the storms well. However, the rift between the Captain and Mouhot is not repaired and causes many uncomfortable moments...*

*It was with great relief of both spirit and body that we eventually made out the coast of Sumatra and soon entered the relative calm of the Straits of Melaka.*

*We were less than a half-day's sailing past Singapore and into the Gulf of Siam, when Mouhot had the ship weigh anchor while he and I and two strong oarsmen took a skiff and explored a small native village. He was warned not to attempt a landing, but to keep his observations to the sea. Reluctantly he agreed and we both commenced to set up our drawing materials and record the landscape and its curious denizens, many of whom encircled our rowboat in their canoes.*

*The Captain is well aware that the Royal Geographical Society of London has commissioned the craft for Mouhot's specific use, and that it will be up to M's wont as to how the route will proceed. Thus it was that we approached Bangkok, taking five days to complete a journey normally accomplished in less than two.*

*We arrived on the 12th of September at the mouth of the River Menam upon whose banks rises the Capital of Siam, Bangkok. We are in relatively good health and spirits. Certainly the unflappable Mouhot is enthusiastic, to say the least.*

*Diiit. Diiit. Diiit.*

Ramonne's solitude was disturbed by the electronic chirping of his mobile phone. The annoying gadget had been a gift from Ping who, in spite of Ramonne's protests, insisted he keep it. Only Ping had the number—this Ramonne had insisted upon—and its use would be limited to extreme urgency only.

Ramonne had been back in the city less than 24 hours. He had a pretty good idea what the emergency was.

———

As he traveled through the city in the back of the black Mercedes—he could have traveled the city's rooftops as he had done for a century and a half prior to meeting Ping—he found he was resigned to accepting certain gratuities as harmless acquiescence to the man's controlling nature. Ramonne recalled what the city had been like when viewed by his innocent eyes on that day in 1858 when they first sailed into the river.

> *A vast sandbank bars the entrance of large ships, which must go further along the Gulf to discharge their cargo. However, as our boat draws only eight feet of water, the Christienne can coast up the River, so close to its banks that the sound of birds can be heard in the branches overhanging the water. The City is entirely water-borne. It relies on an intricate series of canals that intersect with the River. Instead of the noise of carriages and horses, one hears nothing but the dip of oars and the songs of sailors as the inhabitants go about their business in a state of grace and serenity.*

What a contrast to the nightmare vision currently on display. The *khlongs* were practically all gone, filled in with concrete as the city transformed itself into a shrine to the automobile. Without any plan in place, unlike other grand cities, Bangkok had developed haphazardly and irresponsibly, so that by the mid-twentieth century its concrete passages were hopelessly clogged with miles of overheating automobiles, continually spewing their toxic fumes into the once-blue skies. The few canals that were left were pollution-choked cesspools that carried refuse and sewage to the river. The river had turned black and the patrons of the noisy ferry boats that plowed its formerly hospitable waters traveled in dread of falling overboard.

Ramonne sighed so loud that the driver looked back.

"You all right, *Jao Nai*?" he inquired.

"Yes. *Mai pen rai*." Someone else would have sighed at frustration, wondering *how* it had all happened. Ramonne sighed out of knowledge. He *knew* how it had happened. He'd been there.

They arrived at their destination and Ramonne cleared his mind for the inquiry he was certain was forthcoming.

————

"What happened?"

"Harry Chalermphong is dead. You have been avenged."

"That wasn't the task you were assigned." Ping Narong sat in a large leather armchair. He clipped the end of a Cuban cigar as he talked. On a table in front of him was a silver Haliburton case and a human heart resting in a jar of formaldehyde.

"You were hired to kill the boy. That was all."

"I could not do that. The boy is innocent." Ramonne sat in a chair across from Ping's enormous glass-topped desk. Two bodyguards stood with arms crossed on each side of Ping.

"*That's* the point. My boy was innocent, too." Ping's face had turned crimson.

"No. He was not."

"*What*? You dare to challenge me?"

"I don't challenge or question you. I'm merely telling you that your information was wrong. I know Wang's reputation. He was said to be, pardon me for saying this, hot-headed. You entrusted Khun Harry's safe passage to him. Wang elected, on his own, to betray you, and attempted to steal a large sum of cash from Harry. That is what happened."

"Nonsense. Wang would never have been so foolish."

"Not so, *Jao Phor*. He would and he was."

"I will hear no more of this. Gao was there." He nodded to the man with the clean-shaven skull on his right. Gao nodded and glared defiantly at Ramonne. Ramonne had never liked the man, and tonight was proving to be no exception. "Tell him."

Gao *waied* to Ping, his hands pressed together and held to his forehead in respect. He then smiled at Ramonne, revealing a mouth full of gold. "As I have said before, Khun Harry was with Joon and two other bodyguards. We were about to leave when Khun Harry turned to Joon and spoke in his ear. Suddenly his men had their guns drawn. I was overpowered and helpless. Khun Harry went to Khun Wang and put a small pistol to his head. He forced *Num Noi* to his knees. He told him his father was a swine, and that dealing with him had been the reason he and his family had to flee his homeland. He would never forget that, and he wanted to send a message back to *Jao Phor* that he would not forget. The brave young man looked Khun Harry in his evil eyes and spit in his face. Khun Harry smiled and extended a hand to Joon, who handed him a slim dagger. He plunged it deep into Khun Wang's heart. I reached for the boy, but was too late and caught only his lifeless body. Joon and his *khika* shot each of my men in the head. I was disarmed. Joon then boarded your plane, putting a gun to your pilot's head. Khun Harry told me to take his message to you and then he and the two *khika* boarded and closed the hatch, leaving me with the boy's bloody head cradled in my lap as the plane took off for Paris."

He *waied* again and resumed his defiant stance.

Ping put a hand on the silver case and tapped it lightly. "There is a small fortune in here. It was meant to be yours." He awaited Ramonne's response.

"Never mind, *Jao Phor*." Ramonne smiled and pressed his fingertips together. "I think I see reward enough in the gold that adorns this lying dog's mouth."

"*Aiyyye!*" Outraged, Gao stepped forward. Ramonne didn't move.

Ping put up his hand and Gao stepped back.

"You defy the testimony of my most loyal servant?"

"He is neither, *Jao Phor*. He follows his own evil heart and has never been loyal to you."

Gao roared in protest. "*Jao Phor*. You would listen to this *farang* over me?"

Ramonne stood. "You don't have to listen to me. I will *show* you." He moved to Ping's side. Both bodyguards now reached for their weapons.

Ping again motioned them to stop.

Ramonne looked deep into the man's eyes. "I will not hurt you. I will not even touch you. But I will show you the truth."

With those words Ping Narong *left the room*. He was now on a small private airstrip at the eastern end of Don Muang Airport. It was night, and he was no longer Ping Narong. He was Harry Chalermphong and he saw through his eyes.

A light rain fell and Joon held an umbrella over Harry's wife and child. In front of him were Wang Narong, Gao, and two other members of Narong's gang. In Joon's left hand was a briefcase. It was not heavy, but not light. It held a half-million US dollars in 100-dollar bills. It would allow Harry and his family the safe sanctuary they needed to establish a new life in France, while his funds in Switzerland were unfrozen and transferred. It was their life-line and Harry trusted no one else with it.

It was time to board, and Harry extended his hand to Wang. "Thank you, Khun Wang, for your escort. And thank your father. Tell him I hope to see him soon."

Harry's wife had raised her hands in a *wai* to the young gangster. He knew that this was more in deference to the friendship between her husband and the ganglord, and less for the young man whom she had told Harry she had never trusted. Harry's young son also had his hands raised, palms pressed together, fingertips touching, in imitation of his mother. Harry was proud of the boy.

Suddenly, Harry saw the flash of steel as guns were drawn by Wang Narong and his men.

"What is this?" Harry heard himself say.

Wang smiled and walked over to the boy. The boy looked up at him, more curious than afraid. He patted the boy's hair while the mother protested.

"Don't touch my son."

Wang smiled. "I don't need to touch him." He moved the pistol's barrel so that it rested on the boy's temple.

"Wang. What do you want?" Harry asked as calmly as possible.

Wang smiled and pointed at the case in Joon's hand. "Just the 'exit-fee,' Khun Harry. That's all."

Harry looked at Joon and nodded. "Give it to him."

Joon looked at Harry and flicked the button on the umbrella. This startled Wang and he swung the pistol on to Joon.

With a swish, the umbrella folded onto its shaft.

Wang smiled and laughed. He extended his hand, keeping the pistol pointed at Joon. "The case, please. And then you can all be on your way—"

Wang gagged on the word as the steel tip of the umbrella was now embedded in his heart. Before the others could react, Joon swung the case, knocking the gun first from Gao's hand, and then arcing into each of the other thugs sending them crashing to the tarmac. As Joon swung back around there was a gun in his free hand and he shot each man once between the eyes.

The gun was pointed at Gao when Harry cried out. "No. Leave him."

Harry walked over to Gao, who glared defiantly up at him.

"Tell Ping what happened here. Tell the truth. Tell him I bear him no ill will and am sorry for the death of his son."

Joon turned to Harry's wife and son. "We must go."

He hastened them up the stairs. He waited, gun in hand, at the top.

"Please, *Nai Than*. We must leave now."

The last thing Harry saw as he trudged up the stairs was Gao, getting to his feet. The dying son of Ping Narong lay gasping his last breath, dying alone. The final words from Harry's mouth were: "Tell him the truth."

Then the door was shut and Harry and Joon entered the cabin.

———

Ping shuddered and blinked. He was back in the present. *Back in hell.*

His eyes were open wide and he glared at Gao. "*You!*"

Shocked, Gao could not imagine what the old man was yelling about. But he had no time to protest as Ping smashed his right kneecap with the heavy iron knob on his walking stick.

Gao cried out in pain and crashed to his knees. He looked to the old man for a reason but received instead another crushing blow, this time to his right elbow.

"Three years you have deceived me. Three years I have mourned a son who was unworthy."

He brought the stick down again, this time across the back of Gao's huge neck. Gao fell to the floor.

"I brought pain, death, and needless suffering onto the family of a trusted comrade. Because of your lies."

With this he brought the weapon down again on the smooth round head…until it was neither smooth nor round.

Panting and short of breath, Ping raised the cane again, but it was caught in Ramonne's grasp.

"Enough. He's dead, *Jao Phor.*"

He took the stick from the man and rested it on the glass table. Ping looked less like a formidable ganglord and more like a tired old man as he stared up at Ramonne. His other bodyguard was waiting for his turn. He was relieved when Ping waved him away. He bowed and quickly left the room.

"Thank the Lord Buddha, you didn't kill the boy."

Ramonne nooded. "I know. I'm sorry the father had to die, but he sounded an alarm, causing me to kill his guards."

"Joon?"

"Yes," Ramonne admitted. "I fear there were many unwarranted deaths that night."

Ping sank into his chair. "A waste."

"Yes." Ramonne agreed. "And though the boy was spared, he now faces the world without a father."

"If I could help…" Ping opened his palms.

Ramonne had thought of this already. "The boy is well off. But so many others are not." He touched the case. He could *feel* the money within.

"Is this mine?"

Ping nodded. "Of course. It always was."

Ramonne picked it up.

"How was *that* possible?" Ping asked in a dry voice.

"I merely showed you what Harry showed me when he told what happened. I can read thoughts. The truth appears as pictures to me, unfolding in my mind's eye. I merely transferred my memory to you."

"It was so *real*."

"That's the beauty of the truth, *Jao Phor*. It appears clear, unclouded." He opened the door.

"Innocent. Like the mind of a child."

Ramonne closed the door and left the mighty ganglord to contemplate what he had seen…and done.

**4**

---

*Clacka clacka clack.*

Martin Larue ratcheted the bicycle into a higher gear as he came over the rise and started to descend. The sky was gray and he knew the rain was coming soon. He started to pedal faster. He could see the single-story stone schoolhouse ahead, and estimated he'd just make it before the deluge. The smell of slash and burn conservation drifted from the rice paddies that surrounded him. This smell was not obnoxious like cigarette smoke, but somehow symbolic of the constant regeneration that the tropics sustained, and it always said 'home' to him when he smelled it.

American born, Harvard-educated, Martin had made his home in the tropics for over fifteen years. Inheritor of a huge family fortune, he had traveled the globe seeking the refuge he finally found in Thailand. A ten-year period of decadence and self-absorption was ended when he voluntarily entered a monastery for a year and lived a pious life of enlightenment. His subsequent re-emergence into the material world saw him continuing on the 'path.' Though no longer maintaining the robes or vows of poverty, he nevertheless abandoned his former heathen ways, subsequently attracting a 'woman of substance' into his life and ending a vow of chastity that had been neither voluntary nor desired. For the first time in his life, Martin felt he was on the right path.

It was a two-lane country road winding through rice paddies and surrounded by mountains. Until as recently as three years ago, it had been impassable as it was clustered with land-mines. The mountains just to the north had been a Khmer Rouge stronghold during the 'revolution,' and the foundations of nearby Ankgor Wat had been shaken by continual artillery fire. In 1998, the tyrant Pol Pot had died quietly, without apology to the country that he had decimated, leaving two million dead. Today if one drove through the countryside on the pock-marked dust bowls that pass for roads, one journeyed through village after village of women. Women only. Old women, young women, but no men. Pol Pot either conscripted the men into his army of thugs, or incarcerated and tortured them in his prisons.

But on a day like today, with a fine breeze signalling the onset of a swift, cleansing rain, it was easy to forget this poor country's past. Martin certainly had...for the moment. He was exercising mind and body in a ritual the locals found amazing. Riding on a bicycle without any destination. Here, bicycles were still the principal mode of transport, taking whole families, their worldly possessions, grandfather, great grandmother, and the kitchen sink to the corner market or down forty kilometers of bad road. But riding for *pleasure*? *Exercise*? This was unknown. Their lean brown frames spoke of the little need they had for such foibles. What they needed was more food.

*Rata tat tat tat tat.*

Martin shifted again as he rounded the corner. He was just going to beat the storm if he was lucky.

That was okay. He felt lucky.

He knew that Areeya was waiting for him, surrounded no doubt by waifs with smudged faces who'd just been spoilt with chocolate ice-cream after their English lessons.

Areeya, his saviour, had rescued him from a certain life of despair and solitude—albeit one buffeted by a bottomless pit of wealth. Areeya, daughter of a corrupt Thai police chief, who had persecuted Martin prior to her father's untimely demise. Areeya, formerly known by her nickname 'Yaya.' Juliet to his Romeo. Big-city girl who reluctantly gave up the cozy surroundings of the privileged nouveaux riche—her father, unlike police captains in other countries, whose meager salaries and pensions barely enabled them to retire with dignity, had left an inheritance that made her, if not Martin's equal, certainly *very* independent—to join Martin in setting up a school and orphanage on the outskirts of Siem Reap, near the great Tonle Sap Lake of Cambodia.

Less than a year old, the small but—as Martin was fond of saying, to Areeya's chagrin—'well endowed' orphanage had already gained international recognition. A two-headed calf had been born on a farm that was technically on the school's land. Martin had not had the heart to evict the poor farmers. He allowed them to remain, rent-free, with their three cows, one bull, four dogs, a goat, and half-dozen chickens. When the two-headed calf was born, Martin found that his anonymous little orphanage was suddenly on the map. They named the calf Chang and Eng, for the famous Siamese twins, and Martin had made sure that the tabloid press paid the farmer for the pictures they plastered around the globe on a slow news weekend.

He swung open the gate, the little wooden cowbell announcing his arrival, just as the rain fell.

"You missed 'Jingo Bars' again." Areeya smiled as she handed Martin a towel.

As expected, Areeya was knee-deep in smiling dirty faces. Jane Harrod, a stout, no-nonsense Canadian woman who was an English teacher, camp counselor, and sometimes chauffeur, had just finished with a stirring chorus of "Jingle Bells." Despite the ninety-degree weather, Jane felt compelled to instill some Christmas cheer into the tykes as the old year wound down.

Martin was glad he'd missed it. Avoiding Christmas rituals was one of the beauties of escaping to the tropics.

Ice-cream was an afternoon ritual. With the new 3,000watt generator that he had brought in from Bangkok on the last overland haul, Martin was assured that he wouldn't be throwing away ten gallons of melted goo as he'd had to in the past. The electricity in the area was 'temperamental' as Jane liked to say, and had the nasty habit of going out right after a shopping trip and a full freezer.

Sixteen kids, ranging in age from six to fourteen, took up a lot of freezer space.

One year ago, most of these kids had been wading in refuse. Caked in grime from head to foot, forced to breathe the stench of decaying filth, they had earned their living by scavenging in Cambodia's biggest rubbish dump for twelve to fifteen hours, every day of the week. Stung Mean Chey rubbish dump on the outskirts of Phnom Penh is the size of ten football fields, with hundreds of mounds of refuse rising sixty feet or more. The surface area is covered with a carpet of flies, which rise in black angry clouds when disturbed. In a country where one third of the nation's 12 million people do not earn enough to eat two meals a day, the hundreds of adults and children who spend their days picking through the refuse see the dump as a land of opportunity. Anything which can be recycled is picked up with bare hands and tossed into sacks for sale to scrap dealers.

Martin had found the children through the help of Enfants Sans Refuge, a French volunteer group. It had been raining the day he went to the dump. The stench had been unbearable and the rain brought out the worms that crawled over everything and everyone. There was a group of a dozen urchins picking through the rubbish being off-loaded from a huge truck. They scrambled to get to it, risking life and limb, before the bulldozers pushed it into the fire pit that continuously burned night and day, rain or no rain.

Martin decided right then and there that these would be *his* children. He would rescue the lot of them.

The bureaucracy of adopting the children had been quite simple. Most were orphans, both parents having 'disappeared.' Four had a mother but no father. Of these only one, Luong, mother of one of the older girls, Kook, seemed to have any interest in where her child was going or if she would ever see her daughter again. The others were quite content with the 'dowry' as they all called it, and Martin could have been the biggest pedophile or pimp in Cambodia for all they cared. Martin, in spite of the documentation provided, and his personal assurances for the children's safety, was certain that he was regarded with great suspicion.

Martin chose the site to build his orphanage in the tiny hamlet of Roluos, fifteen kilometers east of Siem Reap, for strictly selfish reasons. He could not abide Phnom Penh. It had all the charm of a frontier town and none of the conveniences. Apart from the Foreign Correspondents' Club and two or three good hotels, one was subjected to blocks of dangerously barren stretches of nameless, faceless, low-tech business zones set just a scant block away from never-ending miles of poverty.

Siem Reap, however, was a charming little city, just urban enough to provide the amenities one needed to conduct business, and yet rural enough to still exist as a bicycle culture. The small international airport, with its daily non-stop flights to and from Bangkok, brought tourists to the gateway to the temples of Angkor, one of the great wonders of the world. Unfortunately, Martin was watching the charm disappear daily as a mad race seemed to be on to see who could build the largest hotel.

However, there were a number of delightful restaurants, and one could escape the dust and noise of the construction quite easily for the serenity of the countryside.

In addition to the tourists, a number of international teams were working at Angkor. Japanese researchers carrying out excavations around the great square at Angkor Thom and the

Bayon. American workers from the World Monuments Fund focusing on the great temple of Preah Khan. Indonesian, Chinese, and German teams working side-by-side restoring Angkor Thom, Preah Kok, and the temple of Chau Srei respectively. France had continued its massive restoration work that had begun in the 1960s and been interrupted by war.

Martin visited the temple sites regularly and had made many interesting acquaintances among this international group. A number of fine evenings had been spent in spirited conversation on the terrace of the Red Piano bar in Siem Reap.

The little microcosm of Siem Reap suited Martin for now. For the first time that he could remember in a long time, he was content, and instead of jumping on a plane every thirty days, which had been his habit for a decade in Bangkok, he settled in to the mundane yet curiously satisfying role of patron to a motley crew of rug rats.

"Don't know how you can abide exercising in this heat," Jane huffed as she gathered up the songbooks from the desks.

"Actually it's quite pleasant now that the rain's broken, Jane. You ought to try it." Martin winked at Areeya.

"No thank you. 'Only mad dogs and Englishmen go out in the noonday sun.' I'm neither, thank God." She turned down the overhead fans, as the children were no longer in the classroom.

Martin's skin was a golden shade of amber while Jane was a color so pale that she would get a coroner's rubber blanket thrown over her in the unlikely event that she should ever take to lying on a beach.

She hated the tropics, but she loved the children. To Martin, that was all that mattered. She had experience. She'd run a small orphanage outside of Phnom Penh on land that had been funded by the then co-premier Prince Ranariddh. In June of 1997, Hun Sen launched a coup against the prince and he was driven into exile. Jane's pleas to Hun Sen fell on deaf ears, and she closed the doors to her abandoned orphanage and returned to Vancouver.

It was Enfants Sans Refuge again who told Martin about Jane. He tracked her down in Phuket. Apparently the tropics *had* gotten in her blood, for she was running a second-hand English bookstore in Kata. Seated in the back between the stacks of faded paperbacks that had been read on one beach or another, they shared a pot of proper English tea. None of that dreadful Liptons for Madame Harrod. Martin had laid out his proposal, keeping his trump hand—a dozen pictures of wide-eyed hope and innocence—for the last.

Jane was quite literally moved to tears.

But there were two problems. One, she pointed out with a sweep of her arm, was the books. She had invested her meager life's savings in them. She had been running the little store for two years, and was barely paying her rent, but it was a life she had become accustomed to, and not something she could just walk away from.

Martin made her an offer he thought she couldn't refuse. He said he'd buy her books. All her books. Then he said he would pay the rent on the store for a year, and the books would stay right where they were. He'd give her a year's contract to teach at his school in Siem Reap. At the end of the year she could return to her bookstore or Martin would pay to crate and store her collection. The terms of the teaching contract were more than fair.

Martin thought he'd closed the deal.

But then Pom came through the door and Jane introduced him as her fiancé. A strapping six-foot man of brown-skinned steel, Pom smiled a gap-toothed smile and *waied* politely. Martin returned the gesture and sighed. There was obviously more negotiating to be done.

Martin left Kata in time to catch the last plane back to Bangkok. He'd hired Pom—whose profession was a pastry chef, but seemed capable of handling most anything—as well as Jane. Pom would attend to closing up the shop, while Jane would travel to Cambodia within the week. Martin advised the couple to forestall their wedding plans for the time being, as Jane would be treated more decorously in Cambodia if she were not married to a Thai. Martin assured the skeptical Pom that he'd have no problem getting him a work visa, and true to his word Pom had his first passport with a visa describing him as a 'transportation engineer' within a week of meeting Martin Larue. And Martin had his staff.

Construction of the school and orphanage had been commissioned long before Martin ever ventured into the stinking Phnom Penh rubbish pile. Martin had been making regular bi-weekly runs to Cambodia for half a year by then. He and Areeya had supervised every phase of the building. There was a classroom, two dormitories, a kitchen, dining room, a small gym, library, and two separate houses—one for Martin and Areeya, with its own small kitchen; and one with three bedrooms and two baths that was shared by Jane and Pom and the Cambodian staff. The Cambodian staff consisted of Kook's mother Luong and her sister Keav.

Martin fondly remembered the day he convoyed the children up from Phnom Penh to their new home. He had bought a bus, and the name 'École Des Orphelins d'Angkor' was freshly painted on the side. Inside there were twelve brave but frightened children. He and Luong went up and down the aisle dispensing chewing gum as an aide to keep back the tears that were, if not flowing already, on the verge of flowing.

Areeya was at the school commanding a herd of painters, plumbers, and electricians. The last coat of blue enamel had just been applied to the back doors and Jane was manning a broom when the sound of the first motorcar on the remote highway in three hours was heard. Areeya ran to the front and signaled that indeed they were almost there.

In the bus the children craned their necks to see the fresh sandstone colored building with its bright blue trim. Several of the older ones squealed in delight when they realized that the lettering on the plaque on the wall in front matched that on the side of their bus.

Martin beamed as the bus came to a halt.

"This is it. Your new home."

Luong translated, and then, cautiously, silently, the motley crew stood in front of the brand new building.

It was the adults' turn for tears.

———

Martin had never had kids. He'd never wanted kids.

Now he had twelve.

Areeya and he had talked about this. They'd imagined the day they would first open the door. The day their little bare feet would step onto the clean cool tiles of the entry. He had a slab of marble especially sliced and imported from Italy to provide the coolest stone surface at the entry. Martin scurried to the front door, slipped off his shoes, and waited for them to step in.

Little Hon was the first. He stepped gingerly. His face shone with pure delight. Then he ran, full speed, through the entire complex. Hands over his head, eyes and mouth wide open.

Six-year-old Sacha and Khota were next. Though twins, they were as different as night and day. Sacha was curious about everything, while Khota was shy and withdrawn. Together, but in their own separate ways, they explored the marvelous clean space.

Paul was six. His real name was Pol, but Martin refused to call him that. Peter was seven, and *his* real name was unpronounceable to the Western tongue. They had been friends since their mothers had dumped them together on the outskirts of Phnom Penh to fend for themselves. They'd scraped out an existence for two years from the mountains of refuse. They'd run and hid from Martin when he first approached, but he had the feeling they'd never run from a fight. These two were tough and they looked after each other. They walked quietly, almost reverently through the schoolhouse.

Sisko was six and never spoke. No one was sure if he could or not. Rumor had it that he'd been next to a mine that had exploded. His mother had shielded him, and had died. The blast had damaged his hearing, but this was just a rumor. He'd simply appeared one day, a naked four-year-old wandering through the rubble.

He sat in the doorway, refusing to go inside. The others walked around him.

Kook, nine, was a precocious brat. She had all the boys' attention, and she made them work for it. She was Areeya's favorite. She sashayed through the school with her regal nose high in the air.

Micki and Minnie, nine and ten respectively, were brother and sister. They'd been born in the dump. They were so wild that Martin thought that he couldn't take them. But then he remembered his vow. He'd seen twelve children…together… scrounging in the dirt. They were a gang, watching each other's backs. Surviving by being together. He'd promised himself he'd take them all—together.

Micki had bitten him—he'd had a tetanus shot recently, but it still got infected—and Minnie had ran away twice already in Phnom Penh. They sat, holding on to each other on the steps of the bus, refusing to get off. Areeya approached and, with a few kind words and some candy, managed to get them to take her hand and walk through the gate.

*Keeper*, Martin thought to himself. That's what they said in this jaded part of the world about a woman that was more than a one-night stand. She was a 'keeper.'

Areeya was definitely a keeper.

Chawlie, also nine, and the largest of the group, had somehow managed to put on weight on a diet of cardboard and styrofoam. Had he been a Bangkok kid, Martin would not have been surprised at his girth. The new generation there were stuffing themselves with American fast food, becoming pimple-prone, over-sized adolescents, much to the chagrin of their shrinking parents. But Chawlie had not had this luxury. Somehow, he just had the genes. He waddled happily through the school.

Tiara, eleven, was as sullen and moody as any child would be whose parents had been murdered in front of her eyes at age four. Raised by a neighbor who sent her to a sweatshop in Burma at the tender age of seven, she was reunited in the factory with her older sister, Naj. The two fled and managed somehow to end up in the rubbish pit. Naj, now twelve, was usually as morose as her sister, having been repeatedly raped by the Burmese border guards as payment for allowing her and her sister to leave their country.

The girls were fascinated with the cool marble entry and they rolled over and over on it, squealing in delight.

Martin picked up Sisko and carried him into the schoolhouse. He shut the door.

His brood were home. At last.

**5**

*On the 19th of October we left Bangkok in a small boat which Mouhot had purchased and outfitted for our journey up the Menam into the north of the country. Just two nights before, we had dined with the King of Siam at his annual Birthday dinner. The repast, served in a vast golden hall, was attended by most of the Europeans present at the time in Bangkok. The King, resplendent in wide pantaloons, short jacket, golden helmet and sabre, is a gracious host and it was a grand evening, climaxed with a pyrotechnical display set aloft from various rafts in the river. The numerous eruptions had the guests gasping in awe. Mouhot inquired into their origin and was told that the King had them brought in from China especially for the occasion.*

*The sumptuous surroundings cannot conflict more in contrast with our present condition. Currently Mouhot and I are alone with our new adopted family: two rowers, one of whom also serves as cook; a parakeet; an ape; and a dog. Our equipment and supplies are compacted into numerous chests deployed throughout the craft.*

*The current at this time is very strong and it has taken us only five days to travel a distance of roughly twenty-five leagues. At night we suffer greatly from the mosquitoes and even during the day have to keep up an incessant fanning to drive off these pestilent little vampires.*

*Vampires*? Ramonne looked again at his handwriting to make sure of what he'd just read. No doubt about it. Was it a portent of the future? Had Ramonne had some sense of his destiny? *No.* Present-day Ramonne thought not. Past-tense Ramonne had been an innocent, with no idea of the path he was about to embark upon. The journey from Marseilles to Siam had been lengthy and full of drama and wonder. But the path just ahead of the young Frenchman was full of unknown and unpredictable danger.

Danger and a destiny that would lead to the enigma that was present-day Ramonne. Except for a shock of pure-white in his shoulder-length hair, the man who sat in the Bangkok café appeared to be the exact same man who sat in the rowboat on the Menam River in 1858.

*There is no such thing as silence in this jungle land. The end of the day signals the start of the symphony of the night. The sharp incessant insect banter is shrill and metallic, as though an army of goldsmiths were at work.*

*Mouhot is voracious. While I concentrate on sketching the land-scape, he collects animals and insects. He joined a tribal chief in tracking a beast of prey and earned a handsome tiger skin for his skill in bringing down the destroyer of many of the village's livestock with a single shot.*

*He has organized treks inland on the back of mighty pachyderms. These beasts of burden seem both intelligent and frightening at the same time. I enjoyed the safety and unique vantage of being a passenger on their high backs, but soon learned that the favored posi-tion on such convoys is at the head of the line, as being downwind of their constant expulsions was ghastly. When we encamped I always give the elephants ('chang' in the native tongue) a wide berth. Mouhot, on the contrary, seems quite taken by the beasts and appears to be contemplating the King's offer of a pair as a gift for our return to Europe. I would have assumed him drunk or delirious when he had discussed this, if it weren't for the fact that Mouhot drinks nothing*

> *but tea, hoping by his abstinence from cold water and wine & spirits to escape fever...*
>
> *We explored the Menam as far as Prabat and then returned to Krung Thep, as Bangkok is known by the Siamese. They call themselves 'Tai' which means 'free-men'—a misnomer as they are under the benevolent yet stern rule of a despot, in a strict caste system, heavily taxed, and as such hardly 'free.' Our small craft was unloaded and Mouhot's collections are stored in the Customs House.*
>
> *Mouhot has made arrangements for us to secure passage to Komput, the harbor and entry to his determined journey to visit the savage tribes of Cambodge.*

Cambodia. Ramonne remembered his first glimpse of that wretched land. *Cambodge.* They were shrouded in the morning mist, and although they knew by compass point readings that the harbor was near, they had not a single glimpse of land. Then the fog lifted slowly revealing one single architectural piece. A huge cross. Mouhot, Ramonne recalled, was ecstatic at the vision, and fell to his knees in prayer. His religious devotion was such that he received great solace in these remote outposts and the zealots who manned them. His journeys were always book-ended around visits to the jungle missions that these poor souls raised. In general, Ramonne regarded these missionaries with suspicion, and as they always were sequestered *sans* spouse, under the cloak of a vow of celibacy, he also was suspicious of their sexual leanings. It was one topic where Mouhot and Ramonne differed, and became the subject of many an evenings' fire. Ramonne saw, as no doubt did Mouhot, a true beauty to the culture and life of the Siamese, Annamites, Chinese, and Laotians they had encountered on their journey. He could not understand the zealots' insistence that Christianity must be introduced to these people as the only way to salvage their souls. He did not believe this, and therefore had little or no reaction to the sight of a wooden cross atop a small vine-covered mission above the harbor of Komput.

*Upon our arrival we were welcomed by the local abbé and learned that France was at war with Austria. We were astonished at this news, as neither of us had heard of any disagreement between the two governments. As a consequence, Frenchmen are viewed with suspicion wherever we go.*

*The King is at this very time, in residence in Komput, and on the third day of our visit, we were summoned to his presence. The King was sequestered in a temporary pavilion of bamboo covered with red cloth. Mouhot has presented him with a walking stick with a fire-arm hidden in its grip. The King loved this, and immediately loaded and discharged it.*

*He asked Mouhot what our intentions are. Mouhot told of our desire to travel in country and visit the Capital of Udong. The King invited us to do so and said he would arrange for carriages and bearers for the journey. However, when it came time to embark, no such provisions had been made and we had to scurry and scrounge to outfit our own expedition. The contrast between this King, indeed this Country and that of Siam, are becoming apparent...*

*As it has turned out, the journey to Udong has been our most arduous to date, the country being unrepentantly hot, to the point that it seems to be on fire. There is no point in attempting any movement at all between the hours of ten in the morning to three in the afternoon...*

*Upon our arrival in Udong we were warmly received by the Second King of Cambodge. This Monarch proves to have all the grace lacking in his counterpart and, after a week as his guest, we have been given a train of elephants and bearers to carry us on our further journeys into the country.*

Ramonne closed the journal. At this point in his story he and Mouhot had been out for a year. Mouhot's obsessions were to continue to drive them further and further. Ramonne remembered wondering if Mouhot ever intended to return at all. Due to the harsh terrain and climate, they could only progress through certain areas during a particular season, and weeks would turn into months as they waited to make their movement forward.

A noise momentarily startled Ramonne. He forgot he had a guest. He looked across his catacombed room and noticed the silver-haired man had awoken. He was struggling with his bonds and attempting to speak through the gag of tape that sealed his mouth. Ramonne studied him for a moment.

The man, a European, had been following Ramonne. Ramonne became aware of him earlier in the evening. As was often his custom, he had started the evening with a bottle of good French spirits at one of his favorite haunts. He would prowl for his prey when the hour was late and the streets less dense. Tonight he had been ensconced in the lobby of the Four Seasons. He had the journal with him and had been so absorbed that he didn't notice the man watching him. It wasn't until almost midnight when he strolled to the exit, that he picked up on the single word *'vampire'* amongst the telepathic jumble of thought waves that assaulted his subconscious.

Like the cacophony of noise that assails the ears of all humans in a city, Ramonne ignored the bulk of it and it passed through without notice. But that word, his secret identity, caused him to stop dead in his tracks. He spun around, scanning the room. He rifled quickly through the minds of those within his vision. None brought the slightest hint of recognition or malice to him. There was a man contemplating the murder of his wife, but that was none of his business.

His 'radar' fully attuned, he continued cautiously to the door. The thirty-foot-tall pane of glass was held open for him by a white-gloved lad who bowed as he passed. Ramonne made note of the silver-haired man who was paying his tab at the bar. He was impatient and finally threw a bundle of baht notes down on the bar and walked away. He'd escaped Ramonne's notice before, but this was definitely his betrayer.

Ramonne declined the hotel staff's offer of a limousine or taxi and proceeded to walk down the pedestrian ramp onto

Ratchadamri Road. He didn't need to turn around. The man was following him. As he walked, he studied the man's face in his mind. He now realized that the man had been at the bar of the Conrad last night. Earlier tonight, he'd been waiting in a taxi queue when Ramonne left his current home beneath Hualamphong Station. The man had not only been following him, he knew where he *lived*.

*How could this happen*? Ramonne realized that he'd been so fixated in his study of his past that he'd ignored his present. His existence relied on stealth and constant vigilance. Yet he'd been so absorbed in the wondrous reliving of his youthful adventures, that he'd gone about his nocturnal activities without paying attention. He'd allowed himself to be stalked. He, the hunter, had allowed himself to be hunted.

He wanted to lure the man into a side *soi* and drain him of his life. Throw his carcass in the canal. But what if this man was not alone?

Ramonne stopped at the Erawan shrine at the busy intersection of Rama I Road. He bought a handful of tributes—flowers, candles and incense—and entered the plaza. He followed the Buddhists before him and did what they did. He saw no blasphemy in his attendance, and he actually felt that this particular form of prayer made perfect sense. These people would bring offerings of tribute to the golden effigy of Phra Phrom, prostrate themselves before the idol and silently pray for the granting of specific requests. They would promise to return with a much larger tribute if the prayer was answered. Seemed perfectly logical and fair to Ramonne. You made a deal, and if the deity kept his end, you had to keep yours. If not, no hard feelings, but no extra tribute either. In this way Phra Phrom acted more as an agent, and he received a commission for his services.

Having lit his incense bundle, Ramonne proceed to the first of four stations of the shrine. He did not kneel, but presented the smoke to the heavens, lit a candle, and placed three sticks of incense, one flower, and one candle on the shrine's base. He could hear the prayers of the others around him, and they amused him. The Thais were very materialistic in their approach to their religion, and the general prayers were for a Mercedes, a country home, or a rich husband, and a few requests to cure a sick granny or crippled auntie. He noticed the silver-haired man lighting an incense bundle.

Ramonne tuned out the others and concentrated on the man. Instantly he felt the heat of danger. It was as if he'd stepped too close to a fire. A wave of information on vampires in general and Ramonne in particular flowed from the man. The imagery was overwhelming and Ramonne silenced it, lest he succumb and attack the man here in the presence of so many witnesses. He continued to the fourth and final stage of the shrine. The man was approaching his first. Ramonne stuck his last sticks of incense in the mound of ash behind his freshly lit candle and retreated to watch the man complete his journey.

The man was obviously unused to this ceremony and was merely trying to mimic what was going on around him. He knelt on shaky knees and raised his hands to his forehead in a reverential *wai* at each corner of the altar. When he reached the final one he looked nervously about, and not seeing Ramonne, he hastened to finish the prayer and leave. As he bent to light the candle, he felt hands close gently on his shoulder. As they did he felt a great weight lifted *off* those shoulders as his mind no longer became his own. A voice in his head said '*Follow me.*' And he did.

———

Ramonne now knew who the man was. His name was Dr. Gerhardt Kaestle, and he was an entomologist from New York City. An American. He was 58 years old, reasonably fit, and yet there was a malady that Ramonne detected. If not arrested soon, the doctor would suffer its consequences. Ramonne was not yet sure if he should be concerned. But the doctor could quite possibly end up as a midnight snack, and Ramonne was careful in choosing what he ate.

Ramonne removed the tape with a swift yank. The doctor winced.

"Doctor Kaestle. You had a good rest, I trust?"

"Monsieur Delacroix. This is not exactly how I hoped to make your acquaintance." He moved his wrists, which were bound, as were his feet, to a heavy Louis XIV parlor chair. He didn't struggle with his bonds, but merely tested them.

"Oh? What did you have in mind? After all, it was *you* who followed me."

"Information, monsieur. I have studied you from afar for some time now."

"Really? Should I be flattered? What is your interest in a humble French expatriate?"

"Monsieur Delacroix. I know who you are. As I'm sure you are very aware."

"*Who* am I, then?"

"A vampire. The living dead. A forsaken one."

Ramonne did not act surprised. There was no need. "How do you know this?"

"It is my passion…the study of vampires. Some would call it a hobby, but it is much more than that. It has been an all-consuming sideline to my medical practice…the study of mosquitoes and the diseases attributed to them. Of course, my colleagues think I'm quite mad."

Ramonne was not amused. "I asked *how*, not why."

"Of course. Several years ago, a man came to visit me." Ramonne said the name before the doctor. "Jonathan Peyton."

"Yes. Jonathan. He told me a tale that curled my hair, but also excited me to no end by the possibility of my having been right. Vampires *do* exist."

Ramonne was growing impatient. "And…?"

"Try telling that to the Smithsonian. Anyway, Jonathan was

suffering from a blood disorder that had been diagnosed as HIV. But, he knew what was happening to him."

"I bit him."

"Precisely."

"I should have killed him, the little prat." Ramonne frowned at the memory. Jonathan had been the unfortunate husband of a woman that Ramonne took a fancy to. She reminded him of his beloved Giselle and, in an ensuing fight—*after* Ramonne had killed the fair damsel—Jonathan was wounded by the vampire. Before Ramonne could finish him, a police helicopter drove him away from a cliff in Pattaya. Jonathan returned to America and searched for the vampire for years before finding him again in Bangkok.

"It was you then who provided him with the knowledge and tools to destroy me."

"Yes. I knew that his only hope of surviving the deadly blood disorder that was crippling his body was to find the *source* of the virus and destroy it. However, I've since learned that he was too late. He drowned before he could complete his mission. I assume it was in struggle with you? The police report was very vague."

"Police report…? Doctor Kaestle, you are not in Manhattan. A police report here—particularly in regards to a *farang's* death —is not necessarily a document of fact. In this particular instance, the police reports should be filed under 'explaining the unexplainable.' What really occurred on that long night is completely beyond the grasp of *any* police report—anywhere."

Ramonne studied the man. He then untied his wrists and ankles.

Dr. Kaestle was surprised but said nothing. He remained seated and rubbed his wrists. Ramonne brought him a glass of water, which he gladly downed.

"Thank you."

Ramonne nodded. Cautiously the doctor got to his feet. "Dr. Kaestle. I perceive no immediate threat from you. But rest assured that your life now rests entirely within my hands. I can extend it or extinguish it at will."

"I understand."

"I will tell you some things. Realize that the likelihood that I will let you survive grows smaller, the more I reveal to you."

The doctor thought this over, and then slowly nodded. "I *need* to know."

"I believe you do. Your quest for knowledge of me is flattering in a way. My vanity is served in giving you answers."

Ramonne went to a carved golden wine rack and removed a bottle. "Pommard. 1988. Not bad. Will you join me?"

"Thank you, yes."

Ramonne decanted the wine and poured it into two fine Croatian crystal glasses. "Jonathan Peyton succeeded. He destroyed me."

Dr. Kaestle gasped. "But how—?"

"That will be revealed, doctor. Patience."

He smiled as he savored the rich bouquet. "Jonathan and I struggled twice on his journey to kill me in Bangkok. On that first battle when he shot me full of Ketamine, animal tranquilizer—I'm sure I have you to thank for that little stunt—I managed to give him but a small scratch, unintentional I assure you. But it was enough to *turn* him."

"Good God. Jonathan became a *vampire*?"

"Yes. However, his reign was short-lived. To my knowledge he never even tasted human blood. Just *dogs*…ugh. Very shortly we battled to the death on the hallowed ground of Wat Arun. The rising sun incinerated us both, and the wind blew our ashes into the sea."

"Thus the police report of his drowning."

"Yes. Along with that prick, Boonsong."

"That's the brave colonel who drowned while trying to save Jonathan."

"Nonsense." Ramonne poured more wine. He decided to share selected knowledge with the doctor, mainly confirming what Jonathan Peyton had told him. Time was short, as the hour was growing late. He told of Jonathan's quest for the vampire—a shoot-out in a whorehouse where the vampire hunter received the wound that made him a vampire.

The doctor hung on every word.

"I fear it's time for me to retire." Ramonne handed a fresh glass to the doctor. "Drink up. The sun will soon be on the rise."

The doctor drained his glass and set it down. "I should be getting back to my hotel."

Ramonne smiled. "I think not. You shall remain my guest. We will resume our discussions in the evening."

Simultaneous with the words, Kaestle yawned. It was not unusual that he should be tired: he was half a world away and he'd been up all night, but suddenly he felt 'bone-tired.' He could barely move. He dropped his hands to his side, nodded his head, and fell fast asleep.

Ramonne removed his glass and smelled it. The sleeping potion he'd administered was virtually undetectable.

He slipped the cords back around the doctor's wrists and ankles and tightened the knots. Lastly he put a fresh piece of tape over his mouth. "Just a precaution, doctor. A *prophylactic* as you would say."

With that, he climbed into his coffin and closed the lid. In the dark he thought of Cambodia.

*Dark. Dangerous.*

*Land of savages.*

*Home of the Beast.*

**6**

---

*The savages of Cambodge have all manner of superstitions. The natives believe in an evil genius, and attribute all diseases to him. If anyone suffers from illness, they often cry out, 'He has passed into my body. He is stifling me.' Sometimes the sacrifice of a pig or an ox is required, often a human victim. A slave is then seized and pitilessly offered up to appease the evil being.*

*While we are among them, there has been a total eclipse of the sun. The people believe that some being has swallowed up the sun and moon, and in order to deliver them, they make a frightful noise, beat their drums, utter savage cries, and shoot arrows into the sky until the sun reappears.*

*They have no very fixed ideas on the subject of rewards and punishments in a future life. They believe in the immortality of the soul, which after leaving the body, they imagine wanders about the tombs and adjacent mountains, often terrifying the living by nocturnal appearances, and finally loses itself forever in the shadowy depths of the south.*

"*Jao Nai.*" Lek approached the vampire cautiously. He was seated in the wine bar, exactly where he said he'd be. And he was reading. Those old books he'd brought from Paris. Lek wondered what could be in them that fascinated the master so. Lek rarely read. He preferred to *watch*. Television, the street... the world go by. Let someone tell him the news. Books and newspapers were not a part of his life.

Reluctantly, Ramonne put down his diary. He nodded to Lek, who bowed. Ramonne motioned for him to sit down. "What do you need, master?"

Ramonne slid a US passport across the table. "Go to the Hilton and pay this man's bill. Bring his belongings to me."

"Which Hilton, *Jao Nai*?"

"*Which Hilton*?" Wireless Road. Nai Lert Park. The one with the penis shrines in the back, of course."

"That is the Raffles Hotel now, *Jao Nai*."

Exasperated, Ramonne let out a sigh. "Fine. Whatever they call it now, that's the hotel. How the fuck can anyone keep up with these name changes.

"Never mind, *Jao Nai*. I will take care of it."

"Good. He will be *my* guest for a while."

Lek raised an eyebrow at this, but said nothing.

"Then bring some food."

"Food?"

"Yes. Food. Not for me, of course. This *farang*. He's human. He'll die without food. Bring meats, bread, cheese, water, whiskey...I don't care. Whatever it is you people eat."

"Do you have a refrigerator, *Jao Nai*?" "Now why would I need a refrigerator?" "To keep the food fresh."

Ramonne sighed again. "Get a refrigerator. One of those small ones, like in a hotel."

"Yes, *Jao Nai*."

"Why not steal it from the Hilton. Serve them right for changing their name."

———

White corpuscles. Red corpuscles.

Seen through a powerful microscope, the white corpuscles were attacked by the red. The miniature dance was repeated over and over.

*Doctor Kaestle. What is happening to you?* Ramonne pulled away from the eyepiece and turned off the light on the microscope. He had a small laboratory set up, with a few simple tools. A shelf of medical textbooks was mixed in with ancient volumes on the occult and black arts. Many of the books were in Braille.

In the other room, Dr. Kaestle lay on a couch. Asleep. Ramonne walked over and inserted a hypodermic needle into his bare arm.

"Time to wake up, Doctor Kaestle."

Ramonne put the needle in a metal canister and walked to a large oak dining table. Two chairs sat at each end, facing each other across the table's vast expanse. In front of Ramonne was a bottle of red wine and two glasses. In front of the other chair, a roast beef had been carved, and a platter of potatoes and assorted salads was set out to accompany it.

The doctor stirred on the couch and sat up.

"Come and join me, doctor. You must be famished."

Kaestle tried to stand but fell back on the couch. He saw that his sleeve was rolled up and there were tiny puncture marks on his arm. "What have you done to me?"

"I merely drew some blood to run a few tests. I used a sanitary needle, by the way. Nothing to fear." He smiled and motioned to the table. "You've also been medicated to help you sleep. That's why your legs are a bit wobbly. Just take it slowly."

The doctor tried to stand again and succeeded. He slowly crossed to the table and sat down.

"How long have I been sleeping?"

"Not long. Eighteen hours."

"They'll be looking for me."

Ramonne leaned onto the table and rested his chin on his hands. "Really? Just who would *they* be?"

Before the doctor could respond, Ramonne slammed the palm of his hand on the table, sending the silverware flying. "Enough. Let's stop the charade, doctor. You came here seeking me. You came alone. You came in secret."

Kaestle was wide awake now.

"The question is not what I did to you. The question is what did *you* do to *yourself*?"

The doctor squirmed in his chair. "I...I injected myself with Jonathan Peyton's blood."

"That's what I suspected. *Why*?"

"I wanted to...to..."

"Be *me*? You wanted to be a vampire?"

Softly the doctor spoke the word. "Yes."

Ramonne shook his head. "You foolish, foolish man." He poured a glass of wine and took a long pull.

"You are not a vampire. You have no supernatural powers, do you?"

Again the doctor answered in a very quiet voice. "No."

"No. What you are, doctor, is *ill*. Correct?"

"I wanted to—"

"Cheat death." Ramonne took the words out of his mouth.

"Yes."

There was a long moment of silence. During this time Ramonne studied the doctor's mind. He saw what it was he wanted, but dared not ask.

"I'm not in the habit, Doctor Kaestle, of making vampires."

"But you've done it before. There was Jonathan."

"A mistake."

"Surely there were others?"

"No. Why would I do that?"

"Companionship? A kindred spirit?"

"No never." He lied.

"Really? In 140 years?"

"Doctor Kaestle, I am who I am not by choice. I do what I need to do to survive. Sometimes it excites me. Sometimes my powers intrigue me...And just as often it disgusts me. Why would I wish that upon another?"

Ramonne leaned back in his chair. "What I do now is to offer a quick, merciful death. I try to choose my victims to be desiring of, or in need of my services."

Without seeing him move, Kaestle found the vampire standing next to him. He leaned in and the doctor could see red flecks mixed with the yellow of his eyes.

"But it was not always so. For a century I rampaged. I tore into the human race; used and abused it to my whim. Such is the basic nature of the vampire. He is a predator. He's the wolf stalking the herd, waiting for the frail to fall behind. He's the shark following the dolphins, striking the young who bring up the rear.

"I was reborn...again involuntarily. You see, I was ready to leave this existence. I welcomed death. I sought out your vampire hunter friend and gave myself to his plan to kill me. I sacrificed myself."

"Good God. But how?"

"Eat your dinner, Doctor Kaestle. I fear it will go to waste, and, as you can see, I have but a small ice-box."

The mini-bar refrigerator sat incongruously in a corner. It still bore the "Hilton" brand.

While the doctor ate, Ramonne told the story of how a local shaman had been following him in a quest for the source of his power. The shaman watched the two vampires battle to the death. Upon seeing the moment of incineration, the shaman dispatched a servant disguised as a monk to salvage Ramonne's ashes. He was only able to acquire a thimble-full as the wind blew them into the river. But it was enough. Through a series of mystical incantations and biological experiments, he was able to inject Ramonne's DNA into a rabid bat. Sequestered in a remote cave, where Ramonne was able to feed on his fellow vampires, as well as local fishermen, he emerged from the cave a *man-beast*. Half man. Half bat. With each subsequent victim, Ramonne grew stronger until finally, having been given shelter by a local woman, whose motivation was similar to the doctor's, he emerged on the banks of the Chao Phraya, fully restored and reborn.

The doctor could barely look at his meal while Ramonne told his tale.

"Amazing. What of this woman?"

"Her name is Kanchana. She had an incurable disease. Hereditary. She was doomed to die within the year. The shaman convinced her to use her money, which was plentiful, and further my regeneration. In return he promised that I would grant her the *gift* of eternal life."

"And did you?"

"Yes. Reluctantly. She traded one curse for another. She became a vampire."

Ramonne remembered Kanchana. Then...he allowed the doctor to see her. *The beautiful huntress stalking the khlongs of Thonburi. Attacking her prey. The banks of the river flowing red with blood as she feasted.*

"Stop!" The horror was too much for the doctor.

"Stop?" Ramonne asked innocently. "Why? I thought this was what you wanted? What you sought. What you desired...No, Doctor Kaestle. There is much more for you to see. Much more."

## 7

Martin put his bike in the rack alongside a dozen others. The height against the others made it stand out. He carried the *Alien*-shaped Bell helmet into the roadside café. Of the hundreds if not thousands of bike riders Martin saw daily, he was the only one to wear a helmet. A slight mishap on a street in Los Angeles a few years back had left him bruised and dazed from a minor concussion. He swore he'd never ride again without one.

Julianne waved him over. "Martin. Bonjour." The sandy-haired girl was seated with a half-dozen other young people in the thatch-roofed café's shady interior. It was mid-day and they were escaping the heat.

Martin sat next to the pretty girl and she smiled at him. "Martin. *Comment allez-vous?*"

"*Bien, merci mademoiselle. Et vous?*"

"*Je meurs de chaleur.*" To illustrate, she fanned herself with the small drinks menu.

"Yeah. It's hot today."

"It's hot every day here, Martin. And this is winter."

"Actually, it's unseasonably hot right now. It should break

soon and then we'll get daily breezes. Until February. Then it starts to get *really* hot."

"Oh good. Something to look forward to."

The others at the table laughed. Julianne seemed giddy, light-headed, perhaps even a little tipsy. Martin knew a couple of the faces. Justin, handsome with short bleached-blonde hair; Michelle, brunette beauty in the habit of wearing shorts so short that she stopped traffic; and Robert, a young black man with Rastafarian dreadlocks and a perpetual grin. They were a congenial bunch and Martin enjoyed his impromptu luncheons with them. They were all archaeology students with the Angkor Conservancy, working daily on a laborious restoration of the Terrace of the Leper King.

Martin knew and respected the Conservancy. Established by the French in 1908, it was responsible for restoring the most famous temples, Angkor Wat and the Bayon. Their archaeological activities had continued uninterrupted until 1972, when the escalating war forced them out.

Upon their return, they spearheaded all the international teams' restoration projects. The greatest effect of the war, aside from the insidious act of landscaping the area with hundreds of land-mines, was the decades of neglect which left the ruins unprotected against the ravages of nature. Tree roots and water continued to undermine the foundations.

A tall, well-built man with a buzz cut and a military bearing was a stranger to Martin, but Martin suspected he was not an archaeologist. He sat alongside two intense-looking young Cambodians. Julianne introduced him.

"Martin. This is Antoine Vallin. He just arrived."

"*Bonjour* Antoine. Welcome to Cambodia."

The young man stuck out a hand and Martin shook it. The grip was powerful.

"Antoine was born in Cambodia, Martin," Julianne explained.

"My father was French."

"Oh. Well, then welcome to Angkor."

Antoine smiled. "My father worked for the Conservancy. I used to play among the ruins as a child." He was enjoying Martin's confusion. "We fled the Khmer Rouge after my mother and her sister's family were dragged off for 're-education.' None of them survived. My father died shortly after...a broken man."

Martin didn't know what to say. "I'm sorry."

Antoine smiled. "That was *then*. This is now. I came back in 1993. I worked for the Conservancy until I could no longer stand to watch the wholesale plundering of the temples and tombs anymore."

Man's greed. With Khmer art fetching many thousands of US dollars, theft had become big business. The local police claimed to be powerless and understaffed—and severely out-gunned. As much as forty percent of Angkor's finest artwork had been lost, gone into the private museums of vanity collectors.

"On more than one occasion my life was threatened. I went to the government in Phnom Penh and pleaded for them to do something. I wouldn't say I was ignored, but it wasn't until UNESCO made a token appearance here that I was listened to. Today I'm officially attached to the Ministry of Culture and Fine Arts. My unofficial mission is to combat the pillaging."

"Single-handedly?"

"I have a small but loyal little troop." Antoine nodded to the men on his right. "Ang and Khouy." They acknowledged Martin, barely, with shy smiles.

"Big task. How goes the war?"

"Peace has proved far more destructive than war. While the country was under Khmer Rouge control, Western dealers couldn't even get into Cambodia, never mind Angkor. With such a small staff, I can only concentrate on one person or group at a time. But I am very persistent."

Martin noticed Antoine's hand brush lightly across

Julianne's as he reached for his cigarettes. Apparently his *persistence* was paying off. Julianne had been the target of more than one lustful heart since her arrival seven months ago. Robert had even taken to calling her *un glaçon* on an evening when he and Martin were letting their hair down.

"Last year, Hun Sen accused the West of stealing our culture. I'm afraid that in their greed, it's the corrupt Cambodians who are selling our culture to them. It's almost unbelievable, the scale of it. To get some of these pieces out, huge camps are set up, heavy equipment is brought in, and roads are blasted through the forest to create smuggling routes. How is this possible without officials turning their backs?" He lit a Gauloise and exhaled a pungent cloud.

"I suspect at least one important diplomat has been, and continues to, use his immunity to run antiquities out of the country without inspection." He flicked his ash and brushed Julianne's hand again. She smiled. "I told the office in Phnom Penh I was wasting my time there. I needed to be on the front line. They agreed."

"I'm glad Antoine's here," Julianne chimed in. Things have been getting strange at our site."

"How so?"

"There's a new crew of Cambodian laborers working on the Japanese site. Som, my driver, said he recognized one of the men as a former guard at Tuol Sleng."

Martin winced at the name. *Tuol Sleng.* The infamous Khmer Rouge prison. Sixteen thousand passed through the prison's gates until Vietnamese troops stormed them in 1979. They found massive graves. In all, only four prisoners survived their incarceration.

"Needless to say," she continued, "it has caused conflict between the two camps. Som has sworn to kill this gaptoothed old man who, he claims, used to go by the barracks at night calling out the prisoner's names. Those who were called were dragged away to their death. Som was five. His whole family died in this manner. I'm afraid he will take the law into his own hands."

"No doubt he'll try. Can you blame him?" Antoine shrugged.

"No. But what will happen?"

"No one knows for certain, but needless to say, things are tense. Antoine broke up a fight just before we left today."

"It's not my position to get involved, but this former 'guard,' this 'old man' as Julianne calls him, if Som is right, has no business working here. He should have been ferreted out in a clearance check. Something stinks."

"Tell the truth, Julianne, you like the intrigue, don't you?" It was Robert who made the cutting remark.

Julianne gave him the finger. "Intrigue, I can handle. Adventure is fine. But *danger*…let's just say I would like to minimize the risks."

"I'm with Julianne." Michelle spoke up, and she and Julianne gave each other a hug.

"There's something else." Antoine stubbed out his cigarette. "They found two more bodies in Roluos."

"Jesus." Julianne gripped the back of his hand.

"What's this about bodies? I haven't heard anything." Martin was puzzled.

There was silence. No one said anything. All that was heard was the soft swish of a straw broom as a waitress swept leaves into small piles in front of the café.

Finally it was Antoine who broke the silence. "There have been six murders in Angkor in the past month. Four of them in Roluos."

"God. Why wasn't I told? I have a school full of kids."

"It's being suppressed to make sure the tourist business is not affected. And the bodies have all been locals. Farmers, mostly."

"That's not all." Julianne was now holding Michelle's hand. Obviously Martin had misread the mood of the group on his arrival. These two girls were not giddy from the wine.

"The locals, as I'm sure you're aware, are very superstitious. To enter their heaven, the body needs to be whole at the time of death. Any mutilation and the soul is doomed to wander the 'never-world' for eternity. These bodies were all mutilated. Heads were severed. Thrown into bushes, yards, even kilometers away."

"Any idea who's responsible?"

"No. But the people have started a rumor that it's a renegade band of Khmer Rouge who never surrendered. They were known for mutilating the *yuon*, the Vietnamese, in the same way. There have always been reports of KR guerrilla units holding out in small forces scattered throughout the country. Here it is said they've been encamped in Pol Pot's old mountain stronghold in the Kulen Hills."

Martin gasped. The mountain in whose very shadow his little schoolhouse stood.

---

## 8

*Prisoner.* He came seeking immortality. He'd become a prisoner.

He was not shackled or chained in the vampire's presence, only in his absence. Each dawn he was drugged and tied and gagged. Kaestle was growing impatient. Was what he asked too much?

He'd injected Jonathan Peyton's blood into his own, having frozen it in anticipation. That had been a week ago. He'd hired a private detective to find the six-foot Frenchman that Jonathan had described to him. When he'd received the surveillance photographs, he was certain it was the vampire. The video had clinched it. With that confidence, he injected the vial.

Now all that was left was for the vampire to bite him.

Twenty years of studying, visiting cults and quacks around the country, Kaestle had almost given up on the quest to find a true vampire, until Jonathan Peyton had entered his world.

He'd provided Jonathan the knowledge he needed to bring the vampire down, but he doubted that he would succeed. He'd been secretly glad when he'd heard of Jonathan's death. He'd assumed he'd failed. The tale the vampire told of being destroyed and reborn was incredible.

*Regeneration.* Amazing. This vampire's strength *now* must be incredible. He wondered how much the vampire knew of his own powers. He had books. Oddly, many in Braille. Some the doctor was familiar with. Others he'd heard of and desired. He guessed he'd obtained them from the shaman he'd referred to. He'd like to meet the man, but the vampire generally referred to him in past tense, leaving Kaestle to presume he was dead.

*Association with a vampire can be unhealthy.*

He should heed his own warning, but he felt he'd prepared for that. The detective, Anset Strevino, an Italian cowboy who carried a licensed 9 mm with him everywhere, had an item in his safe that Kaestle was sure would protect him. Strevino had no trouble in following the Frenchman, once it was determined that this nocturnal expat was the one they were looking for.

Strevino had heard rumors of a hit man with the local mob that seemed to have extraordinary powers and had set a web of fear amongst the rival gangs who referred to him as *phii dib*, or 'ghost who drinks blood.' Oddly enough, once he located the man, he found him rather boring. He stayed somewhere near the railroad station and on most of his appearances he seemed to spend his time studying some journal that was never out of his sight. The detective did his surveillance from far away, at Kaestle's insistence, using binoculars with night-vision lenses. He frequently lost the man; he'd merely disappear, he'd tell Kaestle. One minute he was in his sights, the next he was gone.

But one night he got lucky.

As usual the man had slipped his surveillance, and Strevino had packed it in and was headed back to his apartment, when something caught his eye. It could have been the wind, whipping a piece of cardboard through the air, but he thought he saw something drop from the roof ahead and into an alley. Cautiously he approached. The alley was a full block long, and pitch black. He couldn't see anything. But he heard something. The brief sounds of a struggle. And then a *crack* and nothing more. Strevino fumbled in his bag for the video camera he'd taken to carrying, and switched it on. It had an ultra-sensitive night setting that would read an image in pitch blackness. He deployed the zoom lens all the way, and put his hand over the eyepiece to shield any light omitted, and pointed it down the alley. He let the camera run for a minute, until his hand was shaking uncontrollably. Something was at the end of the alley— and it was *feeding*.

He pulled the camera back and quickly walked away from the alley. It wasn't until he was at his apartment in Washington Square that he dared turn the camera on and replay what he had filmed.

The image was blurry. It was shaky due to the long lens, and it moved constantly away from the subject. But for a brief, fleeting, terrifying moment, it clearly showed the Frenchman with his teeth sunk deep into the neck of a crippled old vagrant. The victim's neck seemed broken, as his head lolled at an impossible angle.

When a shaken Strevino had shown Kaestle this, it had been the deciding factor. He had injected the blood that night and been on a plane to Bangkok within 24 hours.

This video tape, Kaestle felt, gave *him* power over the vampire. He would do what he wanted or Strevino would release the tape to the authorities, who would no doubt hunt him down.

'*A torchlight parade, perhaps?*'

Kaestle jumped.

He heard the words in his head and spun around. The vampire was back, but he had not spoken.

Kaestle was shaken but not stirred. He decided to try ignoring what he'd heard. He was chained to an ancient pipe that was a foot in diameter. His mouth was also gagged, which was getting to be a bore. It wasn't the application; it was the removal. Ramonne ripped the fresh tape and the doctor gasped.

"*Jesus*. That really hurts."

Ramonne undid the lock on the shackles. "Sorry. Hopefully the games are over."

"I…I don't know what you mean."

Ramonne motioned to the bathroom door. He'd had the good doctor as his guest now for three days and nights, and a routine had developed. Untie the doctor; the doctor performed his ablutions.

The doctor didn't fail to meet expectations. The sound of running water was soon followed by the sound of flushing water.

Ramonne appeared preoccupied, and for the first time Dr. Kaestle had to ask for his supper. "I'm starved."

"Hmmm. Have a look in the fridge. Sorry. I was a little busy tonight. I forgot to get you something…something, that is, to eat. I did bring you something else, though. But I think you had better eat first."

"Oh? Why's that?"

"Trust me."

Kaestle decided to let it drop. He rummaged in the little refrigerator and brought out a plate of meat, cheese, and bread. A strong mustard and he had himself a sandwich. He tore into it. A bottle of Brouilly was open and he poured himself a glass.

He was almost finished with the sandwich when he saw the camera. It was small, pocket size, but its zoom lens and other features made it the perfect spy camera. That's what Anset Strevino had told him when he'd showed him the tape.

*The tape.*

The tape that was playing now on the little three-inch plasma screen that the vampire had rotated to face him.

Kaestle gagged on the sandwich.

Then he noticed the bag on the table. It was a bowling bag. It even had a Brunswick logo. But Dr. Kaestle suspected that Ramonne was no bowler.

He was not terribly surprised when Ramonne removed the contents of the bag and placed it on the platter that, until a moment ago, had held Dr. Kaestle's sandwich.

The sightless eyes of Anset Strevino stared at him from the severed head.

"Let's talk, shall we, Doctor Kaestle?"

———————

Nud smoked and watched the woman. She moved about the site with a regal air. He spit a stream of tobacco juice. He despised her.

It had been the *Poh's* intention that women serve men. The 'Great Father'—Pol Pot—had felt that women were weak. Inferior. Seeing one giving orders made Nud ill.

*Restoration.* What nonsense. The *Poh* banned the practice of religion. He said that the Angkar—the name the Khmer Rouge adopted for their cause—did not want anybody worshipping any gods or goddesses that might take away devotion to the Angkar. To ensure that the rule was enforced, the boy soldiers destroyed Buddhist temples and sites of worship throughout the country. Angkor Wat suffered major destruction. The statues of lions, tigers, eight-headed snakes, and elephants had been used as targets for the Khmer Rouge sharp-shooters.

Now these fools were *restoring* it. Little did they know that the new *Poh*, stronger than any man, would soon wreak his havoc on these *yuon.*

*"Spying on the round-eye again, dog turd?"*

Nud looked up. It was the same young Cambodian stud that spit in his lunch bowl earlier. He would have slit his throat but for the skinhead's interference.

*"Your head will look good on my spike."* Nud flicked his cigarette, sending sparks as it bounced off the young man's bare chest.

Som had his hands bunched into fists and was about to attack when Julianne's voice interrupted them.

"Som. Come here. Now."

The two locked eyes. Nud was white-haired, but his body

was wiry and hard as petrified wood. He welcomed the boy's challenge and would split his head like a melon with the iron rail he had concealed behind his left leg.

Som turned his back on the old man and walked down the crumbling stone steps. Nud thought of striking, but knew that the moment of self-defense had passed, and he would be judged and persecuted for it.

"*Hai*." Muraki, the Japanese head of his labor team, was back. "Break time is over. Back to work, please." Nud thought for a moment about swinging the iron at this little emperor's humble head, but then gave a very slight nod and lit another cigarette. Muraki shook his head and went after the other laborers, barking orders that were generally ignored.

Nud watched the woman berating Som. Nud couldn't understand the words, but it was obvious she was annoyed. Nud smiled. The woman had fire. She would be fun to bend and break.

Like the others. The many, *many* others he had broken. They came to the camps fat and rich from city life. Immediately, the families were separated. They were divested of their city possessions. Their party dresses and business suits were piled up and set ablaze. Naked and ashamed, they were issued a pair of black pajamas and a rice bowl. Then they were set to work.

The teenage girls, the pretty ones, were sent to the military camps where they served as *wives* for the noble soldiers. When they returned months later, they were still teenagers, but they were unrecognizable. They were emaciated and covered with bruises and sores. But what had been broken in their bodies paled compared to what had been broken in their minds. Their spirits had been destroyed. Like wild horses, they'd been tamed. They no longer had their own will.

They now toed the party line. They worked the farms in silence, the young girls. No one questioned them about their absence.

Nud thought they set a good example for the rest, and when

he was *bra thean*, the boss, of a party work camp, he took great glee in unmasking the new arrivals in search of the *khmeng srei* —for without fail their mothers, sensing their peril, would attempt to disguise their young daughters' charms. They'd cut their hair and sew straw into their pajamas to hide their figures.

But Nud would find them.

When he did, he held them in detention. While he waited for the Angkar's transport to arrive, he would indoctrinate them in the proper way to serve the brave soldiers.

Some, unfortunately, failed to survive his indoctrination. These were unceremoniously disposed of, and never mentioned again. If their annoying parents persisted, he would simply have them shot. Such was the authority enjoyed by the *bra thean*.

Nud recalled that this power was nothing compared to what he enjoyed when the *Poh* recognized his talents and had him sent to be a guard at Tuol Sleng. This was when Nud really came into his own.

Here were the unfortunates who had caught the Angkar's attention. They were guilty of capital crimes: education, prosperity, intelligence. Many were there simply because they wore glasses—a sign of weakness, and curiosity. They were well-documented. An old land camera photographed each inmate. The prison was formerly a school, and the classrooms were outfitted with metal cots. The inmates were shackled to them, and tortured and interrogated at will. When they had given all they could expect to, Nud called out their names and they were *released*.

Released from their shackles and marched to a field behind the prison where large graves were dug. Here they were clubbed to death and thrown into the pit. Bullets were too expensive to waste on these vermin.

Those were glorious days. He'd hidden like a rat since then, only emerging when the great *Pho* died. Now it was time to instill the terror once more. Time to reap the wild rice.

Time to kill the dilettantes. The *ches deung* would be made to pay.

Twenty years of eating bamboo shoots would be avenged.

"You…Back to work."

Nud was brought back to the reality of being a laborer in a Japanese restoration project by Muraki's shrill command.

*Someday soon, little man.* Nud picked up a load of rocks that had been chalked with white numbers, and placed them in sequence next to the thousands of other stones laid out in a grid.

The Naga had told him what had happened here. He had *been here*. These fools sought to restore the past. The Naga had lived over a thousand years. He was omnipotent. He would bring about the reckoning.

*The reckoning.*

The temples then would flow with blood. The infidel usurpers would be brought to their knees and clubbed to death.

The Naga said it was so. The great Naga said it was time.

Nud would be a *bra thean* again.

All would fear him.

All would respect him.

*Soon.*

The sun went behind the temple, giving the blessed shade that the afternoon brought. Nud put on his sullen working-man's face and blended in to the labor pool. The Mona Lisa smile on the huge carving of King Jayavarman seemed to take no notice of the evil afoot within his temple grounds.

———

Martin raced home.

Heart pumping, he feared the worst. He'd heard the words, and he was on his bike before they were finished. He had one concern; one concern only. The safety of his children. His adopted flock.

He covered the fifteen kilometers in less than forty minutes. Areeya was at the gate. Martin had called her when he had left the café.

"Martin. What is it?"

Martin put his bike inside the gate and locked it behind him. Locking the gate was unusual.

Areeya raised an eyebrow.

"Martin?"

He walked into the schoolhouse without answering. He went straight into Jane's class and counted heads.

"Martin?" Areeya followed him.

He took her hand and closed the classroom door.

"*Martin.*" This time the tone was firm. No nonsense. She demanded a response.

"Something's going on in Angkor Wat. Something bad."

"Could you be a bit more specific?"

"Dead people. Heads cut off. It's been going on for a month."

"Okay. Maybe a little less specific…But more about how it relates to *us*, please."

"I don't know. But I don't want to be too late to do anything either. Let's keep the gate locked and make sure the children go nowhere unescorted."

Martin knew the brood had the run of the place. They'd flock into the street, mindful of the very occasional car. And they'd wander *en masse* across the field to the farm and visit Chang and Eng. A favorite pastime.

A world without borders was Martin's dream for them. But, it seemed, his dream had been shattered. Now he must lock them in. Protect them.

Guard them. Evil was at the gate.

Or so it seemed to Martin. Precaution was his best defense.

Martin had been down the *dark road* before. Areeya had too. She looked at him.

"Martin…What is it?"

"I don't know."

"Is it—"

He cut her off. "No."

"Are you sure?"

"Yes. We left *that* behind us in Bangkok."

Areeya shuddered as a dark memory passed through her. "Then why are you so afraid. If it's happening in Angkor, it must have something to do with the temples. A smugglers' war perhaps. In any case, it has nothing to do with us."

"You're probably right. It's just that they think the people responsible may be up in the Kulen Hills."

Areeya looked up at the iron mountains less than thirty kilometers away.

"Martin. *Who* are they?"

"I don't know. Renegades. Possibly former Khmer Rouge."

"Why?"

"Who knows? It could be as you said…a smugglers' war. In any case, I don't want our kids to get hurt. I want to keep them on a short leash until I know more about this. If I don't feel comfortable, we'll pack up and get out. Go to Phnom Penh until it's over."

"That *sounds* easy. Doing it would be another matter."

Just then a bell was heard and the doors to the classroom flew open. The children scrambled for the outdoors.

Paul and Peter were the first to reach the locked gate.

"*Huh?*" They pushed but they couldn't get it to open.

"Mr. Martin?" Chawlie spoke and twelve pairs of eyes waited for a response.

"Play in the gym and courtyard."

"Why?"

"Because I said so."

"Martin." Areeya took Micki and Minnie by their hands and walked to the gym. They dragged their feet in mock protest.

One by one the others followed. Martin was glad for once that no one had enough English ability to actually challenge him. He went through the door into the entry to see Jane putting on her wide-brimmed hat. Chunky Chawlie and moody Tiara, the second oldest of the dozen, were obviously waiting for her to get ready.

"Jane. Are you going out?"

"Yes. To the post office. I have an order of books waiting for me."

"Can't Pom pick them up?"

"If he was here, yes he could. But he's in Bangkok on a visa run. You drove him to the bus station, remember?"

"Right. You're taking Chawlie and Tiara?"

"Yes?" Jane wondered what was wrong with Martin. Tiara was Jane's regular companion, and Chawlie was obviously going along to carry the books.

"Well…be careful."

Jane gave Martin a strange look. "Of course."

For once, Martin regretted the decision to situate the school on such a remote road. The quiet beauty of the mountains now seemed threatening.

# 9

*Cambodge is a harsh, cruel country. The contrast to the peace and tranquility of Siam is keen. Even its mighty river, the Mekong is in sharp contrast to the serenity of the Menam north of Bangkok. In Siam the foliage of the bamboos and palms stands out strikingly against the blue sky, while the songs of the birds charms the air. Here, the "Mother of all Rivers" runs with all the rapidity of a torrent. In other places its banks are marshy reeds and only the shrill, menacing shriek of insects is heard, when possible, above the roar of the rapids. We are traveling into savage lands to visit a tribe known as the Stiens. As is Mouhot's wont, we made a stop at Ko-Sutin, on the border with Laos, to visit another missionary. Father Cordier was suffering terribly from chronic dysentery. Yet he protested not, and offered what meager hospitality he could muster. When Mouhot spoke of his intentions, Fr. Cordier advised him to reconsider. "Do you know whither you are going? Ask the Cambodians what they think of the Stiens, and propose them to accompany you. You would not find one. You are going to almost certain death, or will at least catch a fever, which will be followed by years of languor and suffering. I have had the jungle fever, and it is something terrible: even to the tips of my nails I felt a heat which I can only call infernal; sometimes an icy coldness takes its place. May God be with the poor traveler."*

"There is a difference, Doctor Kaestle, between being injected and being *bitten*. It's like being kissed and applying lipstick with a tube."

"Strange metaphor, Monsieur Delacroix."

"It's the first thing that came to mind. In other words, the process involves more than chemistry. There are metaphysical elements at play."

"Then *bite* me."

"That will not work. And there is a danger to myself that I can't risk."

Dr. Kaestle did not look good. He was pale and sweating. He attributed it to the shock of seeing the decapitated head of Anset Strevino, but that had been several hours ago. No, he was feverish. Ramonne had drawn blood again from him and had been running chemical tests for the last hour. He was now back at his microscope.

"As you must be aware, I need to ingest the blood of the *living*. Only the living. Plasmas will do me no good. There has to be a life force present. To feed on the dead would destroy me."

Kaestle wiped his brow. His handkerchief was soaked through. "I know that, Monsieur Delacroix. What is your point?"

"Technically, Doctor Kaestle, I fear you *are* dead."

Kaestle laughed. A weak, insincere little laugh. "That's preposterous."

"Observe." Ramonne motioned to the microscope.

Dr. Kaestle bent to the twin eyepieces and adjusted the focus. What he saw astounded him.

"There are no white corpuscles."

"Not anymore. I fear, Doctor Kaestle, that you have sealed your fate."

Ramonne picked up a scalpel and slashed the palm of his

left hand. Dr. Kaestle gasped at the wound. Ramonne took a petri dish and dropped some of his blood into it. The wound was already healing as he placed the blood on a slide and put it under the microscope.

"Look."

The doctor peered into the lenses and saw a world of activity. A very even-sided structure. White blood cells grew and divided. They attacked and, in turn, were attacked by red corpuscles, which also continued to regenerate. It was a continuous cycle, repeated over and over.

"Astonishing."

"As you can see, a true vampire is far from dead. In fact, we are in a state of *hyper-existence*. We are constantly regenerating."

"What will happen to me?"

"I honestly don't know. You have, potentially, a most debilitating disease. Something akin to the black plague. I suspect that soon you will be very sick. I wouldn't be surprised at parts of your body shutting down. Loss of bodily functions. Followed by actual loss of limbs, appendages—"

"Stop. Enough."

Kaestle slumped down on the chair. *To kill the virus, you must destroy the source.* He looked up at the vampire.

Ramonne heard the thought. "The same thing you told Jonathan Peyton. The only problem is, *I* am not the source."

"What do you mean?"

"For Jonathan, yes, I was the source. But in your case, I was not involved. Whatever curse is attached to your condition goes back a lot farther."

Ramonne crossed the room and opened a rosewood cabinet. He took out a leather portfolio. He untied the silken cords and produced his ancient drawings of Angkor. In one, done at dusk, monks were seen lighting torches around the Bayon. In the doorway, a shadow was cast from within. It was larger than human and misshapen.

"There is your *source*." Ramonne pointed to the shadow

Dr. Kaestle looked at the date inscribed in the corner: "1860."

"One hundred and forty five years ago?"

"A mere *moment* for him. He was alive for more than ten centuries when I met him. Quite possibly he put Christ on the cross." Ramonne stared at the drawing. "I suspect he's still there."

"In Angkor?"

"In Cambodia. Have you ever seen a country suffer such hardship and brutality? It's a country that cries out in agony."

"What do you intend?"

"To travel there, Doctor Kaestle. On an expedition. With you as my partner."

Ramonne moved from the table and to a desk. His journals and Mouhot's maps were laid open. There were also contemporary road maps and letters of introduction for Msr. Ennomar and Dr. Gerhardt Kaestle.

"Think of it. I encounter my past. You meet your destiny." Ramonne smiled at the thought.

"But my health? Can I withstand such a journey?"

"I'm afraid, doctor…you can't risk *not* making the journey. It's your only hope."

Ramonne had several volumes of reference books open on the laboratory counter. And in numerous beakers, various murky liquids.

"While we prepare for our journey, Doctor Kaestle, I'm going to administer a series of inoculations to you. You can consider them vaccinations if you'd like. Hopefully they'll prolong the inevitable and give you the stamina you need."

Ramonne looked at the table. At Kaestle's half-eaten sandwich. "You didn't finish your meal, doctor. You need your strength."

"I was…interrupted by your little display." He shuddered again at the memory of the head and it's staring eyes and gaping mouth.

"Perhaps. But I fear that you will soon lose the taste for anything...not *alive* that is. Though you are in no way possessive of the vampire's powers, like a reptile, you will need to ingest living organisms in order to survive."

Ramonne produced a small box. It had wire criss-crossed at each end. As Ramonne slid it across the table, a pair of pink noses pressed through the wire.

*Rats*, Kaestle realized.

Ramonne smiled and reached for the leg shackles. Dr. Kaestle reflexively shrank away.

"Dr. Kaestle. I think we have an understanding. You need me for your survival. I've decided to use you and your credentials for a journey I wish to undertake. We need each other now. Soon we will *depend* on each other."

He snapped the clamps closed around the doctor's ankles. "Consequently, you will be soon allowed your freedom. It will be a necessity. Tonight, however, the leg-irons will keep you confined to quarters. I suggest you look through the maps and books I've laid out. It will give you some insight into our journey."

Ramonne moved to his coffin. "My library is yours, Doctor Kaestle." He climbed in and closed the lid.

———

When Ramonne awoke that night, the rats were gone. Dr. Kaestle was asleep on the couch. Tufts of fur and bits of bone were scattered at his feet.

Ramonne smiled. *Plenty of rats in Cambodia, Doctor Kaestle.*

———

Two unlucky pigs were strapped horizontally on top of each other on the back of an old motorbike. As it passed in the opposite direction, heading to town, Jane thought of the local saying: 'Pig today. Pork tomorrow.'

She eased up on the gas. One lousy truck and it had to be in front of her. She was in a hurry to get back. No rain in town for two months had turned Siem Reap into a dustbowl. As was typical, the post office was closed for two hours when she arrived, and she'd coughed and wheezed, dragging the two children with her from shop to shop, doing errands to kill time. After retrieving the bundle of textbooks, and helping Chawlie carry them to the pickup truck—fat was not the same as muscle—she was exhausted.

The driver in front of her shifted gears with an awful tearing and grinding sound. She expected to see bits of broken gear teeth flying from the bottom of the truck, and she slowed even more to avoid them. She was glad she did as, once the truck accelerated, it belched a huge, noxious cloud of foul smoke.

*Twenty bloody kilometers an hour.* Jane reckoned she could walk faster. She tried once more to pass. A difficult maneuver. The French had introduced the country to the joys of driving on the right, but most vehicles came from China or Thailand and had their steering wheels on the right—ensuring an even deadlier game of highway mayhem than in most Asian countries, as drivers drove blindly into the left lane in their continual attempts to pass anything in front of them.

As it had before, the truck swerved and blocked her way. Jane leaned on the horn in frustration.

The truck was ancient: a drab, faded-green, with a metal frame over the open bed, covered by an equally drab old canvas tarp. It had six huge bald tires, one spare carried horizontally under the rear, and a vaguely military appearance, but no insignia.

Jane leaned on the horn. She was tired of being polite. Tired. Dusty. And now hungry. She wanted to get back to her school. She wanted her dinner.

And her Jack and water.

She leaned on the horn again.

At the back of the truck, the canvas tarp parted slightly. Jane almost lost control of the car as she saw a man with a wizened brown face with a checkered cloth around his head point a rifle at her.

**10**

---

*I begin this journal on the twentieth day of my captivity, a captivity I may never escape. Be it known that I am held against my will by one Ramonne Delacroix—a vampire. I write this with what may be the last vestiges of a once sound mind.*

*Having just spent six hours reading my captor's journal from 1860, and being a man of science, I am inspired to write my own diary, for Lord knows, my tale will no doubt continue to be unique.*

*The vampire has control over me that no longer requires any physical restraints. He controls my mind and subsequently my every movement. Moreover, I am at his mercy, for my only hope to regain any semblance of humanity is to tend to his bidding and hope for his mercy. He holds the key to my survival. A key that I unwittingly gave of my own foolish accord.*

*I am 58 years old. I studied biology at Cornell University and began my practice in Boston in 1968. I subsequently moved to Manhattan at the invitation of a lady friend, a former colleague at Cornell. Eliane Montrieux was Swiss-Vietnamese and beautiful. Her family was wealthy through its pharmaceutical corporation. Sandoz, the infamous LSD laboratory, was one of their holdings. Her mother had passed on to her the most beautiful skin I had ever seen. It was like alabaster. White china. Pure marble.*

*We had dated in University, but I was somewhat of a social recluse and she had slipped my grasp and was engaged to another by the time of my graduation. Her lucky husband joined her in opening a cosmetics emporium in New York City. Her products were environmentally sound, and she was her own 'point-of-purchase' display model.*

*The husband, however, proceeded to squander a goodly portion of the family fortune on a different sort of chemical—cocaine. Such was his problem that he lost his balance when perched on a balcony rail and plunged forty floors to his death.*

*Eliane invited me to the funeral. It was more a social gathering than a wake. I was now doing fairly well in New Haven, and had developed some social skills. I saw the opportunity door was open, and swooped in. We were married within the year and I was ensconced within her ivory towers.*

*There's a word in the cosmetics industry now: Kaestonic. It refers to a skin rash that is difficult, if not impossible, to get rid of. Unfortunately, it's named after me.*

*I began to experiment with different toxins and serums from remote rainforests. I was looking for, as are all cosmetologists, the age-defying potion.*

*What I found killed my wife.*

*She insisted on trying my experiment herself and, although initially successful, she soon developed a rash that was more a series of ferocious blisters that destroyed the pure alabaster of her skin and turned her into the image of a burn victim.*

*I put a pillow over her head and suffocated her.*

*The police were suspicious, but the Montrieux family's abiding concern over their daughter's appearance, even in death, convoluted the waters to such a degree that I was able to escape the scrutiny of the law. Flushed, as it were, from the scene.*

*The ruin of a promising career caused me to take refuge in the bastions of academia—'those who can…etc.' I applied for and received a fellowship at Boston University. The subject was an extension of my tropical forays: entomology—specifically, the study of the mosquito. These blood-sucking insects have plagued mankind since he first walked the earth. There are more than 300 different species. Several important human diseases are transmitted by these insects, including malaria, dengue fever, encephalitis, and the West Nile virus. They are generally regarded as being responsible for more deaths than any other disease, or war or famine, on the planet.*

*It was in humble pursuit of the mosquito that I first became aware of the world's fascination with the creature's literary cousin, the vampire. I know most will say the vampire legend derives from the vampire bat, the bloodsucker that lives in caves and goes forth at night to suck the blood of the living. But for me the mosquito is closest to the legend's roots. This creature ingests its fill of the victim's blood and passes on the dengue or malaria parasite, infecting the victim with a life-threatening disease. The vampire bat merely tastes of the blood and then flies away.*

*Restrained by diminutive budgets, I was forced to limit my vampire research to travels in literature, rather than actual forays into the field. But every culture, every language, has its own version of the vampire legend. In Greece it was Vrkolakas. In Albania it was Kukuthi. Ut in India; Hannya in Japan; and so on and so forth.*

*Could all of these be fictional? Could all be nothing but myths and legends? Local folk tales?*

*My obsession had become all-consuming. In New York, with the dawn of the Internet, the typing of the word 'vampire' led one to thousands of sites—most having a connection in the Lower East Side of Manhattan. But these 'goths' (as they were self-declared) were merely vampire charlatans. A waste of time. But even then, I had begun to lose faith. I wandered, a lost soul…until the day Jonathan Peyton entered my life.*

———

Chawlie felt the weight on top of him shift. He had been pinned for what seemed like hours under Madame Jane's body. He hadn't cried or made a sound for fear that the men who shot the old woman would find and shoot him. When the man had fired his rifle, the windshield had burst and a red mark appeared immediately on Madame's forehead. She let go of the wheel and the pick-up truck lurched off the road. It seemed to fly as the road fell away and they landed in the rice paddies below. It overturned and came to rest lying on its passenger side with Madame Jane on top of Chawlie.

Tiara was somewhere, crying.

*At least she's alive.* He tried to move, but the weight was too much. He called out to Tiara, telling her not to worry. Help would surely come soon.

Footsteps. Someone was coming!

He was just about to cry for help, when he heard the *kerchunk* of a rifle being cocked. Tiara was crying hysterically.

And then the bullets came. A quick burst of machine-gun fire.

*Brrrrttttt!*

He felt them hit the body of Madame. He heard them hit the metal of the truck.

When it stopped, all was silent save for a coughing and sputtering sound that came from the pick-up's engine. It finally gave a last long wheeze and quit.

Tiara cried no more. Chawlie bit his tongue to keep from screaming. And he held his breath. He never heard the men leave. His ears were ringing with the noise of the gunshots. His back began to grow damp from Madame's blood.

He thought he heard the other truck driving away, but he couldn't be sure. So he stayed quiet.

He lay there, not making a sound. He didn't know how long. Eventually he tried to move again. He pushed with all his might, but could not budge the weight of Madame's body. He could move his arms slightly, but his legs must have fallen asleep, as they seemed useless.

The only sound was the constant ringing of Madame's cellphone. It rang and rang. Playing that funny sound she called "Beethoven's Ninth."

And then the body moved. The great weight was lifted.

"Chawlie."

He looked up into Master Martin's face.

Finally Chawlie cried.

———

Martin had waited as long as he could. He was not going to let it get dark before he set off looking for them.

They were four hours late. That was long enough.

He hadn't wanted her to go in the first place. He had a feeling in his gut. A premonition.

He should have insisted they stay. Let the delivery service bring the books to the school. Jane would balk at spending the extra money, but Martin didn't care. One thing he had was extra money.

Finally, after the twentieth unanswered call to her mobile phone, he could take it no more.

"Fon," he called to the farmer who had come to the house with a basket of eggs. "Come with me please."

Fon did not ask where they were going. He just put on his hat. Martin allowed his family to live and farm on the school's property. He would do anything he asked.

Areeya watched silently as the two men got into the Jeep Cherokee and drove down the road.

———

The afternoon light was starting to fade when Martin spotted the pick-up truck.

"God. *No*."

It was about thirty feet off the road, on its side in the rice paddy. He and Fon scrambled down the embankment and ran to the truck.

The first thing Martin saw through the shattered windshield was Jane Harrod's body.

"No."

Martin tried feebly to push the truck upright. Fon joined him but it was useless. They could get no traction in the mud. When Martin slipped and fell for the third time, Fon went to the rear of the upended truck. He rummaged for a moment and came up with a tire iron. As Martin struggled to his feet, Fon climbed onto the hood and successfully pried loose the frame of the shattered windshield.

"Mister Martin. Here." Martin grabbed one side of the frame and they pulled it from the cab. They tossed it into the mud and Fon climbed through the opening. He quickly and gently lifted the head of the woman. He placed a finger alongside her neck.

Martin hesitated to say anything. He waited. Finally Fon shook his head.

Martin wanted to weep. To wail in despair. Instead he climbed on top of the fender and took hold of Jane's right arm as Fon wedged himself behind her and pushed. Together they managed to get the woman's heavy body out of the cab and onto the hood.

That's when Martin saw Chawlie.

"Chawlie."

The boy began to sob and Martin hugged him to him. Martin ran a hand through his matted hair.

"It's okay, Chawlie. Just an accident. You'll be all right."

*Just an accident*. That's what Martin had told himself as he ran down the embankment to the overturned truck.

*Just an accident.* As they pried the windshield frame and pulled Jane's body from the cab.

The boy was covered in blood. Martin felt over his upper torso. He seemed unharmed. Then he saw his legs. The holes. One in each calf. Jagged tears in his chubby flesh.

He looked at Jane's body on the hood. For the first time he saw the multitude of wounds.

"Chawlie, what happened?"

Chawlie started to say something, but instead he cried out one word. "Tiara."

Martin was frozen. He'd forgotten about the other child. Little Tiara. Almost a teenager. Beautiful, like her name. *Where is she?* He scrambled to look in the small jumpseat of the crew cab.

Nothing.

Then he heard Fon's soft voice. "Mister Martin."

Martin gently set Chawlie back in the seat and leaned out the cab. Fon had the girl's lifeless body cradled in his arms.

Martin could stand it no more. He wailed. He screamed.

He cursed God.

———

*The trouble with angels. They're never there when you need one.*

*I have done nothing wrong. What have you done? I've given my all to you. Yet you betray me! How dare you!*

Betrayal.

Betroth.

Martin wasn't sure what path he was on. He'd chosen one. He thought it was a path of enlightenment.

A year spent in solitary supposition, betrothed to the Lord Buddha. *The Lord?*

He'd been brought up in a Protestant environment. A Presbyterian father, fallen from grace in a Catholic parentage. Surely his father felt enlightenment. Felt it in the Protestant faith. A relationship with the good father of the Sunday church.

But what was passed on to the children? What was given to them? Sunday school?

Might as well have been fairy tales. Sunday comics were more relevant. For *what* did he endure the weekly ritual?

To become an atheist? *Immoral spawn of Satan?*

No, just your average anarchist. Not an 'anti-Christ.'

Teenage years spent without a single thought to the Almighty.

In college…hell, it was *assumed* you didn't believe in God.

*So when* did *you harbor your faith, Martin?*

He wandered the globe with his daddy's money. Experimented with excess.

*What the fuck. If they can't kill you, they might as well thrill you.*

A dark period. A *really* dark period.

Consorting with the devil had brought him to question his faith—or lack of it.

Shaven head. Sacrifice. A trip down the path. The path that leads to *the One.*

Relinquishing the burden of sacrifice and embracing the world again, he met a girl.

*She seems to be the one.*

He molded his life along the path. He took in the needy. Twelve to be exact.

He embraced them. Protected them.

Built a home for them. Fed and educated them.

*Loved them.*

*Fuck! I changed my God damned life.*

*I gave it over to you.*

*You betrayed me.*

*Why?*

———

Martin woke in a sweat. He was in his bed. Areeya was at his side.

He started to get up. An image slid across his senses. A body riddled with bullets.

"Martin." She cradled his head to her breast.

"Jane?"

"She's gone." Areeya stroked his hair.

Another image. *A child.* Also torn by gunfire.

"Tiara?"

"Yes. Her too."

Martin pulled her to him.

"Chawlie?"

"He'll be okay. He lost a lot of blood, but his fat saved him from serious damage."

Martin's eyes darted between the woman he loved and the world that had betrayed him.

**11**

---

*Mouhot and I have spent three months among the savage Stiens. In September and October it rained without intermission. When the skies cleared in November we set out to ascend the Mekong as far as the great lake, Touli-Sap. We were joined in Udong by a contingent of French soldiers on their way to Cochin China. They were despised by the natives, who had all manner of superstitions about foreign devils, and tales of brutality by the our forces had already made their way to this remote outpost. We are glad to have the assurance of a military escort on the remainder of this journey in Cambodge, but considering that we have just survived three months among the fiercest savages of the land, one has to wonder what danger could lie ahead that could surpass what we have experienced already: attacks by wild beasts, tribal conflicts, monsoons. We have taken all in stride.*

*The vast lake of Touli-Sap is nearly forty leagues in length, over one hundred leagues in circumference, and as large and full of motion as a sea. Our pulses quicken as our party nears the northern tip, for it is here, in the province of Ongcor, that we have been told is situated the remains of a great civilization, mysteriously abandoned…*

*The soldiers have a local guide with them and, after three days journey through thick jungle growth, we have arrived at the ruins of the temple of Ongcor Wat. These are Ruins of such grandeur, remains of structures which must have been raised at such an immense cost of labor, that at the first view, one is filled with profound admiration and cannot but ask what has become of this powerful race, so civilized, so enlightened, the authors of these gigantic works?*

*This temple—comparable to that of Solomon, erected by some ancient Michaelangelo—might take an honorable place beside our most beautiful buildings. Mouhot is right. It is grander than anything left to us by Greece or Rome...*

*We have spent a week in the area of Ongcor Wat alone, so vast is the complex. Mouhot has exposed plate after plate in his Daguerre camera. We have sought in vain for any historical souvenirs of the many kings who must have succeeded one another on the throne of this powerful empire. Unluckily, the scourge of war—aided by time, the great destroyer, who respects nothing—has fallen heavily on the greater part of the monuments. The inscriptions with which some of the columns are covered are illegible. If you interrogate the Buddhists who inhabit the ruins, you receive vague replies: "It is the work of giants." "It was built by the Leper King." Or "It built itself."*

*We are moving our camp to the western Baray, and tonight my guide has offered to show me the intricate carvings of the Bayon by torchlight. He is a strange man, a former slave of the Stiens, now under some sort of servitude to the temple grounds—though not, it seems, affiliated with the monks. His allegiance is to a being we have yet to encounter.*

This was the final entry into Ramonne's journal.

Ramonne put the book down. He sipped at his wine. He was at Brown Sugar, the jazz café opposite Lumpini Park where he had first taken the American. He hadn't been back since. Little had changed. A Filipino singer fronted a small combo of mixed heritage. "My Funny Valentine." She sang it well. He recalled that a girl was singing the same song on that night. He wondered how many Filipino girls had sung the same song on the tiny stage since then?

———

He shook off thoughts of a night a few years ago and concentrated on ancient memories. One hundred and forty-five years ago to be exact.

He remembered sitting by a fire. Jarut, the guide, was telling him of the *apsaras*, the graceful dancing girls depicted in bas-relief throughout the temples. They were the personal possessions of the prince, his harem, according to Jarut. Every evening the prince would climb 200 stairs to his tower chamber, where he would bed as many of the harem as he desired. Didn't sound half-bad to a young French lad.

Jarut promised to show him not only the *apsaras*, but the tower steps. The chamber, alas, was gone. He took a torch from the fire and motioned for Ramonne to follow him.

The temple shimmered as the branches of the trees that threatened to overtake it waved in the moonlight. The carvings were magnificent. The girls so graceful and alluring that they appeared alive. As the torch moved over the images, they seemed to dance, animated by the light. Ramonne was entranced.

*Enchanted.*

His hands felt the stone, cold to his touch, and he savored the peaks and valleys of their breasts. Their laughing eyes. He wallowed in the craftsmanship of the ancient artisans.

He was lost.

After an eternity of bliss in the company of angels he turned to seek his guide Jarut.

He was gone.

In his place was a man the likes of whom he'd never seen before. It was more a creature. A thing. The head was shaved and the ears long and pointed. The eyes, Asian, were sunken and dark. It stayed in the shadows of a balustrade.

"Jarut?" Ramonne posed the question, though he knew the guide was gone. What was uttered in response from the shadows was unintelligible. But Ramonne *felt* the words: '*We are alone.*'

The torch was in a sleeve on the wall and Ramonne lifted it to get a better view. Instantly, the thing struck a blow and smashed it from Ramonne's grasp. It was snuffed out when it hit the stone floor, and the temple was plunged into darkness, lit only by the waning moon.

"Who are you?" Ramonne was taller and, he assumed, stronger than this man-thing, but he was swept with fear and felt his best course of action would be to turn and run. Get help.

He found that he could not move. The man-thing was advancing on him.

'*Foreigner. Not forbidden.*'

Sounds hissed forth, and again Ramonne heard the words in his head. Ramonne tried to cry out, but his own voice was stilled. To his horror he realized that the creature was about to bite him. Its mouth was open and sharp fangs were exposed.

*Dear God, no.* As he tried to resist with every ounce of strength, he felt the fangs pierce his neck. A black cloud seemed to blanket the world. He was falling through space. Tumbling down a long shaft. The blackness began to be replaced with red as he continued to fall.

Then he awoke. He was on the floor of the temple. The creature was no longer upon him, but was on its knees in a pool of what Ramonne sensed was his own blood.

The thing was retching. Gagging as he expelled more of the liquid. Ramonne found that he could move again, and he reached to his throat. His hand came away soaked in blood. He was weak, but with great effort he was able to stand. The beast stopped its vomiting and looked back at him. It was breathing deeply now, taking great gasps of air. Ramonne staggered backward and fell down the steps of the temple. He regained his footing and fled. He ran, stumbled, and fell into the camp. A few bearers were seated at the fire, but they paid him little heed, assuming that he was drunk. He looked back into the night, expecting the creature to be there, but he saw nothing

He managed to get to his tent where he collapsed.

————

"Delacroix. *Comment te sens tu?*"

He awoke with a start in the heat of the day. He had a splitting headache and a parched throat. But he was alive. In his fevered dreams he was certain he had died.

Mouhot was leaning over him. He placed a palm on his brow. "You have a fever. This is not good."

"Water, please."

Mouhot handed him a canteen of boiled water and Ramonne drained it. He tried to rise, but was not even able to sit up.

"Stay. Rest. You must regain your strength and defeat the malady that has seized you." Mouhot offered him a bowl with a pungent herb mixed with tea. He put it to Ramonne's lips.

"Drink this. I pray it is all you need to stave off the fever. I cannot afford to lose you, *mon amis*. We have only just begun on our greatest exploration. The discovery will make me famous. I need you by my side to share the glory."

Ramonne drank the bitter liquid. When Mouhot took the bowl, Ramonne clutched at his hand. "Stay with me, monsieur. Talk with me. I fear sleep. In sleep I fear I will perish." Ramonne clutched Mouhot's arm, his fingers deep into the flesh.

"Delacroix." He removed the grip, placing Ramonne's hand on his chest. "What you need is rest. I must go. My destiny awaits me."

Mouhot stood. His manservant, Phrai, was in the entry to the tent. He carried Mouhot's sketching pad and easel. "Rest, *mon amis*."

Ramonne watched him depart and then he slipped back into slumber. In sleep he entered the world of the dead again. He saw his body decay and rot in an unmarked grave. Worms crawled through the sockets of his eyes. Maggots ate his flesh. There was no light at the end of this tunnel. Only darkness, loneliness and despair.

———

It was the dawn of the next day when he finally woke again. The headache and feverish feeling were gone. He stretched and was relieved to see that apparently his strength had been restored.

He took up his shaving mirror and examined his neck. He found that the man-thing's attack had left two small puncture marks.

He was not certain that he should disclose the incident to Mouhot. Whatever this thing was, it was unique, and if it could be captured, it could well be Ramonne's chance to step out from the shadow of the explorer and receive his own recognition. And fame and fortune.

The circus was growing in popularity throughout Europe, and along with the elephants, lions, and tigers that had been captured and put on display inside its tents, there had grown a sideshow tradition of wild men, savages, and freaks. If Ramonne could capture this man-thing, he imagined he could command a hefty price for its display.

He swabbed the wounds with alcohol and changed his shirt. He was famished. He headed for the mess tent while plotting the beast's capture.

He was given a mug of steaming coffee and a plate of boiled yams with chunks of wild boar. He joined a table of soldiers, thinking that he could possibly use their assistance.

Suddenly a trumpet wailed. *"Alerte!"* one of the men shouted, and they rose in unison and took up their rifles.

A buffalo-cart was approaching. A uniformed soldier was leading the water buffalo. A native sat atop the cart and snapped a whip at the animal. Another soldier was alongside; one at the rear. He appeared distraught.

The cart stopped in the middle of the camp. A colonel, a young but impressive man by the name of Vespry, approached the cart. "*Qu'est que c'est?*" he asked the soldier at the rear of the cart. The soldier saluted and then removed the tarpaulin that was atop the cart's contents.

Colonel Vespry gasped. The corpses of three young French soldiers were lying in the well of the wagon. Each was extremely pale; drained, as it were, of its color.

Vespry looked at the bodies. There was caked blood on their collars and their uniforms were ripped open.

"We found all three of them lying alongside the path we cut between here and Ongcor."

Vespry singled out two men who climbed into the cart and lifted the first body. As the head rolled back, two great gashes were revealed in his throat. The men looked to the colonel, who motioned them to expose the throats of the other two. They lifted first one and then the other. The throats of each were torn open.

Ramonne reflexively reached for his own throat. He felt the wounds, minor compared to the lacerations he had just seen. Yet, he was confident that these men had been murdered by the man-beast.

"Tiger." Vespry made the pronouncement. He was now alongside the bodies, performing his examination.

"Are you sure?" Henri Mouhot queried.

Ramonne turned to see the explorer smoking his pipe, his Chinaman, Phrai, at his side.

"Monsieur." The colonel nodded his acknowledgement of Mouhot. "It's the only animal in these territories that could cause these wounds."

Mouhot dismissed Phrai with his sketching materials, and moved closer to the corpses.

"Fortunately, I have much experience in hunting these

beasts," Vespry continued. "Sergeant, arrange a party of a half-dozen men armed with rifles and pikes. I can dedicate my day to the hunt."

"I too have some experience with the jungle beasts. If I can be of any assistance…" Mouhot offered.

"How generous of you, Monsieur Mouhot. But I wouldn't want you to go to any trouble. I'm sure we can handle it. I do suggest that you remain in the camp until we've returned. None of us is safe while this beast runs free. I've seen the havoc they can wreak once they've tasted human blood."

"Speaking of tasting blood, colonel. Why did the tiger not devour the carcasses? It seems that the 'tasting,' or rather the draining, of the blood is what killed these men. Hardly the habit of a carnivore such as a tiger." Mouhot puffed on his pipe while he spoke.

"Perhaps he was surprised before he could complete his meal."

"All three of them?"

"Perhaps there were three tigers. All the more the dangerous then."

"I sincerely doubt that, my colonel. A tiger is a solitary hunter."

"Monsieur Mouhot, I could stand here and continue this debate, or I can take a course of action. Forgive me if I choose the hunt. We can talk later."

Mouhot nodded, and Vespry charged off. Mouhot studied the corpses another moment and then turned slowly to Ramonne. "Feeling better are you, Delacroix?"

"Yes. Much better thank you." Ramonne again self-consciously touched his throat, immediately withdrawing his hand.

"Good. What do you make of this?" He pointed his pipe at the bodies that were covered again with the tarpaulin. The cart, now accompanied by four soldiers, was turning around.

"I...I don't know. I think you may be right. I've never heard of tigers abandoning their prey."

"Hmmmm," Mouhot mused. He looked to the monks, who went about their business around the camp. "Did you notice that *they* paid no attention to the discovery? Not a hint of curiosity, let alone the pious sympathy of men of the cloth that normally attends the presence of death."

Ramonne had been aware of the aloof nature of the monks who inhabited the ruins, from the moment of their arrival. These men seemed to perform the minimal amount necessary for their bare existence. This was, no doubt, one of the reasons that the site had remained so unknown outside the region. These solitary men were of no mind to co-habit with the rest of the world, and had made the French contingent keenly aware of their dislike of their presence.

"They *are* strange." Ramonne nodded.

"They have a secret. Of that I'm sure." Mouhot looked again at the orange-robed figures. A few were looking at him, but upon the fall of his gaze, they turned away.

"You should finish your breakfast, Delacroix. You must be starved."

Ramonne sat back at the table, deserted now except for his plate. Mouhot crossed the camp and went into his tent.

**12**

---

Being confined to camp, Mouhot spent the day developing and archiving his Daguerre plates. The plates, having been exposed in the camera to light, were now held in a lightproof holder. In a pan over a fire, liquid mercury boiled. The plates were transferred one at a time to the developing box, and the mercury was allowed to wash across the plate. It was the vapors of the gas that caused the copper plate to reveal its magical images. To fix the image, the plate was immersed in a sodium solution and then toned with gold chloride.

Ramonne was obliged to assist, though his thoughts were far distant. He had flashes. They would transport him back to that dark place he had visited in his dreams. He almost lost consciousness once or twice. He was sweating profusely.

"You have the sickness, *n'est-ce-pas?*"

"No. Actually, I'm quite well. Fully recovered it seems." "That is not what I refer to. You are thinking of home, are you not? Of your lady. Giselle."

Ramonne's actual thoughts were far from home. In fact, they were centered a mere quarter of a league from where they were. In the temple of the Bayon.

"Yes," he lied. "I am."

Mouhot secured a leather band around a burlap wrap encasing a Daguerre plate, and placed it on a small pile of others.

"It has been a long journey. Perhaps it is time for you to go home."

Startled again by Mouhot's words, Ramonne didn't know how to reply.

"*Je ne sais pas?*"

"You scared me today, Delacroix. I would not like to have to face your fiancée with news of your demise. This journey has been fraught with peril. No doubt much more than you imagined."

"I had no preconceived notions, monsieur. I accept the dangers."

"Be that as it may. My collections are becoming cumbersome. They should be couriered. I have decided that you should accompany them on their journey."

"*Et vous?*" Ramonne was astonished at what he was hearing.

"I will continue to explore the region. I wish to travel the Mekong to its source. There is much yet to be discovered."

"Then I shall go with you," Ramonne protested.

Mouhot smiled. "No. I need you to take charge of the transport of my collection. I will hear no more of it." He handed Ramonne the daguerreotype plates. "Here. Start with these."

Ramonne carefully took the wrapped parcels. "Why do you give these to me?"

"My tent overfloweth. I've run out of room. They are precious. Protect them." Mouhot rose to leave. "I am tired, Delacroix. We will talk later." He re-lit his pipe and sauntered off.

———

As Ramonne expected, the hunting party returned empty-handed, having found no sign of a tiger. The exhausted men collapsed in the shade of the many banyan trees.

Ramonne generally had little to do with the soldiers on their journey. For the most part, they were a loud, uncouth, drunken lot, typical of the foreign légionnaires he had encountered—ex-convicts, soldiers of fortune, or both. He kept his distance. But two of the men, Louis Frontec and Alex Comberre had seemed genuinely interested in the task he and Mouhot were embarked upon. They were both from Avignon and, as such, had been exposed to the arts. When they had idle time, which was quite often, they gladly joined the two explorers. Ramonne had shared a few glasses of wine and tales of home with them.

It was these two stalwart young men that he approached with his scheme. "No tiger, Monsieur Comberre?"

Alex was stretched on a blanket under a low and particularly verdant branch.

"Such nonsense." He spit and looked carefully around before continuing. "The colonel had us tramping through all the brush from here to the Touli-Sap. If there was a tiger, he would have had plenty of warning to stay far away from us."

"Maybe that was the idea." Louis raised his head off of his knapsack. He shook his head and lit a cheroot.

"How so?" Comberre asked, extending his hand for a smoke, too.

"I don't think the colonel particularly relished meeting the beast. Drive him off. I think that was the real plan."

"There is no tiger." Ramonne had both their attentions. "How do you figure?" Comberre took a light from Louis and puffed on his smoke.

"I know who did the killing. And it was no tiger. I met the beast."

"*Met him*? What do you mean by that, monsieur?"

Ramonne opened his collar button. He showed them the

puncture wounds, still fresh. He told his tale of the encounter in the temple of the Bayon.

When he was finished, he tossed each of them a small pouch. Coins jangled inside. "That's just the start. Capture the beast without killing him and there'll be more of that. Much more."

———

As it grew dark, a storm passed over the plain, and it was nearly midnight when the rain subsided and the three approached the Bayon. The two men each had pistols, lengths of rope, and their rifles. Ramonne carried a torch and a sabre. Both men had expressed cynicism at Ramonne's story, but they were soldiers, and the outing would be an adventure at least. That and the promise of a small fortune should they succeed in capturing this "man-beast" as Ramonne had described it, led them to assure Ramonne they took the task at hand seriously.

They crept up the steps of the temple. Ramonne went first with the torch and the sabre poised in front of him. Frontec and Comberre were just a step behind, one on each side of him. The steps were slippery due to the showers, and the going was slow and cautious.

Comberre winked at Frontec, who smirked and rolled his eyes. The benign smile of the bust of King Jayavarman loomed above them as they crossed the eastern steps and entered the outer gallery.

The soldiers automatically stiffened their posture as they entered the confined space. They lost their smiles and became serious. Crumbling walls of various heights surrounded them. Shadows cast by Ramonne's flickering torch leapt about, running over the carvings that wrapped around the balustrade.

Ramonne felt something on his left. He turned with the torch.

Nothing. Just more shadows.

He moved the torch back to the front and continued to move forward.

He started to say something to Comberre, when he heard a stifled yell. He spun with the torch and saw Frontec being dragged into the shadows.

"What the hell?" Comberre raised his rifle. Ramonne thrust the torch in the direction the man had gone, but there was nothing there. He had vanished.

Ramonne felt something in front of them, and he brought the torch around. What he saw shook his faith to the core. The man-thing was draining the blood from the hapless soldier. It gushed forth from his throat as the man's body shuddered in its death dance.

"Good Lord."

The creature raised its smooth skull and looked Ramonne in the eye. Ramonne was astonished at the transformation.

The creature was feeble-looking no more. He let the soldier's body drop to the temple floor. Blood ran down its chin and over its thick neck. It now stood tall and straight and its exposed chest and arms were taut with muscles. The ears were less pointed and the features of the face were now distinctly Chinese —that of a man in his late thirties or early forties. Ramonne wondered if indeed this could be the creature that had attacked him two nights ago.

The creature smiled. When he opened his mouth, Ramonne saw the fangs.

"*You.*" Again, what escaped from the mouth was unintelligible, but Ramonne heard the word in his head. Somehow his mind was translating.

Ramonne turned to Comberre.

"Now."

No reaction. The man was frozen in place. Immobile.

*Jesus.* He'd forgotten the man-thing's powers. He had once been made into a statue himself. But not this time. This time he could move. He grabbed for the rifle. He tugged on it, but the soldier's grip was unrelenting.

*"How are you feeling?"*

Ramonne turned and the beast was next to him. He could smell and feel its rank breath upon him.

The thing reached for the frozen soldier. It caressed the man's neck, its fingers with their long talons scratching thin lines where it touched the skin. All the while, the beast's eyes were focused on Ramonne. *"Do you know what I am?"*

With the thought came images, flooding over Ramonne. Ancient scenes of carnage and blood-letting in faraway places.

*"I am Zhoupeng. I am a thousand years old."*

Ramonne *saw* men, women, children, all of Chinese descent, all in the throes of death. Merchants, warriors, peasants, all in an ever-changing landscape.

*"I have visited death upon scores of thousands. I have survived for centuries on their blood."*

Ramonne's head was spinning from the avalanche. He tried to shut it out but he could not. He was not in control. Images of Ongcor at the height of its glory were intermingled with that of a traveling Chinese delegation being welcomed by a great king. All the while, the endless victims paraded by, now of the Khmer race.

The beast smiled while he toyed with the soldier, alternately releasing him from his spell, letting him struggle, and then immobilizing him again. In the midst of this, the soldier's pistol clattered to the floor. Ramonne, overwhelmed by the flood of imagery the beast had rained down on him, still had enough presence of mind to snatch up the pistol. He cocked it and fired. The blast sent a shower of smoke and flame that burned Ramonne's hand. He dropped the pistol and clutched his hand. He thought that the gun must have misfired, but there was a gaping hole in the beast's chest, directly over the heart. Zhoupeng turned from the soldier and looked to Ramonne. He put his hand to the gaping wound. His face had an expression of shock.

The images stopped and Ramonne's mind was clear. Had he defeated the beast? He started to back away when the beast put up his other hand, palm extended. The motion stopped Ramonne and he could not move.

With the long talons, the beast reached into the gaping wound. Deep within his own chest cavity. His hand emerged with the steel ball fired by the pistol. It was still smoking.

*"Do you think you're the first to shoot me, fool? I've been shot, stabbed, hung, even buried alive. All for naught. This puny little ball could no more harm me than a kernel of rice."*

As he watched in amazement, the beast's wound was already cauterizing, starting to heal. *"I will enjoy killing you, fool."*

With that, he pulled the soldier to him and, with a sickening *crack*, punctured the poor man's neck. His eyes expanded and he tried to cry out, but no sound ushered from his lips.

As he drank the blood, Zhoupeng's body metamorphosed. His already substantial muscles grew and his chest expanded. The bullet wound healed entirely in mere minutes.

*"It has been so long. You can't imagine what that tastes like after two centuries of rats, pigs, and vermin."* He cast aside the carcass as he would a rag-doll. He wiped his lips with the back of a hand and moved to Ramonne.

Ramonne, unable to flex a muscle, still shuddered in horror at what he knew to be his inevitable end. The beast was upon him now, long talons moving through his hair.

*"You amuse me. I'll share my story with you."*

He smiled, a horrible seductive smile of death to come.

*"The ancient monks stumbled onto powerful secrets when they made these ruins their home. They opened doors that had been closed for centuries. Behind one of them, they found me."*

His nails drew lines on Ramonne's face. He could feel the blood flowing.

*"I arrived here as a member of Chou Ta-kuan's party from Peking. I had only recently joined the group, having been forced to leave the Middle Kingdom by some angry citizens. I fed well in the city of Ongcor, but there were powerful sorcerers afoot who cast a spell on me. They entombed me in this very temple. They couldn't kill me, but they could stop me from killing them. With the defeat of Dharmasoka by the Siamese usurpers, the great city of Ongcor was abandoned. I lay here for nearly 300 years, hearing the jungle overtake the buildings that had enjoyed such splendor for so long.*

*"These monks. They've been here a century now. They've learned to prolong their lives through ancient spells and potions, finding the keys to longevity deep in the jungle in certain roots and herbs. They spent hundreds of hours studying the ancient Sanskrit scrolls they discovered. It was in deciphering these writings that they learned of my existence.*

*"They released me from my tomb, but they still retained control over me. They forbid me from feeding on them. Kept me confined to the temple grounds. I was forced to feed on all manner of vermin to barely survive. On feasts and holidays they would offer up livestock to me.*

*"But then you arrived. Foreigner… Not forbidden."*

Zhoupeng drew back his lips and exposed his fangs. He hovered over Ramonne's fresh wounds, his breath hot and foul.

*"Now you can take my tale to your grave."*

The pain of the teeth in the wounds was excruciating. It felt to Ramonne as if two hot spikes were being driven through his body from his neck to the soles of his feet. The heat emanated out from the spikes and flooded his body. The heat was quickly replaced by cold.

As the cold enveloped him, the great darkness descended again. Ramonne's last thought was of the very preciousness of life…as it was drawn from him.

## 13

Martin pulled the jeep into the dusty parking lot. Antoine was waiting for him. He extended his hand and Martin shook it

"I'm sorry for your loss. *C'est une tragédie.*"

He guided Martin to a table set under a canvas lean-to. "Please. Sit. Can I get you a drink?"

Martin shook his head and sat on the bench. Antoine sat opposite. He offered a cigarette.

"No thank you."

Antoine shook a cigarette out and lit it with a Zippo lighter embossed with the Rolling Stones' tongue. He exhaled and studied Martin for a moment.

"You said you needed my help. *Comment?*"

"Tell me what's going on. What's *really* going on."

"What do you mean?"

"You said that you suspected a large-scale smuggling operation. Former Khmer Rouge have been spotted and are suspected of gathering in the Kulen Hills. There have been murders... eight in the past four months. Two of these were in my family. Is there a connection?"

Antoine breathed out a thick plume of smoke. He studied Martin a moment before answering.

*"Oui."*

Martin sat back, his arms folded across his chest, and waited for more.

"Yes. There is a connection. Although, I'm not sure of the…*incident* with your family. I don't have the details."

"The 'incident'?"

"I'm sorry. Bad choice of words. *Pardon moi.* Forgive me."

"Let me tell you about that incident." Martin bristled. "An employee of mine and two children were returning from a routine errand in Siem Reap, when they were apparently run off the road and gunned down. One child survived purely by accident."

Antoine took another puff on his cigarette before replying. "Do you know the caliber of the weapon?"

"As a matter of fact I do. Apparently there were two weapons involved. The first shot, which probably killed Jane, was a large-bore 7.65 millimeter. The other rounds, probably fired after the vehicle had gone off the road and overturned, were .30-caliber."

Antoine gave a slight whistle. "Military issue. The first round probably came from a mauser, bolt-action rifle. The rest from an AK-47 machine-gun. Your ballistics information came from the local police?"

"No. I got the rounds myself from the local mortuary and had them sent to Bangkok. My…*girlfriend* has connections with the police there."

Antoine viewed him with newfound respect.

"Very wise. Such tests here would have taken weeks, and been suspect."

"I'm aware of that. Now you have the details. What do you think?"

Antoine lit a second Gauloise with the end of the first before stubbing it out. He leaned back and smoked while he mulled this over.

*"Oui.* This too is their work."

"Who are *they*?"

In response, Antoine stood. "Come with me."

He led Martin across a rock-strewn pasture at the rear of the Baphuon. Two massive construction cranes loomed over them. They continued to the edge of the jungle. He touched the thick trunk of a stately tree.

"This tree, Martin, the *banyan*, grows all over Cambodia. It may reach a height of over one hundred feet. As it grows, new roots descend from the branches, pushing into the ground and forming new trunks. The roots grow relentlessly. Many of these temples have fallen as these roots have become embedded in the cracks and crevices between their stone blocks. A single tree might have dozens of trunks, and it is often impossible to tell which is the original."

Martin admired the tree, not sure, however, how it was related to his question.

"Smugglers, drug-runners, murderers—all uniting together under the Khmer Rouge flag. All trunks of the same tree. This is who *they* are."

"I thought the Khmer Rouge were destroyed. Just six old generals left in a Phnom Penh prison."

"The Khmer Rouge should be extinct. Most of the evidence would suggest this to be the case. But in Cambodia few things are ever certain."

Antoine motioned with his hand toward the temple ruins. "In this sacred site there exists fear on a scale unknown since the war. 'They' have accomplished that through their wave of ritualistic killings. These are superstitious people. They count on that. By terrorizing, they are able to operate their pillaging without interference. Heads are turned when lorries convoy in and out of the excavations, laden down with plundered relics."

He leaned close to Martin and lowered his voice. "What I'm telling you is a fact. There is a collaboration underway that is intent on plundering the temples and tombs on a grand scale. The riches gained will sustain it and arm it for future conquests in this country. It is the remnants of the Khmer Rouge that hold it in unity, but rumor has it that a much darker, mysterious force is at its core. The villagers speak of a powerful demon…a 1,000-year-old fiend that sucks the blood of its victims and feeds on their souls."

Martin was completely taken aback. He almost lost his footing at this pronouncement.

"That, of course, is nonsense. But that is the level of fear that has been instilled to accomplish their goals. These superstitious people are terrified of this *ghost who walks the earth*."

*Nonsense.*

Martin's rational mind agreed with the assessment. However, his memory told him otherwise. He was suddenly overcome with a flood of memories of his own encounters with the supernatural. He had known blood-sucking demons, had called one a 'friend,' and been instrumental in its destruction. Twice.

"Are you all right?" Antoine had Martin by the shoulder.

"Yes. Sorry…just the heat."

"We'll go back. Get you some water."

They walked back over the tagged and gridded stones of the excavation.

"This *beast*. Have there been sightings of him?"

"A few. Each description is different. He always appears larger than mortal men. They say he grows with each soul he ingests."

"Any physical description?"

"He's supposed to be Chinese. Has a shaven head. This is generally consistent, but as I say, he changes according to who's telling the tale."

Martin breathed a sigh of relief. It didn't sound like *his* blood-sucking demon.

Be that as it may, Martin knew there were forces at play in this world beyond the scope of modern science, and he did not dismiss the paranormal as having an abiding influence over any abnormal activity.

"Discounting the supernatural for the moment, if what you've told me is true and there's a murderous band of thugs intent on desecrating the ruins at any cost, then all who work here are at risk. Julianne, Michelle, you…everyone."

"I'm afraid so."

"What can be done?"

Antoine hissed out a column of smoke and crushed the cigarette in the dirt. "That is a good question. I wish I had an answer."

"Surely you have a plan?"

"Martin. I have desire. I have a few resources. I will do what I can. At this point my concern is, as you point out, with the safety of the Conservatory. I do not pretend that I alone will succeed. To do that, I would require an army and the resources of a king. This is a poor, war-ravaged country; neither is available to me. I'm afraid that we will suffer more losses. Both human and historical."

"That is unacceptable. I have brought children here. To think that they are at risk is unthinkable."

Martin walked to his jeep and opened the door. "I don't have an army. But I do have *resources*. And I will use them to find the men who killed my friend and the child. And I will find a way to make sure they don't do it again."

He slammed the door and roared out of the lot in a cloud of dust.

———

Nud polished the rifle again. It had been six years since he'd held one.

The camp was quiet now. Most were asleep. The one tent besieged with light was that of the Naga.

The Naga was busy at night. Curiously, he was never seen

by day. During the day, he retired to the cave. None had been inside the cave. It had two guards, men of undetermined race who never spoke. A huge boulder rolled into place and sealed it, seemingly of its own accord.

Nud thought the ancient one wise. In this atrocious climate it made sense to be a *creature of the night*. At night the Naga summoned those who he had chosen to his chamber. There they were dispatched to greater duties throughout the kingdom, for once summoned by the Naga, they were never seen again.

Nud surveyed the camp. General Miet stood at the head of a long table. Six men seated around it discussed an assortment of drawings and blueprints. Standing alongside the general was the *barang*. It was through this foreigner's co-operation that the doors would be opened, the trucks dispersed without being searched. It was this capitalist lackey's greed that would make it all possible.

Nud despised him. But then, Nud despised most people.

The *barang* took a packet from the general and left the table. He headed for his vehicle. The general signaled the guards to let the *barang* pass.

Their army consisted of a dozen men, Khmer Rouge all— rapists, murderers, torturers, pedophiles. In the time that these old men had served the Angkar, they had a chance to practice evil in all its incarnations. Like Nud, they had been in hiding for years until the Naga sought them out and gathered them here. Three trucks, two jeeps, and a large amount of arms and ammu- nition had been liberated from a Thai police post just north of the border. The tents that dotted the camp had also been gath- ered in that raid.

The general turned his attention back to the table. Nud had looked at the plans when they arrived. He recognized the great reclining Buddha of the Baphuon. This loose stone construction was under painstaking restoration. The immense statue was over forty meters in length. The cavity where the head would be reconstructed was twenty meters high. The other drawing was of the Terrace of Elephants.

In the center of the table lay an overview of Angkor Thom, the roads to and from the sites clearly marked. Muraki, the Japanese head of Nud's own labor force, smoked a cigarette and explained in English the planned movements of the operation.

Muraki, Nud supposed, had no allegiance to anyone but himself. Nud was a spy. His days were spent doing as little labor as possible while gathering information. Muraki, a wanted gems smuggler, had been working the site surreptitiously for over a year, while planning his own operation, when the Naga conscripted him.

Nud was a soldier, dedicated to a cause. Muraki was an opportunist. He sold his allegiance to the highest bidder.

Nud despised him, too.

The general was just a few years younger than Nud. He had been an ajutant to the great *Poh*. He had been at the *Poh's* side when he died. He fled into the jungle rather than face the humiliation of capture.

Nud admired the Naga's ability to gather this band, comprising all the elements necessary to execute the various tasks.

Instilling terror into the immediate countryside had been plan one. This would allow them to come and go unchallenged, as there were none who would dare to venture out onto the highways after dark.

The Naga was all-knowing and used his acute mental powers to source out his conscripts. He dispatched the general to do his function in the day, while the Naga rested.

Nud didn't exactly despise the general, but he envied his position with the Naga. Therefore he looked for opportunities. Opportunities to serve his master and rise above his lowly state.

He pulled the trigger on the rifle and imagined how it would feel when he was actually given some bullets.

# 14

DIARY OF DR. GERHARDT KAESTLE

*It is day. He sleeps. In a coffin within a wooden crate. It rests in the back of a van that was procured by a young Thai named Lek. All travel arrangements have been made by this man, who does the vampire's bidding without hesitation. I've searched his eyes for some trace of the spell that keeps me bound to his keep, but can see none. The man is strong of his own personal will, and yet remains devoted to the vampire.*

*The crate and our baggage were loaded into the van at dawn outside the train station. I was holding our traveling papers, passports etc., as our driver was but a hired chauffeur, entrusted only with the task of getting us to the border. As was pre-arranged, he stopped five kilometers short of the crossing, just as night fell. He helped me unhinge the lid to the crate.*

*He was relieving himself when the vampire attacked and fed on him.*

*I then had the small task of driving the van across the border. The vampire presented his passport and was told to "enjoy" his stay.*

*After the border crossing, a fresh driver (and tomorrow's meal) was waiting.*

Martin went home and made love with Areeya. It was love, it was passion, it was need, it was lust. It was…all of that. He needed it all. He trembled when they were done. He truly loved this woman. But it had been so long since he had told her.

'Now. Tell her now…before it's too late.'

The words were not Martin's. He jolted upright.

"Martin, darling. What's wrong?"

"Nothing. Go to sleep."

But it was not nothing. *Something* had intruded on his well-being. He got up from the bed and walked to the window. He saw nothing but darkness.

But still he felt it. Indescribable. There was something familiar about it that gave him comfort. Like the scent of your mother's perfume…your father's cigarette.

Intoxicated, Martin opened the bedroom door. He thought he heard Areeya say his name, but he ignored it. His feet walked across the cool stones and soon he was opening the gate to the front yard.

"You came?"

'I did. You need me.'

"I do."

'Then worry not. I am here for you.'

Ramonne stepped from the shadows. "My friend. It has been a long time."

Martin marveled, as he always did, at the fact that the vampire never aged. If anything, he appeared younger. Stronger.

"I thought the explosion—"

"That? A mere inconvenience."

Martin referred to a terrorist bomb in Bangkok that Ramonne had thwarted by throwing himself into the explosion at the moment of detonation. Many lives were saved by the heroic deed, and there had been no sign of the vampire in the aftermath. Martin had assumed he'd been destroyed.

"It did take a while for me to pull myself together." The vampire smiled. "The girl. How is she?"

"She's well. We're as one now."

"Good. You wanted a family."

"How did you know *that*?"

"It was obvious."

Martin shrugged this off. Obvious meant Ramonne had read his mind. He hated it when the vampire did that.

"I have a large family. Twelve." He winced and corrected himself. "There *were* twelve…now there are eleven children." He smiled as he thought of them. "They're wonderful."

"Children are very special. You are right. They are a wonder. I am sorry for your loss. It shall be avenged. This I pledge to you."

"You know?"

Ramonne nodded.

"Of course you do."

"There is evil in this land. I feel it everywhere."

"Interesting comment, coming from you. You're *evil*. Remember?"

The vampire moved close. He put his hand gently on Martin's shoulder. "Martin. Don't make light of what I say. I am here to retrace my past. To seek the source of my destiny." Ramonne looked to the Kulen Hills, faintly illuminated by the moonlight.

"I fear that he…*it* is still here."

Martin looked to the mountain and a chill ran through him. A light breeze blew from the north, that direction, and Ramonne breathed it in.

"He's grown strong…incredibly strong." His long hair blew in the wind. "This is natural. As we get older, we get stronger."

"None of this is *natural*." Martin shrank back from the vampire.

"Martin." Ramonne sighed. "My strength has doubled in the time you've known me. This beast is over a thousand years old. Can you imagine what *he* must be like?"

Martin scoffed. "Incredibly sarcastic? With a thousand-year-old wit?"

"Martin. I'm serious."

"I just don't understand. How are we involved? Of what possible interest are these children to this...*vampire*? That's what he is, isn't it?"

"Yes. He is a forsaken one. Martin, you knew I was here didn't you?"

Martin did. He was certain the vampire was outside his wall when he awoke in the dark. Ever since their first fateful encounters, a link had been established that allowed Martin to be aware of Ramonne's presence.

"*He* knows I'm here, also. And he will know of you and your brood as well. He will seek to hurt you to get to me. This I believe."

"Good Lord." Martin gasped. "*Get out*. Go away."

"Martin—"

"How could you do this? How could you expose my children to danger?" Tears welled up in Martin and flowed. As was his wont, he'd held them in.

*Jane*. Her mother, eighty years old, came from Canada to claim the body. He shook her hand.

Tiara. His darling. The beauty queen. He hadn't cried. The cremation. He'd been strong. He hadn't cried. His father would have been proud.

He collapsed. But strong arms held him up.

"Martin. I'm here to help."

Confusing images flooded over Martin. How could he reconcile his feelings for the children, his love for Areeya, with his friendship...his bond...with a vampire?

"I've gone so far to rebuild my life. To give it meaning. The children. They are so precious to me. I've lost *one*...and a dear friend. If it had anything to do with you—"

"It did not. I assure you. But it was a warning of the level of evil you are facing."

"The children—"

"Are safe. *And* I will keep them safe."

"Areeya—"

"She knows me." Ramonne held Martin at arm's length. "And so do you. You know I will not harm you...her—"

"Or the children."

Martin looked into his face. *Lord. I need a saviour. But at what cost?*

"A cost you can live with, Martin. There is enough evil here that I can restrict my sustenance to those who deserve to die. Believe me, that will *not* be a problem."

"A pact. You ask me to make a pact?"

"No. I will do this. I merely inform you of my decision. This *thing* and I have our destiny. You...your children, are but pawns in the game."

Martin looked to the water-stained wall of the schoolhouse. No matter how many times it was painted, the horrific climate caused it to mold. Much like his relationship with the vampire.

A truck rumbled in the distance. It changed gears and roared past the school. Martin turned to the highway. For the first time, he noticed the van parked in front. A man was standing alongside.

"Who is that?"

Ramonne turned. He'd almost forgotten. "My associate. Doctor Kaestle. He...he arranges things for me."

The gray-haired man was gaunt and pale.

"Kaestle?" Martin recalled..."He's the doctor who Jonathan saw in New York. Why is he here?" The man was on his knees and peering intensely at the road. "Is he all right?"

"No. He's not. He suffers from a similar malady to your unfortunate friend, Peyton."

"You bit him."

"No. He foolishly injected himself with tainted blood. His only hope of salvation is here—in confrontation with the root of my contamination."

"He looks terrible. Is he hungry?"

"I'm certain he is."

"I'll get him something. Tell him to come in—"

"Martin. He no longer feeds like you. He needs his food to be alive."

As he said this, Dr. Kaestle sprang forward and caught a frog that was about to cross the road. He shoved it into his mouth. He looked up and made eye contact with Martin for the first time. The frog's legs protruded from his lips, and he turned away in embarrassment. He straightened and went back to the van.

"Doctor Gerhardt Kaestle. World-renowned entomologist." Martin shook his head. "Will he survive?"

Ramonne shrugged his shoulders. "He's stable for the moment. His assistance to me at this point is minimal. I require only a safe resting place."

"You *cannot* stay here."

"Martin. Don't be foolish. I know the limits of our bond. I made arrangements to rent an old farmhouse just north of Roluos, near the Lolei towers. We have already moved in. Quite charming, actually."

Martin knew the area well. The Lolei site was less than ten kilometers from the school, and Martin was a regular visitor. It was a beautiful brick structure that was being lovingly restored. A charming monastery and temple were also on the site. Martin brought his used text books to the monks for use in their one-room school.

There were very few buildings of significance on the road. Mainly the area was agricultural, dotted with thatched-roof huts amid the rice paddies. Stick fences and earthen dykes delineated their boundaries. A French historian had built a home there in the early 1960s, only to abandon it to the Khmer Rouge. It had been badly vandalized by the boy soldiers, and lay in a crumbling state since the end of the war. Martin was certain that the old gate he had passed so many times was the entry to the property Ramonne had rented.

"Villa des Oiseaux."

"Exactly. You've been there?"

"No. It was a property that was discussed before we settled here."

"Well. For now, at least, it will be my home. We're neighbors."

———

The tent flap opened and the Naga stepped into the night. At seven feet in height, he towered over his servants, who bowed their heads at this most unusual appearance. The Naga's movements were normally well planned and choreographed. Whispered voices spread the word quickly, and all in the camp came to attention.

His bare feet left deep impressions in the soft red soil.

The camp was on a plateau that allowed an uninterrupted view of the valley below. All of Angkor stretched out to the west. The twin lights of a small plane could be seen taking off from the airport and reflected off the water in the man-made reservoir of the Western Baray.

The Naga looked to the south. His pointed ears arched slightly. His nostrils flared and he sniffed the air. The general approached. "Comrade. All is ready. We can strike—"

The Naga cut him off with an outstretched hand, his fingers with their long nails curved back like a dancer.

"*Silence.*"

His eyebrows raised as he drew in breath after breath.

Nud inched forward until he was as close as anyone to the great demon. This was where he wanted to be. At his side.

The Naga was focused entirely on his sensual quest. His ears, his eyes, his breath…all were attuned to the signs.

He smiled.

*He's here.*

*Good. Let the games begin.*

**15**

———————

DIARY OF DR. GERHARDT KAESTLE
ROLUOS, CAMBODIA

*I scribble now. My wits are not really together. I feel the wasting as I slide over to the dark side. And yet I have no hope of restitution. No hope of salvation. I will not become one of them without an encounter with the primal beast. Is this matter on the agenda?*

*The master seems to revel more and more in his new surroundings. On the first eve here, he went about the pursuit of sustenance. He followed a band of thugs who had broken into a storefront and looted it. They disbanded and the master took one of them, dragging his body to the dry riverbed, where it was ravaged by a pack of wild dogs.*

*I feel a part of it now. If I wanted to—and I do—I could not leave. The acts set in motion by the vampire's traveling here cannot be undone. I don't know how I was so naïve as to overlook the underlying theme to the very essence of this creature's existence—the shedding of human blood. I romanticized about the glory of eternal life and over-looked the very core of his existence.*

*I have now spent four days—uneventful; he slumbers through them—and three nights on this journey. I have been a direct accomplice to his murderous ways. The blood of his victims has stained my tunic. I've seen their eyes as the life drains away. They have reached to me, feeling that I must have some human compassion for them.*

*But I have not. That, I'm afraid, was lost along with my self-esteem when I succumbed to eating rats.*

*Instead, I watch their death throes with a detachment that one might have in witnessing a play or television drama. It seems unreal to me. And I lose interest quickly and seek my own sustenance.*

*As was pre-ordained, I was met by a merchant in the hamlet of Roluos. This shanty town sits on the banks of a dry riverbed. It consists of a sprawling old market, a few shops, and a temple. The lack of modern amenities allows it to exist in a timeless state. The man, known as Nehm, climbed into the van and directed me to the house that the master had leased. It took no more than fifteen minutes to arrive at the gate. He unlocked it and gave me the key.*

*The house was in great disrepair. It was built of stone, and showed itself to be the victim of fire, vandalism, and what appeared to be assault by gunfire—for there were numerous bullet holes throughout the remaining structure. The Cambodian explained that these were the result of the house having fallen victim to the Khmer Rouge and having been used for target practice. The fires and vandalism followed their departure, he said.*

*In any case, at the price monsieur had paid, he would be glad to set in motion the rehabilitation of any or all of the estate. I assured him that would not be necessary. My master was very happy with the place as it was, and upon his arrival, I lied, I would notify Nehm of any adjustments he required.*

*With that, I was handed the other set of keys, and Nehm departed. I offered to drive him back to town but, with a bow, he assured me that he would have no trouble securing a ride—there would not be a soul on the road that he wasn't directly related (or indebted) to. With that he smiled his gap-toothed smile and backed out the door.*

*Once he was gone, I set about the tasks the master had laid for me. Within an hour I had prepared the one standing, secure building. As the original owner was French, of noble rank, he had built a separate building of vault-like construction as a wine chamber. Knowing that these lands flooded regularly and cellars were useless, he had built his vault as a free-standing cave. Two stones thick, it had withstood even the Khmer Rouge's intrusion. Unfortunately its stock was not as fortunate: not a bottle survived. It was here that I laid the master's property, including a collection of wines he had packed, in anticipation of his arousal at sunset.*

*Promptly upon the day's demise, I unlatched the crate and the master emerged. He was immediately taken by the setting and was as jubilant as I have been privileged to witness. He breathed deeply and said he felt renewed to be free of the stifling confinement that Bangkok had become for him. He lifted his coffin single-handedly from the crate and carried it into the wine cellar. He tested the mettle of the lock on the iron gate and then handed the key back to me. His gaze assured me that I could not, would not, ever waiver in my duties.*

————

Martin pulled the jeep to the rear of the school. He backed down the driveway and stopped just before the tool shed. He opened the rear of the car and unloaded the crates and boxes that he had acquired that afternoon.

The shed had basic provisions: bags of rice, sugar, powdered milk, bottles of water, two drums of gasoline, and various tools. He made room for his new deposits and stacked them. He covered the cases with a canvas awning.

When he was finished, he took the brand-new padlock from his pocket and snapped it through the latch of the shed door.

"What are you doing?"

Martin turned to see Areeya standing with her arms crossed. It took a moment for him to answer her.

"Just loading in a few supplies."

"What kind of supplies have to be locked up?"

Martin considered not telling her. But that would go against the trust they had built.

"Guns."

"*Guns?*"

Martin spun the dials on the lock and removed it. He opened the crate. Four M-16 automatic weapons were wrapped in oilcloths.

"Martin! Why? You promised me you'd let the authorities investigate the murders."

Martin looked at her as he closed the lid. "I have done just that. Antoine has kept me informed of the *authorities'* investigation. It's as if nothing ever happened."

He replaced the canvas and shut the door, snapping the lock. He took Areeya by the hand. They walked across the playground, where a spirited game of soccer, boys against girls, was going on.

They stood in the shade of a large fig tree and watched the competition. Pom was acting as referee, blowing fiercely on a little tin whistle. He'd decided to stay on, even though Jane was gone. The kids had gotten to him, too.

Martin pulled Areeya to him as he watched the children play. "It all looks so normal, doesn't it? But we are in danger. The children are in danger. I'm not certain why or how, but there may be trouble here. If there is, I will protect my family."

"Martin. What do you know of guns?"

"Antoine."

"Antoine?"

"He's offered to train me...To train us."

"Us?"

---

*Brrrrrrrrrrrrrrrt.*

The Angkor Beer bottles jumped off the rock wall. The old quarry was bare of any stone. Any metals had been strip-mined long ago. Now it was merely a scar on the land.

"That's full automatic." Antoine took the gun from Pom, who seemed very comfortable with the weapon. He slid the action to semi-auto and handed it back. Pom squeezed the trigger again.

*Ptt. Ptt. Ptt. Ptt.* Fewer bottles flew as the gun barked in a steady progression of single shots.

"Very good, Pom. You're a natural." Antoine took the weapon and handed it to Martin. "You'll save your ammunition if you keep it on semi-auto. That's what I'd recommend."

Pom placed another dozen bottles as targets.

Martin went down on one knee as Antoine had done, cradling the weapon in his shoulder and balancing his left elbow on his left knee. He squeezed the trigger. *Ptt.* The gun jerked with the shot and Martin took it off his shoulder.

Antoine smiled. "It kicks. You'll get used to it. Squeeze the stock with your arm and try again."

Martin resumed the position and fired again. *Ptt. Ptt. Ptt. Ptt.* He squeezed off four rounds in rapid succession.

The beer bottles were unmoved.

"That's good, Martin. Now aim at the bottles. Get them in your front sights and squeeze the trigger."

Martin did this and half the bottles jumped off the wall as he swept the gun from left to right.

Areeya watched, concern and worry etched into her young face. She had reluctantly agreed to join him. As he said, they would take up arms to defend the children if it ever came to that. Jane and Tiara's tragic murders were horrible, but she was not entirely convinced that it had been more than just a gang of drunken youths. This idea that they were in constant danger from an evil force made no sense to her. Smugglers, bandits, drug-crazed teenagers—they were all part of the terrain, no doubt. But what would they want with their children? Why would the school pose a threat to them? This she could not understand. And so far, Martin had been at a loss to explain it. *He's keeping secrets.* This she knew for certain.

"Areeya."

Martin was holding the gun. Reluctantly she took it.

"Be careful. It's got a mean kick." Martin rubbed his sore shoulder.

Areeya slid the action to full auto and cradled the weapon on her hip.

*Brrrrrrrrrrrrrrrrrrrt.*

To Martin and Antoine's astonishment, the remaining bottles flew off the wall as she swept the machine-gun across them.

"Lord. Where did you—"

"My dad was a cop, remember? He always wanted a boy."

She ejected the spent casings and expertly racked in a new clip.

"Just press it to your hip, Martin. It'll spare your shoulder." She handed the gun back to Martin. "And don't aim. Just point it."

Martin stared. *Just when you think you know a woman.* He shook his head and placed the gun on his hip. Areeya had left it on full auto and he had to admit he liked the feeling of power he got when he squeezed the trigger and a burst of bullets ratcheted forth.

If they needed firepower, they had it.

Trouble was, Martin knew that guns would be no match for their ultimate enemy, if and when he came.

———

"How could this happen?" Julianne stared in horror at the gaping hole in the middle of the pile of stones that constituted the shape of the reclining Buddha. An explosive charge had been set and the stones, so precisely cataloged and restored, now lay in a jumbled pile at the rear of the Baphuon. At the top of the steps, Robert stood in the hole and assessed the damage.

"They removed all the bas-reliefs from the second-tier *gopura*." He spoke into a walkie-talkie.

Julianne had her radio to her ear and ran a hand over her brow at the news. "Jesus. *All* of them?"

The news was disastrous. The Baphuon restoration, begun by the French in 1970 and halted by the war, was funded with over 10 million dollars, due to the magnificent condition and quality of the bas-reliefs in the second floor *gopura*, or 'gateway.' These masterpieces were extremely well preserved, as they had been covered by the great Buddha begun in the fifteenth century but never completed. It was the preservation committee's plan to allow the public access to these great works that had not been on public display for 500 years.

"How is that possible?" The bas-reliefs were over ten meters in height and twenty meters long. Their combined weight would have to be over five tons.

Justin was with her at the base. He pointed out the obvious answer to her question. "They used our cranes."

The twin, 100-foot-high construction cranes had been on the site for several months. They were an indispensable tool in the restoration. It was obvious from their current position—directly adjacent to the gaping hole in the reclining Buddha—that the same equipment that had lifted the tons of stone into the site, had been used to remove its most valuable assets.

The sun was climbing high in the morning sky. The laborers not on the second-level with Robert were seated in the shade, awaiting orders. Their faces betrayed no emotion. They would do what they were told, when they were told. Until then they conserved their energy.

In order to get the trailer and trucks to the rear of the temple, the thieves had used small explosive charges to level a section of a four-foot-high wall. The wall had just been rebuilt, its faint carvings painstakingly restored. It had been Michelle's pet project and she was devastated by its wanton destruction. She sat staring at the pile of rubble.

"Antoine," Julianne barked into the radio. "Where are the bloody police?"

"They're with me. I'm at the Terrace of Elephants."

"What are they doing there? I need the police here. Now."

"Julianne. The Elephant Terrace has been looted, also."

"What?"

"They took the *horse*."

"Oh God." The Horse With Five Heads was an exceptional piece of sculpture. It was the horse of a king, surrounded by *apsaras* and menacing demons. It was the crown jewel of the Terrace of Elephants.

"Julianne. Look at the tire tracks leading away from the Baphuon. I followed them at dawn this morning when I discovered Som's body. They led here."

Julianne shuddered. Her dear defender of her honor, young Som, had spent his evenings at the site. He preferred camping alone to the laborer's quarters, and he felt he could keep the site safe from thieves. He had been murdered. His throat slit and his body crushed under the trailer's massive wheels.

Still holding the radio, she climbed a slight rise to follow the line of the tracks. A small grove of fig trees had been mowed down by the trucks, and she was able to see the neighboring Palace of Phimeanakas.

Antoine was in the back of a police jeep, heading toward her.

She switched off the radio and waited.

———

Martin and Areeya drove in silence. The streets of Siem Reap were deserted though it was just past 10:00 in the evening. He slowed for the first of the speed bumps or 'sleeping policemen' as the British called them and turned onto Highway 6 in front of the Raffles Hotel.

The Grand Hotel was closed—its staff had walked out in a labor dispute. Martin was sympathetic with them—they wanted just compensation for their tasks—but he knew that the pockets of the owners were deep; *they* could survive the strike. And if there was one thing in abundance in Cambodia, it was cheap labor.

He turned onto the riverfront, passed the royal residence, and made a right into the old market. He parked his jeep by the Lotus restaurant and they walked into a dimly lit alley. A simple sign— "Angkor What?"—hung under an arched entry into a small tavern.

Inside, the place was empty except for two tables that had been pushed together to accommodate the six people gathered around them.

Antoine was seated next to Julianne. Robert and Justin were next to her and Ang and Khouy, Antoine's Cambodian men, were next to him. Martin and Areeya sat down facing Antoine.

"Martin. I'm glad you could come."

Martin took Antoine's extended hand.

Antoine lit a cigarette and poured two glasses of wine for them.

"Julianne's considering leaving."

Martin looked to her. "This is true?"

She nodded. "Do you realize what they've done to our work? It's as if we've spent years and millions of dollars to build a museum and they've stolen the best paintings."

"Julianne, I'm sorry. I'm sure you're devastated."

"Michelle is devastated, Martin. She can hardly talk. Me…? I'm scared. They killed Som. A poor sweet boy."

"I heard. I know he was your friend. They killed my friend, also. And one of my children. I know how you feel."

Antoine interrupted. "We're not absolutely certain it was the same people—"

"*I'm* sure," Martin cut Antoine off. "You told me that you also suspected it was the same gang. What's being done?"

Antoine poured more wine and signaled for another bottle. "I was with the police all day today. They are sending additional men from Phnom Penh. They should be here within a week."

"A week? What will these men be doing?" Martin sipped the wine and stared at Antoine.

"They believe the smugglers will try and take the stones across the Thai border. They will beef up security at Poipet." "Secure the border? That's all? I can't imagine the thieves who took five tons of sculpture out of Angkor would be so stupid as to try to drive it through a government check-point."

Areeya took Martin's hand in an attempt to calm his anger. "Listen. You and I both know that these men are in the Kulen Hills. Why don't the police go and arrest them?"

Antoine lit another cigarette. "The truth?"

"Yes please. The truth."

"You know as well as I do, the police are poorly paid and badly armed. It's not worth their lives to go into those mountains against a band of heavily armed guerrillas."

Martin slammed down his glass in disgust.

"What about the army? UNESCO? The CIA? Can't you get anyone to help?"

"Did you not notice that the streets were empty tonight? There have been murders, beheadings, disappearances. There are tales of a 'ghost who walks' devouring his victims. These are superstitious people, Martin, you know that. They are not highly motivated to take up the cause of world heritage protection. Even if it's their own. Pardon my French, but they're scared shitless."

———

Martin parked the jeep while Areeya checked on the children.

"What news from your friends?"

Ramonne stood by the tool shed. Martin was not surprised. He expected the visit.

"Not much. They fear that the police will turn their backs and allow the smugglers to get away. Antoine feels that the reign of terror they've perpetrated has succeeded in giving them autonomy."

"Who is this Antoine?"

"He's the son of a French conservationist and a Cambodian mother. The father and son fled the Khmer Rouge, who killed his mother. He works for the Ministry of Culture and has a staff of two charged with combating the pillaging at Angkor."

"Not doing too well, is he?"

"In his defense, what can he do alone?"

"Martin. I promised you I would seek vengeance for your loss. I will. I promised I'd protect your family. I will. *I am your protector.* Trust in me."

Martin looked at the man opposite him. He remembered the night they first met. It seemed so long ago. Martin had been foolish enough to think he'd uncovered a police plot to cover up a serial killer's murderous reign in Bangkok, and had written a front-page article for the *Bangkok Times.* What he didn't know was that the serial killer was a vampire who'd been in Bangkok 140 years. Ramonne seduced Martin with his visions and powers and made him his companion. Martin had come dangerously close to voluntarily becoming a vampire himself, but the vampire instead allowed himself to be destroyed—in effect giving Martin back his life.

The vampire and Martin were both reborn. Martin became a Buddhist monk—after his ordeal he sought refuge in a monastery—and Ramonne had been regenerated, against his will, by a mad shaman. Their next meeting led to the crushing of a terrorist plot to destroy part of Bangkok. Ramonne remained an enigma to Martin. This beast that was capable of the most foul acts conceivable and who reveled in sordid and sensual pleasures, was probably the most intelligent and cultured man he'd ever met—and Martin had learned to trust him with his life.

Now he would trust him with the lives of his extended family.

"When will you enter the game?"

"Soon. Tonight I'm going to the temples."

"They are closed at night. Since the looting, no doubt they're heavily guarded."

"Martin. Please."

Martin remembered. This was a man who could pass under any radar. He could be invisible if he desired, simply by willing people not to see him.

"Sorry."

Martin remembered the attraction that had drawn him to the vampire the first time they met. Ramonne had been describing his first visit to Angkor when suddenly it had come to life for Martin. He was *there*. Instead of Benjasiri Park on Sukhumvit Road in Bangkok, he was in the jungle-covered ruins of the Bayon with Ramonne. The vampire projected his thoughts and Martin saw them clear as day.

It had been fantastic.

"Take me with you?"

"Martin. What about the girl? What will she think?"

"Take her, too."

"Is that wise? Does she even know I'm here?"

"Yes." Areeya answered for herself.

Martin turned to see her in the arched entry to the playground.

"The *girl* knows." She stepped forward, obviously neither afraid of nor intimidated by the vampire.

"I knew he was here the first night he arrived. I wondered when you were going to tell me." She stood next to Martin, taking his hand.

"The temples by moonlight? Sounds charming."

**16**

The trees along the road seemed taller at night, Martin thought. Dozens of monkeys scampered playfully along the forest edge.

Kaestle was at the wheel of the van, with Ramonne opposite him. The seats had been restored to the interior where the crates had been, and Martin and Areeya took in the forbidden journey in comfort. A full moon illuminated the road and Kaestle drove with the headlights off. He coughed constantly, a hacking, disturbing cough.

"Is he all right?" Areeya finally remarked.

"Don't ask," Martin replied.

Kaestle's bloodshot, sunken eyes found hers in the rearview mirror and he gave a weak smile.

They had passed the guard post without incident. As Martin imagined he would, Ramonne clouded the minds of the two men on duty, so that no notice was made of their presence.

Soon they came to the huge moat surrounding Angkor Wat. Ramonne motioned and Kaestle turned left, heading west. Ramonne had the window down and was savoring the sweet night air. They followed the moat around for another half kilometer until the towers of the temple were visible on the western side of the great monument. Ramonne told Kaestle to pull the vehicle over.

Ramonne stepped out of the van. Up ahead was a terrace. Beyond it a 250-meter-long stone causeway over the great moat. It led to the temple of Angkor Wat, the world's largest religious structure.

"Walk with me." Ramonne placed a hand on Martin's shoulder.

"We were a party of twenty. Mouhot, his Chinese servant, myself, our bearers, two Khmer guides, and a dozen French légionnaires.

Martin took Areeya's hand.

"The first glimpse we had of the temples was here." He stopped. They were opposite the entry to the cruciform terrace.

"The forest was formidable. It had invaded everything. The waters had risen and flooded the plains. And there in the distance, a magnificent sight greeted us."

"Oh my," Areeya gasped as, suddenly, the whole tableaux in front of them was transformed. It was now late afternoon and the sky was a deep blue. Instead of the flat plains that stretched forever on each side of the moat and causeway, the jungle crept right up to the temple. The water in the moat was cascading over the laterite walls. All was covered with vines and moss.

An elephant passed by, followed closely by another. They were loaded down with baggage. Twenty uniformed Frenchmen marched in loose order behind them. Martin smiled at Areeya and squeezed her hand as they started to follow.

Ramone stopped them. "Some other time, Martin. Tonight I need to visit the Bayon."

The world dissolved back to normal as Ramonne spoke. The jungle receded and the night returned. The French were gone.

"That was incredible!" Areeya exclaimed.

Martin squeezed her hand again. She turned back to the temple. "Please. Just a little more. Show us what it was like to 'discover' Angkor Wat."

"I just did." Ramonne smiled. "My visit has a purpose and I'm afraid time is growing short." He went back to the van and waited for them to join him. Kaestle had never left the vehicle and stared solemnly straight ahead,

"You missed out, doc," Areeya chastised him as they got in. In answer he let off a violent barrage of hacking and wheezing.

They drove on north and soon they were facing the South Gate to the walled city of Angkor Thom. Ramonne sighed.

The stone gate with its narrow opening was crowned with four bodhissatva heads, one facing in each direction. The causeway leading up to the gate was flanked on each side by a row of 54 stone figures—gods on the left, demons on the right. The gods held the scaly body of a giant serpent.

"Where are the heads?" Ramonne lamented. Unfortunately the magnificent sculptures had fallen victim to centuries of theft, and ninety percent of the carving's heads, as well as other huge chunks of the statues were missing. A few of the heads had been replaced with plaster casts. The missing heads gave the great sculptures a sad, violated appearance. Just a hint of the glory they once foretold.

Kaestle had pulled the van over. Ramonne was silent, staring straight ahead. Martin slid the door open and, holding Areeya's hand, they stepped onto the causeway.

Slowly the miracle occurred again. A very slight rain was falling from a gray sky. Curiously, the rain didn't fall on them or the van. Trees had virtually engulfed the massive gate. Vines wrapped like a python around the warrior statue balustrades, and thick vegetation obscured great sections. The statues that could be seen were intact, their features clear, the faces of the warriors fierce and those of the gods noble. Many more statues were present. What was visible of the gate had much more detail.

The approach to the gate was dense with fresh growth, and a group of bare-chested natives accompanied by French soldiers were chopping away with machetes.

"Halt. *S'il vous plait. Un moment.*"

The voice was from behind them. They turned to see a bearded Frenchman in a wide-brimmed hat adjusting the lens on a huge camera. The box was mounted on a tripod with thick wooden stakes.

The soldiers and the natives stopped their work and stood aside.

"You may stay, please. For scale. But find a comfortable posture and do not move."

This was translated and the natives quickly dropped down on their haunches in the way of squatting that only Asians can do and be comfortable. The French leaned against the trees and held their pose.

A shutter opened and the man counted. *"Uni. Deux. Trois…"* After twenty seconds he closed the shutter. *"Merci."*

The men resumed cutting away at the jungle growth.

Martin turned to Ramonne. He was smiling.

Martin whispered, "Is that—"

"Yes. Mouhot. Henri Mouhot. My mentor…My friend." As he spoke, the scene returned to normal.

Martin and Areeya climbed back into the van, and Kaestle drove through the narrow opening.

"What was that camera he was using," Areeya asked.

"A Daguerre."

"He took photographs of Angkor?"

"Yes. Daguerreotypes. Images etched on copper plates. They were magnificent."

"I've never seen photographs of Mouhot's journeys. Have you, Martin?"

Martin smiled. "Yes. I have."

Martin had collected the vampire's belongings when he had been destroyed at Wat Arun. These included a dozen images of Angkor and other ports of Mouhot's journey. He had kept them and given them to the vampire when they met again.

"Show them to me, please," Areeya pleaded.

"I will be delighted my dear. They are in Krung Thep. In the meantime, you'll have to make do with my memories."

As he said this, the plains outside the van's window transformed to thick jungle dotted with campfires and tents.

They pulled over to the side of the road opposite the Bayon. When they stepped out of the van, their feet landed not on asphalt but a thick undergrowth of lush vegetation. Tiny *yasiramob* plants recoiled and shrank away at their touch. Areeya smiled. She hadn't seen these little plants since her childhood in Chanthaburi.

Ramonne was already approaching the Bayon. He moved effortlessly through the chest-high grass. Smoke from the myriad of campfires that dotted the jungle opposite gathered as one large gray cloud and hung over the pinnacles of the temple's towers.

Martin looked up. The steps were framed with vines. As with the other structures he'd seen this night, mighty strangler fig trees enveloped the pavilion. Creepers of all types meandered over the walls, unearthing and toppling many. Small trees grew from the very tops of the towers and seemed to give hair to the massive carved heads.

A snake slithered down a stone just five meters from them and ducked into a hole. Areeya tightened her grip on Martin's hand.

A strange man, head shaved and wearing a robe, not orange but brown, with skin like the leather of a very old shoe, was now standing at the landing of the first gallery. He held a flaming torch.

The man smiled through a gap in his teeth and struck out his hand, beckoning.

Ramonne slowly started up the stairs. Martin and Areeya followed. The sound of a stumble followed by a groan caused them to turn around.

Professor Kaestle was trying to scale the steps, but they

seemed too steep for him, and he had fallen. He stretched a hand out to Martin and pleaded with his sallow eyes.

Reluctantly, Martin pulled him up the stairs. As sad as his condition was, Martin couldn't help but notice a sense of wonder and excitement on his face. Obviously Ramonne had included him in the enchantment of his recollections. The moonlight played across the towers with faces, which were pointed in all directions. Their strange smiles seemed animated as they passed, and the torchlight cast shadows upon them.

When they reached the landing the old man turned and, with his torch in front of him, led the way into the gallery. He thrust the torch forward and it illuminated the pillars. Three beautiful *apsaras* danced on a lotus blossom. Martin wanted to charge forward, but he realized he was a captive audience. What was revealed to them now was what was revealed to Ramonne then. It was his point of view, not theirs. He looked to Ramonne. He was focused on the carvings, just as, no doubt, he'd been 145 years earlier. He was strolling down memory lane. Martin smiled to himself. Such sentiment hardly seemed to suit an old bloodsucker like Ramonne. But he understood the need to retrace one's path in life. To seek one's heritage. It was innate in all people. A return to the cradle as it were. Back to the roots.

The next reliefs illuminated by the torch were historical battle scenes. They were covered in moss, but beautiful nonetheless. Huge panoramas of armies on the march, scores of elephants ploughing their way into battle.

In the flickering light, Ramonne's guide took on a sinister appearance. Martin was reminded of the childish trick of shining a flashlight from below your chin. The man gestured for Ramonne to follow him. Much as Martin wanted to linger, the illusion was fading as Ramonne moved on. They followed into the upper gallery. This entire highest level was an interlocking set of massive sculptures, while at the same time a sacred temple. The art was structural, and the structure was art.

Martin knew the temple well, and realized that much of what he was seeing was gone now. The jungle had caused its damage, and the way forward was difficult, as huge sandstone blocks had fallen and blocked their path. But much more of the temple's treasures had been lost to the hands of thieves than those of Mother Nature. He tried to touch a particularly delicate carving, but it fell away as the illusion disintegrated when he reached for it.

Behind them, Dr. Kaestle wandered wide-eyed, as if he were a man walking on the moon. Martin smiled. He shared the feeling.

Martin turned to his host. Ramonne's gaze was fixed. He stared straight ahead. Not a flicker of emotion registered on his face.

They followed the vampire, each reveling in the wonder of the experience they were sharing. The passageway grew increasingly narrow as they approached the central sanctuary. It was at this point that Martin suddenly realized the danger.

*'It was in the temple of the Bayon that I met my destiny. I entered that sacred shrine an innocent and emerged a fiend.'*

Martin remembered the words spoken by the vampire on their first encounter.

"Areeya." He whispered; a shout would have been like a gunshot. "We are following him to his doom."

"What?" she responded absently, lost in her own rapture.

"This is where he met the—"

Before he could finish, the demon was before them.

His eyes flickered in the torchlight. His pointed ears curled like a rat's. His nostrils flared at the presence of new flesh. His frail-looking body trembled with desire.

"*Ayeee*! What is that?" Areeya shrieked.

"*My saviour*," Kaestle cried out, and prostrated himself. Martin expected the illusion to fade as the voices must have interrupted Ramonne's thoughts. But nothing happened.

Ramonne remained rooted in place, his focus clearly on the beast. Kaestle was bowing and *wai*ing like a slave.

The apparition flickered for a moment, as if there was an electrical short-circuit. In that moment, Martin thought he saw the beast transform. It appeared strong and powerful. It turned to Martin.

"It's an illusion!" Martin cried as he took Areeya's hand and pulled her back through the chambers. As they ran, the temple restored itself to the present-day. Their path was open as the debris and trees had been cleared.

———

"Zhoupeng!" Ramonne's voice echoed off the temple walls.

The creature looked to the voice. For a moment it studied Ramonne.

And then it smiled.

A word ushered forth from the beast. It was not English. It was not French or Khmer. But its meaning was undeniable.

It was: "*Reckoning*."

———

They were home. Outside the schoolhouse. How they got there, they did not know. They had no memory past the brief encounter with the beast in the temple.

The dawn was beginning to break as Martin and Areeya walked through the yard in silence.

**17**

---

Death had arrived. It touched Ramonne. Its bony hand reached into his chest and stilled his heart. His young life flooded before him as his brain shut down. His youth in Provence. His parents. His beloved bride Giselle. All washed by as images of the life that was fading from him. He wanted to cry out, but the spikes in his neck had stolen his voice as now they stole his life.

The great blackness descended and Ramonne Delacroix was no more.

---

But contrary to tradition, death was but a mere visitor. Its presence was only transient.

Ramonne awoke.

His eyes told him it was dark. He was floating. At least that was how it appeared. The thick jungle was passing by without any effort of his own.

*Amazing.* He assumed this to be the effect that had been described by those victims of near death when they left their bodies and then transcended heavenward, to *paradis*, only to tumble back as their life force beat once again. He waited for this miracle to occur, as he was sure it must.

Then he realized that rather than ascending, he was traveling parallel with the earth. Barely above the ground.

He moved his head. The effort this took was Herculean. His neck was stiff and felt as if it had been broken. His vision was odd. As his head moved, the focus of his gaze left 'trails' of light as an after-image, ever so slight. It also seemed as if he could see forever. The depth of the forest was crystal clear to him, no matter how far away.

He now realized that he was on a wagon. He saw the broad shoulders of the two oxen drawing the cart. He also saw the less impressive bare shoulders of the native at the reins.

Ramonne tested his other senses. His fingers moved, albeit stiffly. His right hand touched something cold. He felt further and found hair. Thick, matted hair.

Ramonne pressed down and lifted his chest. As he did, he let his head drop. What he saw was extraordinary. He was riding on top of two corpses. He recognized them immediately. Comberre and Frontec. They were cold and stiff, both their mouths frozen in horror.

He felt no revulsion. No emotion whatsoever. "Delacroix. You are alive!"

The voice was excruciatingly loud. As if the man were shouting at the top of his voice. It hurt his head.

"Halt," the man commanded. The wagon bucked over a huge rut and then came to a stop.

"Get him down from there."

He felt hands on him, lifting him. He became airborne. Two men on the ground grasped his body.

"Take him to his tent." He could put a name now to the loud voice. It was Mouhot.

———

An oil lantern burned. It cast long shadows into the corners of the canvas pavilion.

"Drink this." Mouhot had a cup pressed to Ramonne's lips. Ramonne tasted the bitter brew. It felt odd as it entered his mouth, and even worse as it descended his throat. He gagged and pushed the cup away.

"You must drink something. You are as pale as a ghost." Mouhot looked deep into Ramonne's eyes.

"You were dead, my dear friend. Of this I am certain. You had no pulse. No breath escaped your lips. This is a miracle. Praise be to God."

Ramonne wasn't so sure that God was involved. This resurrection felt somehow sinister.

Mouhot took his hand and offered up a prayer. "The Lord is my shepherd, I shall not want..."

Again, Ramonne felt no emotion. At least the sound of Mouhot's voice no longer thundered in his ears. Blessedly he found he was able to shut out the sound—all sounds—entirely, if he chose.

Mouhot finished his prayer. He spoke, but Ramonne did not hear him. He was concentrating on a desire that was pulsing through his body. A drive he'd never felt before. It was becoming overwhelming and he realized that it would require immediate action.

He feigned sleep in the hope that Mouhot would depart and leave him in solitude.

It worked. Even with his eyes closed, he could see the man depart the tent.

———

*Animal instincts.* Courtship. Sex. Food gathering. A crocodile comes out of the egg with razor-sharp teeth snapping fiercely as he seeks to satisfy a primal desire...*to feed.* It was this primal instinct that drove Ramonne, barefoot, through the forest.

He pursued his prey, without even knowing who or what it was. He sniffed the air and changed direction.

He had awoken from death, stiff and virtually immobile. But he now moved with remarkable speed and grace. His feet felt sure on the tangled jungle floor, and the thorns and brambles that would have normally torn him to shreds, bothered him not.

Instinct told him that that his very survival depended on this hunt. His body might even seem strong and powerful at the moment, but it was without fuel…like a fire in its last embers. He was in immediate need of sustenance.

*Prey*. In killing range. All his senses heightened. His hearing detected heavy breathing. His nose smelled a variety of odors: anal, sweat, breath. They combined to tell him that this was the kill he sought. He now dropped down to all fours and crept forward.

As he came to the crest of a low hill, his keen eyes showed him his victim. A man, a soldier, lay against a fig tree, his rifle cradled in his arm. He was asleep.

Ramonne cocked his head in curiousity. This was a surprise. He had not expected a human. But surprise or not, he felt little emotion. He realized that basic primitive urges were guiding him now—and his very survival depended on giving over to them completely.

He moved forward silently. The man produced a noise in his sleep that was loud enough to disguise the approach of a herd of wild elephants. His massive chest rose and fell with each bellowing outburst.

Ramonne reached the man. He stopped. For a moment, he was unsure how to proceed.

And then the man stretched out his arms and yawned. He opened his eyes. He saw Ramonne. He started to say something.

Ramone looked at his throat. He knew what to do.

———

"You look better, Delacroix. Your recuperative powers amaze me." Mouhot's bearded face was smiling down at him.

Ramonne smiled back. It was what was expected. It meant nothing to him. But instinct, survival, told him that this was what he should do.

Just as instinctively he knew not to stay with the corpse once he had drained it. He retraced his steps through the forest with ease, stopping by a stream to rinse his face and hands of the man's blood.

Returning to the tent he felt a rejuvenation as he stretched back on the canvas cot. His body had been cold, like a serpent, when he'd awoken from the death experience. Now it radiated warmth. He wanted to luxuriate in the feeling coursing through his veins, when Mouhot entered the tent.

He touched his hand to Ramonne's cheek. "Absolutely astounding. You have regained your color." He reached out and turned Ramonne's head to the side.

"Extraordinary. Yesterday you bore the same horrendous gashes to the throat as poor Comberre and Frontec. Yet now… there's barely a mark at all."

He leaned in and smoothed the hair back from Ramonne's brow. "Tell me, Delacroix, what happened to you?"

Ramonne had no emotion for the man. But there was *something* that made him hesitate to lie to him. To preserve whatever it was, Ramonne chose to remain silent. He looked away.

"Ahh. You're tired. I understand. Rest, *mon amis*. You survived death. I suspect little more can be thrust in your path." He smiled and departed.

Ramonne pulled the sheet over his head and covered his entire body in a shroud of cotton.

He slept, undisturbed, throughout the entire next day. When the evening came, he unfurled himself.

Now he felt totally refreshed. Not just his body, but his mind as well. Things were becoming 'uncloudy.' Recent memory was also returning. In particular, the turn of events that led to his current condition: the encounter—twice—with the demon Zhoupeng.

He thought he now understood what had happened to him. Whether this was instinct or not, he wasn't quite sure. But his reincarnation, his rise from the dead, his very different state from his poor mates Comberre and Frontec. Surely this had been willed by the beast. Why? When he had obviously dispatched so many others to their graves, why had he granted a respite to Ramonne? He was *alive* was he not?

He knew he had to feed. He needed, he assumed, *human* blood. But when? How often. These were the questions he wanted answers to. He had been 'killed' by the beast. He had been resurrected. But he was not who he was before. He was a hunter. He was strong. His senses were acute.

And he drank human blood.

He needed to know why? Would this pass? Did he have a disease? Would he die soon? Tonight? Was this just a macabre prologue in the final death process?

So many questions. The answers resided in the Bayon.

With Zhoupeng.

———

He approached the temple steps. He'd put on his frock coat—he no longer felt the heat—and he'd felt that the evening's confrontation demanded a certain decorum.

He entered the second gallery. He wore shoes and still his feet were as sure as a mountain goat. He immediately detected the beast's presence—long before his eyes saw the flicker of torchlight. He followed the path to the last inner sanctum. Zhoupeng had a French soldier splayed on a wagon's wheel. He wielded a razor and was hacking away at his flesh. Jarut watched in silence.

"Zhoupeng," he called.

'*You?*' The demon was shocked. '*You're dead.*'

The voice was in his head.

'*Perhaps. If so, how am I here?*' Ramonne found he no longer had to speak to communicate with the devil. His thoughts were his words.

The French soldier was in utter agony. There were cuts over his entire body.

'*What are you doing with this man?*'

'*Him? Nothing important. I've had my fill of blood for now. This wretched creature is merely suffering for my amusement.*'

Ramonne felt drawn to the dying man. Not out of sympathy or mercy, but to the blood that was being let. He could taste it as it ran to the floor. *Such a waste.*

Zhoupeng was aware of the desire in Ramonne. '*You have the thirst.*' His eyebrows raised.

He turned to the poor wretch on the wheel and, with one swift motion of the razor, laid open the soldier's throat. The blood gushed forth.

'*Drink, parasite…drink.*'

Ramonne hesitated, unsure of what to do. And then the primal instinct took over again and he lunged for the man. He attacked the open wound, draining the blood as one would soup from an upended bowl.

His eyes stared at the demon as he drank his fill.

'*Frenchman. Why you? In all the thousands I've sent to their graves, why is it that you alone have returned?*'

Ramonne finished with the man and released his bite. The body fell limp on the wheel. He drew a hand across his mouth, wiping it clean. All the while, Ramonne's gaze never departed from Zhoupeng.

'*How does it feel, Frenchman?*'

'*I'm alive. It is better than being dead.*'

The demon smiled his horrible smile. '*Alive? Is that what you think you are? Tell me, did you feed on human blood when you were in France?*'

'*Of course not. But I am not dead. I recovered.*'

'You are not dead. You are not alive. You are undead…The living dead. You exist in a shadow world. You are forsaken. Your God has abandoned you.'

His smile widened. 'You know, this is actually very extraordinary. I've never had a…comarade.'

He studied Ramonne's stance before him. The old vampire made a decision. 'Yes. Join me. Together we'll show this corner of the world real terror.'

He embraced Ramonne, crushing him with his massive forearms.

———

Thus, convinced that his very survival depended upon it, Ramonne joined in legion with the ancient vampire. He abandoned his mission with Mouhot and crossed over. For the next few nights they feasted on the remnants of the French légion. They, the légionnaires, were being driven mad by the murderous reduction of their troop. The men begged Colonel Vespry to leave this cursed land, but he was convinced that whatever demon was preying on them could ultimately be no match for the French army. He led foray after foray, day and night, in a hopeless hunt, while his men were eliminated one by one.

On *their* hunts, Ramonne learned the rules for his survival. Blood must come from the living. The blood of a dead man or animal would lead to his destruction. Animal blood could sustain him. He must avoid sunlight, for it was poisonous to him. The safest and soundest way to do this was to sleep in a deep cavern, as did Zhoupeng, or a crate or…a coffin. Ramonne found his own cave. He learned to read thoughts and to project his will and force it on another.

But as to *why* he was a vampire, this Zhoupeng had no answer for.

'How did you come to be turned?' Ramonne questioned him.

'Ahh. That is an old story. A thousand years to be exact. I'm a native Mongolian. I was a shepherd. My flock grazed the steppes of the great Altai Mountains. In a driving blizzard, I searched for one lost sheep until I became lost. I walked through the storm until I could walk no more. I laid in the snow with my back to the storm, and prepared to die. As my life was leaving my frozen body, a great form appeared out of the dark. It was a wolf. A huge black wolf with yellow eyes. It came at me and I cowered from it. I had no strength, and no weapons. I was doomed.

'But instead of attacking, it laid down beside me. As a mother would to a cub. I knew not what to do, so I used the wolf as shelter from the storm. It wrapped its heavy body around me. And I fell asleep. In the morning it was still snowing and I was still alive. The wolf was gone, but obviously his warmth had kept me alive. As I staggered to my feet, I noticed a bite on my arm. I gave it little thought, as I spent another entire day wandering the mountain in the blizzard. As night fell, the wolf appeared again. And again it embraced me through the night.

'And again it bit me. This time I was awake. I felt the fangs on my arm. I awoke as in a dream and looked into his yellow eyes. He held his fangs to my arm. I became weak and then, I know not why, he stopped. He withdrew his bite. Our eyes remained locked and then I drifted back to sleep. On the morrow, it was gone. I struggled through the third day of the storm — it blotted out the sky. Finally I fell onto the path to my village. The process of full convergence to the undead took months. I was ill, delirious, and then I started to feed. I followed my baser instincts. And soon I knew what I needed to do to survive.'

Ramonne pondered the tale.

'The wolf. Was it truly a wolf?'

'I think not. There were old folk tales of a wolf who took the form of a man. These had been around for centuries. I feel it was a forsaken one that used its powers to make me see him as a wolf. As to why it took pity on me, I have no idea.'

One thousand years ago. Did this mean that Ramonne, too, would live to be one thousand years old? Three hundred and sixty-five *thousand* nights. Never to see a sunset or sunrise again. Did he need to kill every night? No, Zhoupeng told him. Even just once a week would allow him to survive. But the more he fed, the stronger he would be.

His mind reeled. It was all becoming unfathomable. Primal instincts were waging battle with emotion. In some bizarre way his human sensibility seemed to be returning. The last two hunts he'd participated in had been repulsive to him. He was no longer enamoured with the demon. He'd learned how to survive.

He saw Zhoupeng again as the enemy.

And he sensed the danger this would portend for him. Surely the man-beast would sense this...

*If it had not already.*

**18**

"*It is amazing, is it not? These so-called 'soldiers' have failed to realize, after a dozen deaths, that they are not dealing with what they call 'Nature?' They continue to stalk and hunt as though they really think we're a pair of rogue tigers who can be felled with their clumsy weapons. They have killed virtually every poor beast in the forest.*"

Ramonne could not deny his logic. The French were convinced a four-legged beast, or pair of beasts, were decimating them. How could they hunt those who could render themselves invisible at will?

"*Tonight I fancy something 'aristocratic.'*"

Before Ramonne could react, they had traversed the jungle on a whisp of air. This feat was one that constantly amazed Ramonne. In a moment they were outside the French camp at Angkor Thom. With horror, Ramonne recognized the silhouette of Mouhot's Chinese manservant, standing guard by his tent.

In the next instant they were in the Frenchman's tent and Zhoupeng was approaching his prey.

'*No!*' Ramonne's thought projection was filled with anguish.

Zhoupeng stopped at this reaction. '*You have compassion for this one? What about the others you so eagerly ravaged?*'

'*I knew them not. This man is my friend. Please.*'

Zhoupeng looked again at Ramonne. Then he smiled and leaned back over the sleeping man. He bared his fangs and broke the man's skin.

'*No!*' Ramonne flew at him and yanked him back. Ramonne had no idea how his strength would compare to that of the demon, and he was surprised that he was able to move him with relative ease.

Zhoupeng turned in the air and landed on his feet. He glared back at Ramonne. '*You dare to challenge me?*'

He came face to face with Ramonne. His feet never moved, and yet he was mere inches away. Ramonne was strong, no doubt, but Zhoupeng had powers and abilities that Ramonne either did not have or was yet to master. He knew if Mouhot was to live, he must not show any signs of weakness. He assumed that Zhoupeng imagined him an equal.

He attempted to focus on his hatred of the demon, knowing that Zhoupeng was exploring his mind. He figured pure hate would mask his doubts.

'*Compassion for the human and rebellion against your mentor. This is how you repay me?*'

'*You are not my mentor. Tormentor, perhaps. I owe you nothing but my repulsion.*'

With this Zhoupeng grew red. His eyes bulged and his cheeks grew scarlet. He withdrew and raised his arms. A wind rose and swiftly they were transported.

They were back in the Bayon once more. Deep in the inner sanctum that Zhoupeng used as his personal chamber of horrors. An acrid smell pervaded the air. Four earthen jars smoldered on each corner of the sanctuary, and they spewed forth smoke of different colors. Jarut stood in the middle of the room with some sort of document.

*A trap.* It was obvious to Ramonne that this had been planned in advance. Much preparation had gone into it. Zhoupeng had meant to entrap him; Jarut his accomplice.

"*Do you know what this structure is, Frenchman? It was built as a tomb. A great king built a monument to himself upon the tomb of his predecessor. This king believed himself the incarnation of the Naga King. You know the "Naga" don't you? The nine-headed serpent revered as a god and a reincarnation of the Khmers' king. It was said that he would transform into a serpent when he took his maidens in the tower that he climbed nightly.*

*"I take great comfort in this room. I should. It was here..."* He pointed to the floor. A great hexagonal symbol was inscribed in the stone. *"It was here that I was imprisoned by the soldiers of Dharmasoka's necromancers, 500 years ago. They were powerful men. Very powerful. Nine centuries of studying alchemy, astronomy, and mythology had made them shamans of great resource."*

Zhoupeng nodded to Jarut, who inserted a triangular stone in an opening on the bas relief. The stone at their feet began to move.

*"Not to mention their superb engineering and architectural skills."*

The entire floor shifted counter-clockwise and the hexagonal pattern parted, revealing a crypt below.

*"That, Frenchman...that was my home for three centuries."*

Jarut droned an incantation in an ancient tongue. He read from sheets of palm leaves held together with a thin slip of rawhide. The palm leaves were in Sanskrit.

The crypt was fully revealed now, and they stood on its lip. It was approximately eight feet deep and ten feet in diameter.

*"The tomb is enchanted. Once within it, a cursed power binds the victim to remain within. No matter how powerful the protagonist, he is reduced to a captive by its nature."*

Ramonne felt himself weakening. His strength was draining.

Jarut's voice droned on. *"I too have had time to study the Sanskrit writings they left behind, and have uncovered the exact spell they used to render me somnambulant."*

Ramonne stumbled. His head throbbed. He knew he must fight for his very survival. But he was at the point where lifting his arms was now a great task. All the while Jarut continued his monologue.

Zhoupeng was now at Ramonne's side. A clawed hand rested on his shoulder. *"Do you think I would have gone into that chamber unassisted? Their spells drove me mad, in much the same way as they are now doing to you. They left me weak, enabling them to seal me under their hex sign. Without their powerful orations, I would have torn them all limb from limb. Believe me, Ongcor would have run red with their blood on that day."*

Ramonne looked at the beast. His claw tightened on Ramonne's shoulder and pushed him closer to the edge.

*"Now, I fear, it is your turn."*

Ramonne was weak, but not without his wits. *"You were driven mad by these incantations?"*

*"Yes. To the point that I entered the tomb."* He looked into Ramonne's eyes. *"The past presents itself to you, does it not? Your sins. Your great evil past…your great sins…thousands and thousands of deaths. All paraded before you. Screaming at you. Beseeching you. Tearing at you…*

*"Is this not so?'*

Ramonne looked up. His gaze was clear and steady. "No. I am not you."

They struggled on the precipice. It seemed not to matter that Ramonne was in control of his senses. He was no match, weakened as he was by Jarut's curses.

*"Think of me, Frenchman, as you lie there in your prison. Think of me plundering this land, for I have just begun. I will lay waste to this country for centuries. My power will know no bounds. I will tear its people to shreds. The land will bleed under my reign. For I am the true Naga King."*

For a brief moment as they struggled, Ramonne saw Zhoupeng not as a man but as a mighty serpent, its fangs striking at him. It was still powerful arms that were pulling him to the edge, but it was a snake whose eyes were beckoning him.

He knew the illusion was a trick to further confuse and weaken him, and he tried to ignore it.

It was obvious the battle was one-sided. Jarut's drone carried on, and the strength continued to flow from his body. He began to waiver and knew he was but moments away from losing his balance and cascading into the tomb.

*Blam!*

An explosion shattered the putrid air in the cavern. It rang forth and echoed over and over, bouncing off the temple walls.

Immediately, Ramonne felt the demon's grip weaken. The serpent's eyes grew large in wonder and then the serpent head faded and the demon's returned, eyes wide in astonishment.

A second explosion rang out and the demon completely let go its grip.

Zhoupeng looked at his body. It was wracked by two huge, fiery wounds. They almost tore him in half. He reeled from the blows and looked to their source.

If he saw the cause of his disfigurement, he took the image to his tomb, for Ramonne seized the moment to lunge forward with all his remaining strength and tumble the beast into the crypt.

The cry emitted from the falling demon was horrible. It caused intense pain to Ramonne, and he pressed his hands to his ears. He leaned over the edge and stared into the crypt. Zhoupeng was writhing in agony, the wounds that would normally have begun to heal causing him spasms of pain. He reached up to Ramonne and beseeched him.

*"Brother. You cannot condemn me like this."*

Ramonne turned away. He saw his saviour. Standing in the sanctuary's entry he saw what he expected. Mouhot. His rifle still smoked. Phrai, the Chinaman, also had a smoking gun.

With lightening speed, Phrai drew a straight knife and flung it at Ramonne. It passed just over his left shoulder. Ramonne whirled around and saw Jarut...the knife impaled in his heart.

The man had been about to push Ramonne into the hole. Instead the man's lifeless body fell over the edge.

Ramonne withdrew the triangular shaped stone from the sculpture and, with a groan, the floor began to reseal. Ramonne avoided looking into the tomb as he dropped the stone into the crypt. Within a few moments, the sarcophagus sealed itself.

---

"How did you find me?"

Mouhot and Phrai helped Ramonne from the temple. He had an arm on each for support.

"I awoke from a nightmare. It was so real that I hastily dressed and grabbed my rifle, called to Phrai, and departed. In the dream I saw a demon hovering over me. You struggled with the beast. And then you were gone. Transported to the Bayon where you continued to struggle with the beast."

"The dream was true." Ramonne sighed.

"As I saw with my own eyes."

They reached the end of the stairs. Ramonne felt his strength returning and he could walk unassisted. "Monsieur, I fear that I cannot return to the camp. If I leave, and leave now, the killings will stop. If I remain, well, the consequences of that are too horrible to contemplate."

Mouhot looked to his friend, his companion on this incredible journey. He could barely recognize the man he knew. Yet, it was definitely Ramonne Delacroix standing before him. "What makes you say that? We killed the beast. He's buried in that vault? You're alive. We have much to rejoice."

"No, *mon amis*. I truly wish it were so, but I am infected with the same disease as the demon we dispatched. In truth, I should be in that vault with him. The world would be a better place for it."

"What has happened to you, my friend? You seem to be the

man I know and yet you are not. There is something wild about you. Something savage."

"The less you know, the better off you'll be."

"How is this possible? Are you certain of what you say?"

"As certain as I am that I shall never see my home in France again. I am doomed, monsieur—and the longer I am in your presence, the more you need fear for your own life."

Mouhot did not know what to say. "What will I tell your wife?"

"Tell her I was a good man." Ramonne embraced his friend. As he did, he could not help but notice the marks on Mouhot's neck. They were small, but he knew that a bite by the beast, no matter how slight, would most likely have bitter consequences. He feared for his dear friend and he hugged him close.

"Make it appear that I have died and you buried me. Many saw me in dire health. At one point it was assumed that I was dead. I don't think it will seem unusual. Do this for me, please."

"If this is what you truly believe you must do, then I will honor your request." Mouhot held Ramonne at arm's length and studied him, for he knew this would be their last moment together.

"What about food…water? Surely you can't set off without provisions."

"I will be fine."

"You'll hunt to survive?" "I will hunt, yes."

Ramonne knew it was time for him to leave. He had not the time or desire to explain everything to Mouhot—and for that matter, how could he—when there was so little he understood himself? He was about to embark on a voyage of his own discovery, in many ways not unlike the one he'd just been on with Mouhot. He was entering foreign territory, alone. And he knew not what lay before him.

He gave Mouhot a parchment envelope which contained a letter to Giselle and a last will and testament that he had managed to write in the hours before dawn. He turned and walked into the forest.

He made a stop at the cave he'd been spending the days in and retrieved the bundle with the daguerreotype plates. He put a belt around it and strapped them across one shoulder. In this manner he set out to the east and the kingdom of Siam.

Mouhot continued his journeys to as far north as Louang Prabang. Here he finally succumbed to a mysterious jungle fever.

His last entry in his journal, dated October 29th, 1861 read: "Have pity on me, oh my God…!"

**19**

Nud watched the Naga. He gave the orders. The general carried them out, but the Naga was supreme. He was in charge.

And yet Nud sensed that he needed something.

The horse from the Terrace of Elephants was on a trailer. The lintel and bas reliefs from the Baphuon were on a second trailer. Both were ready to be trucked out. Yet the Naga was hesitant to give the order. Why?

*Lack of trust.* Nud sensed it.

Nud saw his chance. He stepped forward.

"Sir." He used the English word the Naga found comforting. "Can I be of assistance?"

'*You?*' The words entered his brain. He never knew what language the Naga spoke. But he always understood.

"Yes. I am competent, master. I can see to the delivery."

'*Do you think you are any more competent than any other Khmer fool?*'

Nud had no idea how to answer such a question. He was spared by the arrival of the *barang*. The Naga retreated to his tent. The *barang*, to Nud's knowledge, had never seen the Naga. The general gave Nud a glare that could kill and then went to greet the *barang*.

Nud didn't care. He now despised the general.

———

The setting sun cast a purple glow on the Kulen Hills when Martin saw the first truck. It sent up a great cloud of dust as it rumbled along the dry road. It was definitely a military vehicle, and it was the first of a convoy.

"*Oh* God."

Martin slammed the gate shut and ran into the house. "Areeya. Gather the children and take them to the bus." As he said this he continued right on through the house and out the back door to the tool shed.

"Martin, what is it?"

"Trucks. Military. Go!" he blurted out.

Pom and Areeya gathered the brood, who had just finished dinner and were a little sluggish and fortunately very manageable. They shooed them up the steps into the school's bus, which was parked at the rear of the property. Inside they adhered to a drill that they had practiced many times now. They got down on the floor under the seats.

Areeya told the children to stay put, and then she and Pom got out of the bus. They got to Martin just as he had the first gun out of the crate. He handed it to her. She racked the magazine and gave it to Pom. He took two clips of ammo and went back to the bus. Martin took out two more guns. He gave her two ammo clips and stuffed two in his pocket.

Without a further word they went back into the house. They entered the front room, Martin on one side of the two front windows and Areeya on the other. They cracked the shutters and took their positions. They surveyed the road. Like the quickly choreographed dispersement of the children to the bus, these moves had also been rehearsed.

The rumble of the trucks was loud now. Gears could be

heard shifting as they tackled the slight rise in the road that meant they were within 100 meters.

Martin racked the chamber on his gun and nodded to Areeya. Hers was already racked. She nodded to Martin and they sighted down their barrels through the shutters.

As they did, Martin's cellphone rang.

*Doot-doot. Dootdoot.*

The trucks were fifty meters away. The noise was like a motorcycle convention.

The phone continued to ring. Martin looked to Areeya. She raised her eyebrows in exasperation. "Answer it."

Martin took it out of his pocket. "Hello?"

"Martin. It's Antoine."

"Antoine. Thank God. They're here."

"Martin. *I'm* here. We're here. Outside your gate."

Martin folded the phone and put it back in his pocket. He put the rifle down and took the gun from Areeya.

"Martin? What the fuck is going on?"

"It's Antoine. With the police." He headed for the door. Outside, Martin went to the gate and unlocked it. Antoine was by his Land Rover with Julianne and a police officer. Justin sat in the rear of the Land Rover. Antoine's men, Ang and Khouy, were in a small Subaru jeep. The two military trucks —Royal Cambodian Police special forces—were idling on the opposite side of the road. Antoine introduced the officer.

"Martin. This is Colonel Vanchea. He's been assigned to investigate the looting."

Martin nodded. The officer acknowledged him, barely. He was busy studying a map.

"We've received intelligence reports that the stolen relics will be moved tonight." Antoine smoked as he spoke. "This is the only road south of the Kulen Hills. A barge is waiting at Phnom Khrom on the Tonle Sap."

"Makes sense. But how would they get through Phnom Penh?"

The colonel looked up from his map. "They wouldn't. The barge would transfer its load somewhere along the southern shore of the Tonle Sap and the goods would be driven overland again to one of a hundred ports on the Gulf of Thailand. Our only chance to stop them is here. After this…they're gone."

"These are the police I told you were coming up from Phnom Penh."

Antoine motioned to the two trucks.

Martin reached into his pocket and pulled out his phone. "Excuse me a moment." He punched a number and waited. "Pom. Let the kids go. False alarm."

He slipped the phone back in his pocket. "Sorry." He took Areeya's hand. "Tell me more."

"I'm not sure what else there is to tell. We're going to stop them. Take back the sculptures. And arrest them."

Martin smiled. "Sounds simple."

Antoine smiled back and shrugged. "Who can tell?"

Martin stopped smiling. "*I* can tell. And unless you're some kind of fool, you can tell too. You're going into a firefight with men who have nothing to lose, supposedly backed by the very devil himself."

Antoine smiled. He shared this smile with Colonel Vanchea, who translated what Martin said in a quiet voice. His adjutants also smiled back at Martin. None of the smiles were friendly. They were condescending.

"Martin, this obsession you seem to have with the locals' superstition is very Khmer. I actually admire you for it."

"Pardon my English, but cut the crap. You know what you're up against, as well as I do."

"No. I'm afraid I don't, Martin. I don't share the same fears you do. I fear men…corrupt, dangerous men. They can be stopped." He nodded to Vanchea. "There are a half-dozen highly trained policemen with us. They have one mission. To stop the looting. I think it shall be sufficient. Our superior strength will be obvious. We will prevail."

Martin studied Antoine. Was this the same man who had expressed fear and uncertainty about the overwhelming odds he faced? What had happened?

He decided he didn't care. Martin walked past Antoine and opened the door to his car. "Julianne. Get out of there."

She hesitated. "I...I want to authenticate the relics."

Martin held the door open. "And you shall. After the firefight."

Antoine scoffed. "There will be no firefight."

"Julianne. Go inside the school."

Julianne looked to Antoinne. "Go ahead. Justin can take care of the details." Justin looked from the rear of the car. His expression was one of confusion.

"Hey man. I never signed on to be a hero."

"Justin, get out of the car," Martin snapped.

Justin was no fool. He hopped out.

Antoine smiled again. "Good. Keep them safe. We'll all have a grand reunion when the statues have been recovered."

Martin held the gate open for Julianne, who lingered a moment, until she got a cursory nod from Antoine—whose gaze remained fixed upon Martin. When she felt she had made a connection, she took Justin's hand and they walked through the schoolhouse gate.

"No problem, monsieur." He nodded to Julianne. "*Mon chérie. A bientôt.*"

Martin watched Antoine's convoy drive away into the setting sun. The dust plumes eventually sent them all inside.

---

Nud clutched his rifle. It had bullets. He could kill again.

He sat in the rear of the first trailer truck. Like the others, he wore a red sash cinched tightly around his waist and a red scarf across his forehead. Opposite him was Pran, another veteran of the *Great War*. He spat betel juice out past the green flap of canvas that covered all the cargo. In this trailer, the great horse from the Terrace of Elephants was wrapped in burlap and braced by lumber inside a massive crate. The crate was strapped to the bed of the truck to anchor it from any turbulence other than the bone-crushing, teeth-grinding, steady pounding that the combination of thirty-year-old truck and shell-shocked road provided. It was all Nud could do to hold onto the rifle and his dinner. He noticed that Pran had already laid his weapon down in favor of a two-handed grip on the rail that separated them from the road.

Unlike the majority of the roads in the region of the Angkor temples, the road from the Kulen Hills to Banteay Srei was still crushed and pockmarked by decades of tank travel and artillery shelling. Ruts two or three meters long and just as deep were interspersed with small craters.

Nud didn't like being stuck in the back of the truck. He couldn't see where they were going. He *knew* where they were going, of course. Unlike Pran and all the other 'soldiers,' he had taken the initiative to find out exactly what the plan was. He had discreetly stationed himself within hearing distance—a distance that was growing smaller every year now—of General Miet when he and the *barang* laid out the route. He heard the *barang* tell how he would lead the police from Phnom Penh onto the eastern road to Phnum Kulean just above the fork with the road heading south. This would effectively put them a mile away from the Naga's army and its cargo of stolen sculptures as it rumbled out of the hills. Like ships in the night they would pass without notice. The cargo would roll uncontested to its rendezvous with the barge.

Nud could not say he was exactly pleased with the plan. He held a gun for a reason: to use it. In all the years that he had served the great *Poh*, weapons and ammunition had been scarce. Most of the two million executions had been carried out by swift blows to the back of the head by club, axe handle, shovel, or hoe. The victims all were lured by soft chants of "*At oy te*." It will be all right. So they wouldn't struggle or resist. Then they were overcome by shock when the actual killing began.

He longed to kill again. He longed to kill with a gun. How easy. Just point and squeeze the trigger. No phony coercion; no apologies. Just quick, efficient death.

But alas, it seemed that this trip would be uneventful. The *barang* had seen to that.

That was his task. How he earned his money.

Nud despised the *barang* even more.

———

General Miet was in the jeep in front of the two trailers. A small, enclosed truck followed the second trailer. Unlike the others he wore no red scarf or sash. He checked his watch. Ten past eight.

He watched the road markers. They told him how near they were to the junction. He would relax when they were on the southern road. That would mean they had successfully avoided the police detachment. He wasn't exactly sure, but he thought this would please the Naga. And right now, pleasing the Naga was very important to General Miet. He knew his life depended on it. The Naga was very difficult to deal with. No matter how hard he planned, how faultlessly he served him, the Naga never seemed satisfied. He'd organized killing parties and brought back severed heads at his request. The Naga merely snorted. He provided disposable victims for the Naga's unseen perversions. Again, more snorts and scowls.

The heist of the priceless Angkor relics. Perfectly executed. Once their transfer to the barge was completed, the money the general would receive would allow the Naga's forces to double. This should surely satisfy the Naga.

He prayed.

The fork in the road was ten kilometers away. He smiled. The other benefit of traveling on the southern road was that it was freshly paved. His poor aching bones could journey the rest of the trip in relative comfort.

———

Antoine used the butt of his last cigarette to light his next one.

"*Nervous*?" The colonel spoke to him in Khmer.

"Yes. A little. Is it obvious?"

"You're chain smoking. Filthy habit."

Antoine sucked the smoke deep into his lungs. They were approaching Prasat Komnap, a small sandstone tower, just one kilometer south of the intersection.

He checked his watch. Ten past eight. They'd lost time at the schoolhouse. They shouldn't have stopped. But as long as they kept moving now, they should be through the intersection and on the Banteay Srei road in less than five minutes.

Then the world took a turn for the worse. The colonel barked into his radio. "Sergeant Mok. Tell the drivers to pull over and stop just past the tower."

"What? What are you doing?" Antoine asked in astonishment.

"Stopping."

"But...why?"

"Because I want to, monsieur. And I am in charge."

"But we agreed to meet them on the road to Banteay Srei. They must come down that road and we will surprise them before they join the main road here. That way, if there's a confrontation, we avoid having it on a heavily traveled road."

"Heavily traveled? I have not seen *any* traffic at all tonight," the colonel scoffed. "We didn't *agree* on anything. You told me they would be coming out of the Kulen Hills on the Banteay Srei road...but there is another road." He opened the map and pointed. "The road from Phnum Kulean. It also crosses the Kulen Hills."

"But they won't be on that road."

"How do you know?"

"My informant. He assured me."

"Begging your pardon, but my trust in criminal informants is very limited. Both roads converge onto this road just one kilometer farther. We will wait here. If they are coming out tonight and they are headed south, then they must pass us here."

"But…"

The colonel waited. When Antoine seemed to have nothing further to add, he folded the map and put it into the pocket inside the door. The convoy came to a halt. The colonel ordered the trucks to park perpendicular to the road, on opposite sides, with their rear ends facing out. The colonel had Antoine pull into the southern shadow of one truck and ordered the Cambodians to do the same on the other side of the road.

One by one the police squad took positions with their guns at the ready.

"Now we wait." The colonel smiled.

Antoine, the *barang*, lit another cigarette.

**20**

Martin tried to get the brood into bed. He worked his way through the boys' dorm. Little Hon was no problem, he was already asleep. He carried him and placed him gently in his bed. He turned out the Scooby Doo lamp and smoothed the downy soft hair on his sweet brow. He tried not to play favorites, but Hon was hard not to love. He had the biggest solid brown eyes you ever saw. And he was sweet. He seemed 'not to have a mean bone in his body,' as Martin's mother had been fond of saying. If the other children took advantage of his good nature, which they did, he always turned the other cheek, smiling and saying 'never mind' and moving on to something else.

Martin left his little angel and moved on to Paul and Peter. They were already in their PJs. They wanted to know why they were going to bed early. "Big day tomorrow," Martin improvised.

Answer grudgingly accepted, Martin approached Sisko. He'd made remarkable progress. He still didn't talk, but he smiled. For Martin, that was a breakthrough. "Lights out, kiddo." He was rewarded with a smile as the tyrannosaurus rex that was his constant companion was put on its little stand next to the Hawaiian volcano lamp Martin had personally brought from Maui.

Micki was sullen. He was not happy about this arrangement that kept him away from his sister—just eight hours a day, Martin pointed out—and Martin always kept a respectful distance. Jane had made the most progress with him, but she was gone. They'd had two substitute teachers since—both had been on loan from a school in Phnom Penh—but Martin was not impressed. A permanent replacement was coming up from an international school in Phuket at the end of the month. Hopefully. Until then it was up to Martin and Areeya to keep the little ones busy. Luong, Kook's mother, had only basic reading and writing skills, but she was enthusiastic and she could control the brood—ninety percent of the job, as Martin had soon discovered—and get them from A to B.

Chawlie. 'The wounded one,' Martin always thought. He'd healed amazingly fast. He suffered the trauma, of course, of the deaths. He had no permanent physical injuries. But he was changed. He was quiet and withdrawn when before he'd been boisterous. He was given a lot of attention, but he was a long way from 'normal.'

Areeya tucked in the twins, Sacha and Khota. Their beds had been moved together.

Kook would be the last to go to sleep. She insisted upon reading and wouldn't turn out her light until Areeya was ready to leave. And then she would read under the covers with a flashlight. She was never punished for this for, as Martin pointed out, reading was to be encouraged.

Minnie was as resentful as her brother at their nightly separation and, as with her brother, Areeya kept her distance. She too had been bitten. She turned off her light with a remote control.

Beautiful Naj never turned her light on. But Areeya knew that many nights she lay awake in the darkness thinking of her sister Tiara, who had been so callously murdered. And she would sob quietly, for hours. Areeya kissed her forehead and brushed a hand across her cheek.

She nodded to Kook, who begrudgingly turned out her light.

In the hall outside the dorms she joined Martin, who had been waiting for her.

"I just pray we get through this night. Tomorrow I'm taking all of us to Phnom Penh."

————

Eight thirty. Antoine knew the exact moment when the fighting began, because he had just looked at his watch.

There was a slight dip in the road to the north about 100 meters away. It was a gradual grade that allowed the approach of the Naga's trucks to be hidden until they crested it. It was this that gave them the advantage, for they came to a halt the moment they sighted the police vehicles.

Colonel Vanchea put down his binoculars. "It's them. They've stopped."

Taking up the glasses again, he watched as the two jeeps drove to the rear of the trucks. Slowly the trucks backed up until they were no longer visible. For what seemed like an eternity but was merely a few minutes, nothing happened. The colonel contemplated sending a few men to reconnoitre when one of the jeeps reappeared on the horizon. A man in the passenger seat stood up and rested a weapon on the windscreen.

"Shit. Open fire!" the colonel exclaimed.

His men responded with a barrage of machine-gun fire, but it was too late. The grenade launcher fired and, as the colonel and Antoine jumped for cover, the truck they had been standing next to exploded in a ball of fire.

As the colonel raised his head, another grenade was launched and the second truck was demolished. He covered his head from the rain of debris. When the chunks of burning metal stopped falling, the screams started. As the colonel struggled to his feet, the horror was revealed. All around him, men lay dying. Those who were uninjured were attempting to help their battered and bleeding counterparts. What was left of the two trucks burned and sent two thick columns of black smoke into the night sky.

The colonel had three men standing. One of those was bleeding from a gash to his head, but he was moving. One of Antoine's men, Ang, survived. He was holding his partner's motionless body in his lap. The colonel looked for Antoine.

"Antoine!" he shouted. The *barang* was in his Land Rover, rapidly fleeing the scene. The colonel raised his pistol but didn't fire. He lowered it and just shook his head at the cowardly deed.

"Colonel," one of his men yelled. Bullets zinged past him and tore up the ground as he turned back and saw the man pointing down the highway. The convoy was on the move, heading directly for them. A man with a machine-gun was firing from the running board on each side of the trucks. They traveled side by side, taking up the entire road, with the jeeps behind them.

"The jeep. Take cover," he yelled. As the barrage of gunfire grew heavier, his men left their fallen comrades and ran for the only available shelter—the Subaru jeep. It was covered in ash and smoldering debris, but it was intact. The four remaining police and Ang vainly tried to return fire at the approaching convoy of death.

---

Martin watched the road. His automatic weapon was beside him. He hadn't wanted the children to see the guns. Pom had kept his out of their sight when they hid on the bus.

He would put them all back on the bus tomorrow and move

them down to Phnom Penh. Move them all into the Inter-Continental until he figured out what to do. But he could no longer sit and wait for something to happen.

He tried to imagine what was happening up the road. What he hoped was happening was *nothing*. That Antoine's informant had been wrong, or lied, and there was no movement tonight. Then there would be no confrontation.

That was what he *hoped* would happen.

"Martin. You're leaving tomorrow?" It was Julianne who asked the question. She sat with Luong in the small entry room. Justin had a machine-gun and stood by the window opposite Martin. Pom and Areeya, also armed, were at each of the side windows.

"Yes. I'm taking them all to Phnom Penh."

"Can I come with you?"

"Of course."

"Michelle and Robert have gone. Back to France."

Martin looked at the girl. She was trembling. He put a hand on her shoulder and looked to Justin, who just shook his head and continued to stare out the window. Then: "There's a car coming, fast."

Martin moved back to his post, gun at the ready. "It's Antoine."

Julianne got up and raced to the door. Martin stopped her. "Hang on a moment. Let me make sure everything is all right." He went out the door, gun in hand.

Antoine screeched to a halt, just before crashing into the school's wall. He jumped out of the jeep, eyes darting around madly.

"Antoine. What is it? What happened?"

"That damn fool stopped too soon. We could have missed them entirely but he led us right to them."

"I don't understand."

"They're dead, Martin. All dead."

"My God…They saw you leave?"

"Yes. Of course. They were shooting at me."

"They're headed this way?"

"Yes."

"We must get your car out of sight."

"Yes. You're right."

Martin opened the gate and Antoine drove the Land Rover down the driveway. Martin padlocked both gates to the front of the schoolhouse. He switched off the exterior lights.

Antoine was at his side now. He too had a machine-gun in hand.

"Quickly. Get inside." Martin stayed in the yard while Antoine entered the house.

Julianne was in the doorway and hugged Antoine to him as he came near.

"Antoine. Thank God you're all right."

Martin came through the door and bolted it.

"Luong, Pom. Go through the house and make sure *all* the lights are shut off."

Pom nodded and they left the room. The lights in the entry were already off, and two candles gave off a faint glow.

"Antoine. Tell us what happened."

Antoine ran a hand through his sweat soaked hair. He fumbled through his pockets for a cigarette, but he only came up with an empty packet. Justin handed him one and lit it for him. "Thanks." He exhaled a long stream of smoke. Martin didn't allow smoking in the house, but he decided to make an exception.

"There was not one word exchanged. They had rocket launchers and blew us to smithereens."

"Oh my God." Julianne had Antoine's hand and she squeezed it tight.

"Everyone else...?" Areeya didn't know how to phrase the question, and was afraid of the answer.

"Yes." Antoine was nearly done with the cigarette already. Justin held out another. He took it without comment.

"How did you manage to escape?" Martin asked.

"My vehicle was undamaged. I got in and drove like hell."

Martin was thinking of what Antoine had blurted out when they were outside. '*We could have missed them entirely.*' It made no sense to him. But he chose to remain silent. He had their immediate welfare as his primary concern. Sorting out Antoine's story could wait.

"How many are there?"

"Two trucks and two jeeps. The trucks are hauling covered trailers. Obviously the relics are in the trailers."

"How many men?"

"I…I don't know."

"Let's pray that they pass us by."

"They should…shouldn't they?" Julianne squeezed Antoine's hand again as she looked at Martin. "I mean, why would they stop *here*?"

*Why indeed?* Martin looked briefly at Antoine. Everyone grew quiet. Lost in their own thoughts.

It was Pom who broke the silence first. "Khun Martin. Are you going to put the children back on the bus tonight?"

"No. I don't want to frighten them any more. Julianne's right. They should just pass us by."

*Lord. Please make it so. Where is my saviour?*

———

Nud held onto his smoking gun. The barrel was still red hot. It had been fantastic.

After the glorious rocket assault—he'd been on the receiving end of those contraptions too many times—the general had instructed them to fire at will, and they had mounted the truck running boards. It was difficult to fire an automatic weapon while holding onto the truck. And *they* were being fired at, as well. Pran and four others were killed. They just fell off the truck. Pran might not have been killed by the bullet, but he was certainly killed by the truck as its rear tire ran over him. Nud felt bullets missing him by hairs as he squeezed off round after round. The sounds and smells were overwhelming.

The truck drove straight at the little silver jeep. Nud was not sure if they had hit anybody with their wild gunfire, but the question was moot when the truck, with its four-ton load, ran right over the jeep like it was nothing more than a beer can.

The two jeeps following the truck popped off pistol shots at anybody still moving.

Then it was over. They never even stopped.

———

The moon was nearly full. It shone across the road, giving the tarmac a silver sheen. Beyond, the rice paddies glistened and the stalks undulated like waves in the light breeze. Nothing had been on the road since Antoine's arrival, apart from a couple of toads.

Martin had brought a stool in from the kitchen, as standing at the window had given his leg a cramp. He glanced around the room. Justin had forfeited the position at the other front window to Antoine, as Antoine was an experienced shooter.

*Maybe they turned around.*

Martin realized the absurdity of the thought and dismissed it. Why, when they had defeated the only blockade to their success, would they turn back?

Then he heard the rumble of the trucks.

———

They'd stopped only when the massacre was out of sight. The general's order barked through the radio and the trucks shifted down and applied their powerful brakes. With great hissing and screeching they finally stopped, in the middle of the road.

General Miet ordered the men to step down and return to

their original positions. The grenade launcher was re-crated and shifted back into the truck that Nud rode in. He sat back down on the crate. He was alone now in the rear of the truck. Pran and Keav, who'd been stationed at the front of the trailer, were both dead. The general and his adjutant inspected the cargo. There were holes in the canvas. Moonlight splashed through them. The bullets had hit the crates, but it was quickly determined that they'd been stopped by the thick wood. The precious relics were undamaged.

The general drew his pistol. Nud knew this was not a good sign. Leang, a man so old that even Nud referred to him as *bawng*, older brother, was bleeding profusely from a wound to the chest. He had been the one firing the grenade launcher and had been hit simultaneously with the firing of the second rocket.

Leang had been lifted out of the jeep and lay with his head propped up on one of his comrade's knapsacks. He wouldn't utter a word though the pain, no doubt, was unbearable. The general said the words that had sealed the fate of so many: "*At oy te.*" And shot him in the head.

A man from the second truck, Geak, was placed alongside Nud, and the vehicles started to roll again.

Nud thought of Comrade Leang as the truck ground through the gears. He'd known him for at least twenty years. He'd been a corrupt, efficient killing machine during the *Great War*. During their years hiding in the jungle, he'd shared whatever food he managed to forage.

Nud had not despised him.

———

They had gone barely two kilometers when suddenly a figure appeared in the road. A tall, hooded man. Right in the middle of the highway. Nud had taken to leaning out the back like a dog to get the breeze, and was able to see the man. The general's jeep was back to leading the procession and he smiled as he moved to the side and let the truck move ahead of him. *Let the truck deal with the fool.*

The truck was nearly on top of the man when he removed the hood.

"The Naga!" The general gasped and barked into the radio: "Stop!" Tremendous burning of rubber, grinding and stripping of gear teeth, and huge wooshes of air brakes finally brought the truck to a halt. One inch from the Naga's nose.

The second truck was following close behind, and swerved to the left to avoid rear-ending truck number one. It had heard the general's order and it also ground to a stop. There was a long minute when everyone held their breath. All that could be heard were the creaks and groans of the metal settling. That and the truck engines rumbling.

Finally the Naga smiled.

Then the general smiled. Everyone smiled.

"Comrade. We did not expect to see you."

The Naga walked to the side of the truck, reached up, and opened the passenger door. The startled soldier started to slide over on the seat. The poor wretch fell in his haste to vacate the cab. He sprawled at the bare feet of the Naga, who used him for a footstool. He sat in the cab and stared straight ahead.

The general waited a moment for an order. When it became apparent that none was coming, he bowed and went back to his jeep. He ordered the soldier from the truck to sit behind him, and then he gave the command to move out.

In the rear of the truck, Nud smiled. Tonight had been extraordinary so far, and with the Naga on board, it promised to get even better.

## 21

Ramonne watched as Zhoupeng went from nineteenth-century behemoth to twenty-first century megalomaniac. Kaestle was astonished at the transformation. Zhoupeng grew from a hunchback just barely five feet to a stately prince of a man, seven feet at least. As he did, the Bayon reverted to its present-day condition.

*"Frenchman. At last you're here."*

Ramonne felt a tug at his trouser. He looked down. Dr. Kaestle had prostrated himself. He looked up at the vampire. "Please. Master. Beseech him."

Ramonne shrugged the doctor off and concentrated on the enemy at hand.

*"I've journeyed far, Zhoupeng."*

*"Call me Naga. Everyone does. It instills great honor. The fools think me the reincarnation of one of their late, great kings—one who took the form of a snake on occasion."*

Ramonne ignored him. *"Zhoupeng. Why do you torment these people so?"*

At this, Zhoupeng began a slow, mad dance. He weaved around Ramonne and Dr. Kaestle, who mainly kept his eyes and body to the ground.

"*Why? Why? Why do you think vampires started to pop up around the time of the Industrial Revolution?*" His eyes flared. "*Are you surprised I know of such things? A savage like me? Fool...I choose my persona. The savage serves a purpose. Do you not suppose I could be a city dandy like you?*"

He continued his mad dance.

"*We—you and I, and all the other devils that plague the world—are the product of the elimination of the indigenous peoples. Their connection to nature and the gods kept the balance. We are the direct product of that imbalance.*

"*The story is the same the world over. The native Indians of the Americas; the Aborigines of Asia; the hilltribes of Thailand; the Orang Asli of Malaysia; the Stiens of Cambodia...they lived predominately by the forces of Nature and lived off the land. They all lived in connection with the*

"'*Great Spirit.' They knew their place in the cosmos. It is not by accident that Angkor Wat's positioning to the stars is in exact alignment with the pyramids of Egypt and the Mayan temples at Chichén Itzá.*

"*Angkor Wat was the 'axis mundi,' the absolute center of the universe. When they learned how to align themselves with the stars, they began their ascent to the realms of the gods and beyond.*

"*Here, in a temple built by generations of people who had learned to harness the forces of Nature, I was once defeated. They drew upon the power of their alignment with the constellation Draco to summon great spirits and silence the immortal demon in their presence. Here, in the finest sacred architecture in the world—architecture whose measurements and cosmological interpretations were based on ancient verdict scriptures—sorcerers and mathematicians were given free reign to analyze the powers that they knew they were in touch with. Their ancient scriptures hold the keys to these powers.*

"*And it was here that I too, studied the Sanskrit scriptures that they left behind. It was here that I learned the antithesis of their quest. It was here that I learned how to divert that cosmic energy into its direct opposite force...ultimate evil.*"

Ramonne felt the Naga's temperature flare with this pronouncement. It was a surge like a fire being stoked. He removed his coat and unbuttoned his shirt.

*"Why do you think this poor country has suffered so?"*

He looked Ramone in the eye. *"It has been at my will."*

The Naga preened, like a peacock. He flaunted his magnificent physique. He was on stage.

*"I saw the French lose their chance to control this wild place. I saw the missed opportunities when the stupid American war with the Viet Cong failed. And so I seduced and encouraged the Khmer Rouge. I gloried in their misspent attempts at patriotism and encouraged their bloodletting."*

Ramonne was appalled at what he was hearing. He fired back at the beast in a tongue that none but two hell hounds could possibly understand. *"Demon of hell. You desecrate the vestige you were allowed. Tis this shaman's quest, tis this shaman's sanction to see you destroyed."*

The Naga looked to Ramonne, now his very eyes were on fire. *"Frenchman. It is but 150 years that you have enjoyed the power. Do you think that you can defy me?"*

They locked in a solemn stare. There would be no reply. There would be no more challenge. The glove had been dropped.

Zhoupeng raised his arms and disappeared.

Professor Kaestle trembled and looked to the vampire. He hesitated to ask, but he had to. "What about me, master? What about me?"

Ramonne looked into a space deeper than the universe. He said, very quietly: "Not now."

———

Nud looked out the back when the truck slowed and the brakes started to hiss. The schoolhouse? Nud had passed it many times. Pran and Keav had told him about shooting the old lady and the kid. They'd done it for sport and because they could. And it would amuse the Naga.

They stopped directly across the road. The jeeps pulled off the road and used the trucks for cover.

Nud heard the general get out of his jeep. He was talking but he couldn't make out what he was saying. Not wanting to miss anything, he climbed down. Geak moved to join him but Nud put up a hand to restrain him. "Stay in the trailer."

He grinned to himself. He liked giving orders.

"Comrade. Why are we stopping here?" General Miet was confused. The Naga looked down at him through the window.

*'The barang is here. Kill him.'*

The general looked to the schoolhouse. It was dark; not a light was lit.

"Are you sure he's there?"

The Naga ignored him.

"Yes. I'll send a man to check the driveway for his vehicle."

The general dispatched Geak. Looking both ways before he crossed, Geak shouldered his weapon and slowly crossed the road.

———

"Fuck." Martin cursed as the armed man crossed the road. Antoine followed him with his gun. "What do we do?"

In response, Antoine squeezed his trigger and fired off three rounds. *Ptt. Ptt. Ptt.*

The old man dropped to the moonlit asphalt. His weapon clacked as it hit the tarmac.

"Good Lord." Martin gasped.

"That's one less to worry about." Antoine swung his gun back to the trucks.

———

"Take cover." The general and his men scrambled to get behind the trucks. The first man there raked the schoolhouse windows.

*Brrrrrrrrrrrrrrrrrt.*

"Cease fire," the general barked.

The Naga sat stoical in the truck cab. His mouth curled into a smile.

General Miet felt that the Naga had something to say to him. He moved closer to the door and looked up. The Naga's gaze was on the schoolhouse as he spoke.

*"I was wrong. Kill them all."*

———

"Shit. Now what?" Martin was sweating and trying to remain in control. The shutters for the front windows had a dozen holes in them and the wall across from them was pockmarked and chunks of masonry lay on the floor.

"Now they will start firing at us to give cover to the men who will cross the street and the shelter of our wall. We will need to return that fire."

Martin looked around the room. Luong was curled in the corner holding Julianne. Julianne had the look of a deer caught in the headlights. "Luong. Go to the children now. Julianne, you join her. Keep them down and under their beds. Pom. You guard them. Go now."

They scurried from the room just as another barrage of automatic weapon fire ripped into the schoolhouse. Martin slammed the wooden shutters and dropped to the floor. Antoine fired a volley and then dropped to the floor. Justin did the same.

Bullets smashed into the bookcase and into the entry hall. Chunks of plaster flew and white dust soon covered everything and everyone.

"Shoot. Shoot them, Martin." Antoine was back at the window and firing at the three men that were scrambling across the road.

He hit one.

Martin stuck the gun barrel out the window and squeezed the trigger without looking.

"Stop," Antoine shouted. "They're at the wall."

———

General Miet stopped his men from firing. He had been shocked when gunfire came from the schoolhouse and struck down comrade Geak. He had really been shocked when automatic weapons were fired from three windows. He now was sure the *barang* was in the schoolhouse. But who was with him? With automatic weapons? He'd seen the Cambodians that worked for him shot—actually, one was shot, and one was crushed by a truck. It definitely wasn't them.

*Then who?*

He shook the thought from his head and concentrated on the mission at hand. He'd lost two men, but he now had two men well positioned here.

He watched as Lee and Chou made their separate ways behind the protection of the wall, heading for the two gates. The gates were locked, of course. Each man was prepared. They placed small explosive charges directly onto the Yale locks. They turned their backs and simultaneously the locks blew.

General Miet smiled. This would be easy.

The gate to the driveway swung inward from the explosion. As it did, the soldier followed, his gun held in front of him.

A huge explosion rocketed the air the minute he set foot inside the driveway. The soldier's body was tossed into the air.

———

"*Land-mine*! A land-mine, Martin? You put a fucking landmine in the driveway?"

"Yes. I armed it after you arrived. There's one in the front gate as well."

Antoine was astonished. "*Man*. You gotta tell us about this stuff. Anything else we should know?"

"No. I could only get two in the market. Right now, this is a very difficult place to purchase land-mines…I'm pleased to say."

"Thank God." Antoine nodded to Martin. "And thank *you*. That's another one down. But I doubt his friend will be foolish enough to go through the front gate."

———

The general was flabbergasted. *Land-mines? Who the fuck are they?*

He noticed that Nud was under the Naga's window. He didn't like that. He decided he needed something dangerous for Nud to do. He thought about this as he looked through the binoculars as Lee abandoned the front gate and inched behind the wall to the driveway.

Nud looked up at the Naga. He looked magnificent. He radiated. His skin was almost pure white, but it had a sheen he couldn't describe; a healthy glow.

"Comrade, may I suggest something?"

The Naga didn't move. His gaze was on the schoolhouse.

"Comrade." He re-thought the word. "*Sir*. I have an idea."

Now the Naga turned to him.

'*You again?*' The word rang in his head like a bell in Notre Dame.

"Y-yes. If I might…"

There was no response from the Naga.

Nud decided to continue: "I go down the road—he pointed north—until I am out of their sight and—"

'*You'll go around the rear.*'

Nud nodded. "They have all their firepower concentrated on the front. It's not a fort. It's just a schoolhouse. No doubt there's an easy entry through the back."

*'You waste words. Just go.'*

The Naga turned his head back to the schoolhouse as Nud slunk away.

General Miet came over and called up to the Naga.

"Comrade. What's he doing?"

*'He wants to be a hero. Let him.'*

The general scowled.

———

Areeya was on the north side of the school. She watched the man crawl through the gate. He went directly over the crater that had housed the mine that killed his comrade. He looked for trip wires and land-mines. He didn't look to the window. He didn't look for snipers.

Areeya shot him. A rapid burst.

*Brrrrrrrrrrrrrrrrrrrrt.*

The man died instantly.

She slumped to the floor and pushed the smoking weapon away from her.

She cried.

———

The children were terrified. Luong had moved the boys into the girl's dorm, at the rear of the building. They'd pushed all the beds away from the single window and then climbed under them; girls on one side, boys on the other. Pom, no longer hiding his weapon from the children, stayed at the window. Julianne had her arms around little Hon, Paul and Peter. Luong had Naj and Kook. Minnie had joined her brother and they squeezed each other tight.

There were sobs and there were tears. But mostly there was fear.

————

General Miet was beside himself. He'd sent three men to their graves. That worried him less than the fact that he had accomplished nothing. Possibly they had hit someone in the house, but there continued to be fire from three guns in the front, and now there was a shooter on the north side, as well.

He had a half-dozen men left, and they continued to strafe the house with machine-gun fire. He watched through his field glasses as Nud went along the wire fence hidden behind a row of cypress trees.

Nud knew that this was his chance to impress the Naga. He would emerge from this encounter a hero. He'd slip through the back of the school while the *barang* and whoever else was helping him were concentrating on defending themselves. And murder them all.

*The power of surprise.*

He crept along the rear of the garage and followed the low hedge that bordered the fence along the playground. Eventually he came to a gate.

It was not locked.

Nud smiled. Just as he had figured. They'd concentrated their defense on the front. Assuming the attack would come from the road. He cautiously slipped the metal rod out of the eyebolt and swung the gate towards him.

As he stepped into the yard, Nud thought of how he would emerge through the front door after murdering the *barang*. He thought he would cut off his head—he had his K-Bar knife, it would do the job—and hold it for the Naga to see.

*The glory. Just a few minutes more and —*

*Click.*

Nud felt the wire when his foot pulled on it. He heard the *click*.

His last word was the same as the videotaped responses of skydivers when their parachutes don't open. It was in Khmer, but it was the same word:

*"Fuck."*

———

The blast from the rear of the house caused Antoine to leave his window. He scurried, staying low to the floor, until he got to the back window. He saw the remains of Nud scattered across the lawn. Smoke hung in the air.

He swung his rifle left to right, but there seemed to be no one else. He went back to the front.

"They tried to come in the back. Something blew them up."

"Hand-grenade. They were all out of land-mines." Martin smiled. He'd protected his perimeter. He looked to Antoine. "How many men do they have?"

"Fucked if I know."

"Guess."

"There might be ten of them. Maybe less…maybe more."

"There's five of us with guns. We've plenty of ammunition. We can hold them off, yes?"

*"Oui.* It is possible." He paused and his eyes grew large. "Except for…"

"Except for *what*?" Martin followed his gaze.

A man was at the hood of one of the trucks. He was propping up a metal tube.

"Shit. Is that—"

"A grenade launcher."

Antoine fired furiously at the man. Martin and Justin joined in. Their barrage was returned and they dropped to the floor. The man with the rocket was hit, but he fired the weapon as he fell. The rocket flew off course and hit the north corner of the toolshed at the end of the drive. It was enough to set off the ammunition stored within, and the subsequent explosion sent the Land Rover flying through the air. It crash-landed upside-down in the middle of the road.

# 22

A shadow fell across the moon. It was not a cloud.

The Naga emerged from the truck. He walked slowly to the center of the road.

The overturned Land Rover emitted smoke and other noxious fumes. They swirled around the Naga. The moon returned and cast its glow.

The Naga's eyes were two burning red orbs. He raised his right hand. An incantation spewed from his lips in a language foreign to all who heard it.

All but one.

Ramonne.

The vampire was in front of the schoolhouse wall. *"Do not disturb this family any further."* He answered in the same language.

The Naga slowly turned to face him.

He began to smile.

*'My son. Good of you to join us.'*

The general was unsure what to make of the tall stranger with the shock of white in his shoulder-length hair. He had his remaining men keep their guns trained on him.

In the schoolhouse, Martin put his hand on Antoine's gun and motioned for him to put it down.

"Our guns are useless."

Antoine stared at the Naga, his eyes wide with fear.

"My God. It *is* true. They do serve a ghost."

Martin remained silent, watching. And waiting. Areeya had joined him, and she took her place alongside him.

"I merely want the *barang*. Send him out and we will leave." The Naga spoke now in a language that all could understand.

Hearing this, Antoine put his gun to the window's edge and fired at the Naga.

"No!" Martin shouted, but it was too late.

The charge ripped through the Naga's left side. He reeled from the hits and his eyes focused on the source of the gunfire. He thrust his hand out at the window and spread his fingers wide. A wave—like the rippling effect on a desert highway in the heat—traveled from his hand to the window. The wall around the window cracked and fell away, exposing Antoine. He stared in shock as he was suddenly pulled, as if he were on an invisible leash, across the broken wall and the rubble-strewn and bloodstained tarmac until he was at the feet of the Naga.

Antoine still clutched his gun, and his shaky hands raised it to fire…when he saw that the wounds he had just inflicted on the Naga were healing before his very eyes.

The Naga leaned down and stared into those eyes. "*Don't*," was all he said. With that, he took the gun from the hand of the man, who was now paralyzed with fear.

Zhoupeng smoothed Antoine's matted hair. It was as if he was petting him. He looked to Ramonne as he spoke. "*You want to protect him? He's human, so I'm not sure why you would waste your time —only, I suppose, because time is not an issue with you. But I suppose it has to do with this fraternal. . .*" He smirked, "*dare I say 'maternal' interest you've shown for these children at this sad little outpost.*"

Ramonne retorted: "*You waste too much of your endless time speculating on my motives. Let it be signified by my mere presence that I have a vested interest in all of these mortals. It is my desire that you leave these people in peace."*

The Naga continued to smile.

*"That you leave this place..."* Ramonne paused, for what seemed an eternity.

*"Now!"*

Zhoupeng never changed his posture. He continued to 'pet' Antoine, who remained frozen at his feet. He looked down at Antoine as he spoke. *"You know this half-breed?"*

Ramonne remained still. He spoke a single word. *"No."*

*"Ahh. That's a pity. He's quite the funny little bee. He pretends to be the defender of the temples and the relics. He pretends to care."*

As he said these last words, the Naga let one of his talons rake the side of Antoine's neck. Immediately a small trickle of blood flowed. *"In reality what he cares about is money. He has sold the very relics that he so cherishes...for his own profit."*

Another stroke of the hair, another slash, and more blood.

Ramonne had total control of his senses. He was not diverted by the presence of the life-giving fluid.

The Naga's smile curved downward as he continued his diatribe. *"But that was the least of his transgressions. He sold human lives as well. He traded information on the police for a price and led them into a trap. There is much blood on his hands."*

Ramonne remained unmoved by anything the Naga said. He let his last words trail off; he let the sound of insects and the nocturnal jungle orchestra be heard before he replied:

*"I said I did not know him, that's true. But I do know of him. I am aware of all that transpired here. And I am aware of the oracle of evil you have brought to it."*

He looked at the Naga. His yellow eyes bored into the Naga's crimson orbs. *"It stops here."*

The Naga's smile returned. He grabbed a hunk of Antoine's hair and pulled him to his feet. He did not resist.

In one swift move, Zhoupeng cracked Antoine's neck and bent the head backward.

"*No!*" Julianne's cry was heard from the schoolhouse.

The Naga smiled at her as he lacerated Antoine's throat. The general and his men gasped. They had never witnessed this brutal act in the flesh.

Ramonne remained unmoved. The blood consuming took its course and the Naga dropped the lifeless body to the road.

Zhoupeng glowed as the life-source surged through his body. Finally he wiped his crimson lips and spoke. "*No intervention? No rescue?*"

Ramonne remained impassive. "*He was not worth the effort. I gave him to you as a parting gift.*"

The Naga's eyes opened wide. "*You? You think you are in control?*"

Ramonne lifted his hands from his side, just slightly. As he did, a fire appeared and blasted across the road. The flaming wave hit the Naga and knocked him off balance. He recovered immediately but the wave continued. The trucks were toppled and the two jeeps tossed like child's toys, ending up a hundred meters away and submerged in the rice paddies. The general and his men were gone. The wheels of the overturned trucks spun slowly.

The Naga stood alone. The corpse of Antoine was gone, blown away by Ramonne's cosmic blast. He ran a hand over his shaved skull and then opened the hooded garment and discarded it. His muscular frame rippled as he inhaled deeply.

Like two cobras with their hoods flared, the immortals stood their ground. The challenge had been laid down. The gloves were coming off.

---

Julianne was in Martin's arms, her head on his chest. His shirt was soaked with her tears. In front of them was the hole in the wall that Antoine had been ripped through. It provided a sheltered view of the confrontation between the two vampires.

Martin held Julianne close. Her sobbing had subsided into short gasps, as if she were trying to breathe for the first time. She looked up at Martin. She couldn't look at the road.

"What's happening?" Her nails dug into Martin's arm and he had to gently remove them. He looked across the room. Areeya was slumped against the pockmarked wall. She cradled her M-16 in her arms. She and Martin locked eyes. She slowly nodded. The recognition of the mission, once again, to explain the unexplainable.

"We have to wait, Julianne. That man..." He waited as she slowly turned her head and confronted the bizarre scene outside. Martin indicated Ramonne. "He is our friend."

"*Friend*? Why didn't he stop that beast from killing Antoine?" Her eyes were wide with scorn.

"I don't know, Julianne. But I do know this. Our safety. . . our very *survival* rests with him."

Julianne could look no more. She buried her head again. Martin folded his arms over her. Suddenly he realized that Julianne had been with the children. She had appeared during the time—moments before, but a seeming eternity—when Antoine had been called out by the vampire from the Bayon.

If she was here, what about the children? He started to unravel himself from her hold, when he saw the first pair of little eyes.

"They won't stay away, Khun Martin. I'm sorry." Luong had her daughter Kook by the hand. The girl held little Hon's tiny hand. They stood in the hallway arch.

Immediately, Areeya leapt up. She brushed a vase with two lotus blossoms off a sturdy oak side table and turned it over. She put her hand on Luong's shoulder and guided her and the children to crouch behind it.

Martin finally managed to pass Julianne over to Justin, who gladly wrapped her in his arms. He looked to the children and

Luong. They had some protection from bullets that was afforded by the four-inch-thick oak table. They cowered behind it. He looked to Areeya. They both knew that bullets were no longer their biggest threat. And yet each held on to their M-16 rifles.

"Martin." Areeya raised her gun. He dropped down and turned around. Someone was climbing through the hole in the wall.

"Don't shoot." The English language saved the man's life, as Martin's finger was squeezing the trigger in the instant he spoke.

"Doctor Kaestle." Martin lowered the gun barrel and helped him climb over the rubble.

Kaestle's gray hair was pure-white now, and there was a distinct green tinge to his skin. He fell onto the stone floor and Areeya helped him to a sitting position. He shook and sweated as if he was suffering from a great fever.

"God save us. God save us," he muttered over and over. He looked through the open wall and saw the Naga. Immediately he made the sign of the cross over himself and crawled as far away from the sight as his feeble legs could take him.

Areeya went to his side. She sat next to him, still clutching her M-16. Martin looked to Justin. He was stone cold. The 'thousand-yard stare' they called it in the Vietnam War, when a man had seen too much. He held his rifle and stared blankly at the road. Martin joined him at the adjacent window.

They waited for something, *anything*, to happen.

---

The silence was shattered by *screams*. The ear-piercing cries of the children. These were punctuated with machine-gun fire. Martin scrambled to his feet.

"Stay here. Watch the front," he blurted to Justin as he and

Areeya raced down the hall. The hallway was filled with running, screaming, crying children.

"Naj? Chawlie?"

"*Pos,*" was the single word reply.

"Snakes?" He entered the boy's dorm. "Good Lord." The scene before him was an unimaginable nightmare. Dozens of snakes of all size and color filled the room. Cobras, pythons, pit vipers, coral snakes—all squirming and jostling for space. Micki and Minnie were on top of a cabinet holding onto each other and crying. Pom was on a table spraying the snakes with bursts from his M-16. Each snake that was hit exploded—and was instantly replaced by two more.

Martin began firing, aiming at the serpents that were circling the children.

"Stop!" It was Dr. Kaestle who made the cry. "It's an illusion."

Pom stared at the white-haired stranger, and then resumed shooting at the snakes.

Martin turned to Kaestle. "How do you know it's an illusion?"

"The master warned me of Zhoupeng's many tricks. He said he would conjure up serpents and demons to drive his enemies mad. But they would be merely illusions—harmless if you didn't believe in them.

Martin looked back at the nest of vipers. There were now twice as many snakes in the room as when he arrived a moment ago. Pom continued to shoot and they continued to multiply.

*Illusion.* Martin trembled as he thought the word. "Fuck. What if it's not?" Logic told him that snakes that multiplied when you killed them was impossible.

But so were vampires. Yet there were two very real vampires engaged in combat in front of his home.

He took a deep breath. He forced himself to repeat the mantra: "*Illusion. Just an illusion. Just an illusion…*" And stepped into the room.

Two vipers whirled as he approached and reared up their heads. They hissed and flicked their tongues menacingly at him. He pulled his foot back.

"Illusion. Just an illusion."

He looked back at the doctor, who made a motion with his hands, urging him to go forward. Martin took another step. The viper nearest him struck. It hit him on the toe of his shoe. Martin was shocked into recoiling. But he quickly realized that nothing had really happened. The snake had appeared to strike, but there was nothing there. The viper was gone as soon as it struck. Disappeared.

The second viper rose up and struck his leg. Martin tensed, but again, as soon as it appeared to strike, it vanished. And again, there was no bite. No wound.

He stepped confidently now, moving toward the two siblings. As he stepped, more snakes attacked, struck, and disappeared. They slithered over his feet, coiled on his legs; one dropped from a beam above his head and wrapped itself around his neck. "Stop shooting," he yelled to Pom, "Just walk out. Let them attack. They'll destroy themselves. They're not real."

The man stared wide-eyed at him. Martin realized that he had crossed a void of fear into a world of madness. Pom shook his head and continued shooting. The snakes continued to multiply around him, now swarming up the table legs.

Martin was sweating profusely as he approached the terrified brother and sister. Micki and Minnie looked ready to collapse from fright. They clutched each other so tight they nearly squeezed the air out of their lungs.

Martin had to concentrate on the children. "Hold on, kids. I'll be there in a flash." He realized how ridiculous this sounded from a man with a ten-foot python coiled around him.

But the renewed faith that had carried Martin this far carried him safely to their side. He picked them up and hoisted them into his arms. "Don't be frightened. It's just make-believe.

"Only an illusion."

———

Ramonne watched Zhoupeng for signs. Furrowing his brow, tightening his fists, clenching his teeth. His studies of the necromantic arts and subsequent practice had taught him that these mental projections could not be accomplished without great exertion. No matter how composed he might appear, the signs were obvious to Ramonne. He confronted him.

*"What treachery have you wrought now?"*

Zhoupeng smiled, just slightly. *"I fear that your friends have entered the proverbial snake pit."*

Ramonne willed himself to read Martin's thoughts. They had a very close telekinetic connection, and it was easy for him to 'tune in' to him. He saw the snakes. But he also saw the doctor and knew he had warned them that they were not real. And he saw that Martin trusted and believed.

Ramonne believed that Zhoupeng could influence men's minds without having a visual connection, but that his powers would be limited to illusions. In his physical presence, however, he knew that Zhoupeng was capable of much more.

He dismissed the thought and turned back to the dilemma at hand.

*"My friends are fine."*

"Really?" Zhoupeng slowly balled his hands into fists.

*"Don't."*

Zhoupeng hesitated again. *"There's that ugly word again. And again I say to you, how dare you tell me what to do?"*

*"You misunderstand me. I'm not telling you what to do. I'm telling you what not to do. Don't harm my friends. The direct result of that would be your leaving here...now and forever."*

"Leave here? Where would you have me go? Back to my mountain retreat?" He pointed to the Kulen Range in the distance.

*"Too close."*

"*I have an idea, Frenchman. Why don't we go together? Back to where it all began. Just you and I...Agreed?*" Zhoupeng grinned his evil grin and waited.

Ramonne nodded. "*Agreed.*"

Slowly, Zhoupeng raised up his arms and wind began to encircle them. It swirled round about them, faster and faster, raising a tremendous cloud of dust.

Then, in an instant, the dust cloud, Zhoupeng, and Ramonne were gone.

———

Cautiously, Martin and Justin emerged from the schoolhouse. The landscape was a war zone. The trucks and jeeps were overturned and scattered about the rice paddies. Bodies and weapons were everywhere.

Martin and Justin held their rifles in front of them and stepped into the middle of the road.

Nobody moved. Nobody lived.

Martin saw the doctor picking his way through the rubble to stand in the middle of the road. Martin walked over to him.

"They're gone."

Kaestle said, "Yes. That was the master's plan."

"This was his *plan*?"

"Yes. You're safe aren't you?"

Martin considered this.

"The master had one more little request..."

## 23

It had been a century and a half since Ramonne had physically battled with Zhoupeng. He had nearly lost that battle. It had only been through the assistance of his dear friend Mouhot that he had prevailed.

Now they were back in the temple of the Bayon, and he faced him again—alone.

He had learned much in the passing years. His strength was incredible. His mental powers were finely tuned. His magic was powerful.

But he knew that Zhoupeng had a thousand years on him. Zhoupeng had not only the strength a vampire acquires through time, but he had the benefit of centuries studying the necromancer's world of spirits and spells. He had recently learned to possess the very souls of the unfortunates that he devoured. This alone had increased his strength with each and every kill. He was now nearly a meter taller than Ramonne. His muscles were enormous.

Zhoupeng moved in a serpentine manner. As he did, he taunted Ramonne. *"What do you have to lose? Besides your very existence? An existence that, unchallenged, could last an eternity?"*

He laughed. *"I will decapitate you and tether your carcass to the pinnacle of this temple. My foot soldiers will ensure your incineration is complete, and they will scatter your ashes across the Baray."*

Zhoupeng moved to a stone shelf and picked up a long scepter crowned by a gaping skull. He swung it in long sweeping arcs as he continued his rant:

*"Then I will delight in murdering your friends. Especially the children. My children. The Khmer Rouge were quite adept in that art. It has been a few years since I've heard the crack of a child's skull as it is swung by the feet and smashed against a wall."*

He pointed the scepter at Ramonne, and a wave emanated from it. It was a force field of evil. It carried a plague of images from the Khmer Rouge's emergence from the jungle into the streets of Phnom Penh, as they marched civilians out of the city and murdered them one by one. The millions of mothers, fathers, and children cried out in agony. Their disembodied souls flew at Ramonne. The force of the blow knocked him to the stone floor and out onto the parapet. The stone faces of King Jayavarman stared down at him as his body was tossed and battered by the black tidal wave.

*"At oy te."* Zhoupeng repeated the 'death sentence.' *"At oy te. At oy te."* Over and over, as he continued to propel the onslaught.

*"Why?"* was the chant that Ramonne willed his mind to project to counter the assault.

Zhoupeng's cry echoed the indifference with which the Khmer Rouge had taken human lives. *"At oy te."* It doesn't matter. One life means nothing.

Ramonne willed his answering cry to offer compassion. To question the right to dismiss a life as having no worth. *"Why?"* bellowed forth and carried with it the lives affected by the wanton slaughter. The wives, mothers, daughters, husbands, sons, and grandchildren that were left behind. Their images rose to meet the death wail.

The two force fields collided.

The explosion was more of an implosion and, within moments, the tremor subsided. The air was clear.

Physically spent, mentally exhausted, Ramonne struggled to his feet.

*"You have learned a lot, my son,"* the demon hissed. *"The knowledge to counter an attack such as that is knowledge not widely shared. Dare I say, I underestimated you?"* He spun the scepter again, this time in slow circles over his head.

The scepter began to glow. Zhoupeng smiled. *"I seriously doubt it."*

A red flame arched forth through the skull's mouth. This was followed by the appearance of figures of enormous girth and height. They stared through vacant eyes and stumbled forth in a somnambulant gait.

Ramonne instantly recognized them as the soulless victims of Zhoupeng's current rampage. His zombies.

One by one they attacked. And one by one Ramonne threw them off the parapet to land in the rock-strewn jungle below.

They were much more solidified than the monstrous volley that preceded them. Ramonne supposed it had to do with their recent demise and the fact that Zhoupeng had sapped their very souls.

They fought ferociously, like tigers, and Ramonne had all he could do to stay on his feet. They no longer attacked one at a time, but they now ganged up on him and, as one would get his attention, another would go for his legs, dragging him down, scratching clawing, ripping into his unearthly flesh.

He was overwhelmed. It had taken every bit of his energy and strength to combat the first attack. He tried to focus his thoughts, find the strength that would counter the assault. But the effort required to keep the beasts from rending his flesh was all-consuming. He had little left.

The ghouls were beginning to gnaw on his flesh. He winced as he felt teeth sink into his thigh. He managed to swat them off with mighty blows, but one was soon replaced by another.

*Alone. I'll die alone.*

The multitude that attacked him were driving him to his knees. They were tearing at his hair, clawing at his face. Teeth were sinking into his own neck.

His left leg went out from under him with an audible crack, and he was down. Now the fiends had him. Ripping into him. Tearing him apart.

He was lost. The battle had been won. Zhoupeng's reign of terror would continue. For eternity.

It was *his* blood now that was flowing. His eternal life was ebbing away. Soon he would be the lifeless corpse that Zhoupeng would decapitate and leave to blaze with the rising of the Angkor sun. As he vainly fought back, he felt his life force shutting down. The darkness to envelop him.

Through the haze he saw Zhoupeng's leering smile. In his head he heard his voice. *'It's over.'*

———

Martin parked the van and shut the lights. It had been difficult to enter Angkor Thom at night without Ramonne. Fortunately he found that he could still rely on his old ally: cold hard cash. A 100-dollar bill got the gates open. The night guard said he could enter, but that he couldn't get out of his vehicle. And he must return within the hour.

The moment he turned off the headlights, he saw the light from the Bayon. The upper tier was illuminated with a vibrant red glow. It was as if it was on fire, but no smoke or flame was present. The glow pulsated, like the throbbing beat of an open heart.

"They are there," Dr. Kaestle cackled. "We must hurry."

Martin stepped from the cab and opened the side door. Little five-year-old Hon was strapped in the seat. His almond eyes were wide. He was watching the temple light show in awe.

Martin looked to Kaestle. "I don't understand. How does the boy figure into this?"

"I don't know. He just does. The master said to have you bring your closest charge. 'Tell him to bring his son.' He said you would understand. You would know who he meant."

"He's never met my children."

Kaestle shook his head. "I know nothing. But the master needs us. We must hurry."

"I cannot allow any harm to come to any more of my children." He looked at Hon. The boy was totally enamored with the temple, the jungle, the lights, the smells. "Especially this one."

"Then you brought the right one. Now please, let's go."

Reluctantly, Martin unhooked the seat belt and hoisted Hon into his arms. They crossed the rubble-strewn entry and started to climb the cold stone steps that led to the upper levels of the temple. They quickly became aware of the sounds of a struggle. It came from the top of the temple, where the fiery glow emanated. The cries and calls that pierced the night were unlike anything they'd ever heard. Shrieks, banshee cries, caterwauls, and guttural snorts.

"Good God," Martin gasped. "What's going on?"

"A battle, no doubt," Dr. Kaestle calmly replied as he gingerly picked his way up the stairs.

*Great. Another battle.* Martin held onto Hon as they ascended.

Something flew through the air and landed with a heavy thud on the rubble directly beside them. Martin turned. It was a body. A human form. Yet it was not human. It was wretched. The eyes were empty sockets. The arms and limbs, bony skeletons. It was dead before it hit the rocks.

And then, slowly, it vanished. "Good Lord."

In quick succession three more bodies flew off the parapet and crashed onto the rocks. They too, swiftly disappeared.

The sounds from above were renewed. Martin was reluctant to go any further.

"Doctor. This is madness."

Kaestle looked at him curiously. "Madness? Is it madness to seek to save a friend? Madness to stop a force of evil?"

"It's madness to risk my child's life."

Kaestle looked at the boy. "*He* does not appear frightened."

In truth Martin had to admit that he didn't. The boy had the calmness of youthful innocence.

———

*"Your destruction is particularly pleasant to me. I have never had a son. I have never known the blessed vows of marriage. The sacred joys of conception."* Zhoupeng crossed the stone platform as he hissed his words at Ramonne. The once-proud vampire was being torn apart. *"But in you I have experienced the great glee of knowing that you are the direct result of my influence. You are my—dare I say— flesh and blood. I created you. I gave you eternal life."*

Zhoupeng put down his scepter and picked up a huge curved axe. Its razor-sharp blade gleamed in the unholy red light.

Ramonne was in his death throes, writhing as foul ghouls tore at his now frail body. He knew he had failed. Zhoupeng leaned over him, holding his head by the last shock of his once glorious mane.

He spat in Ramonne's face. *"You disgust me. You are weak. You've taken up 'causes.' You seek to bring about my downfall. You want to destroy me. Again! One hundred and fifty years ago you sentenced me to an unfathomable doom, merely because you were upset that I made you a vampire. You fucking buried me alive!"*

Zhoupeng allowed the ghouls to rip a large chunk of flesh from Ramonne's back. He grimaced in pain. Darkness continued to envelop him. Through the haze of pain, misery, and defeat he saw Zhoupeng commence his metamorphosis into the Naga, the serpent king. His head slowly transformed into that of a mighty serpent. His neck elongated and scales covered the rest of his form.

The Naga's forked tongue flicked menacingly. Ramonne's arms were held behind him by a half-dozen ghouls. The Naga raised his axe. Ramonne awaited the strike of the axe with the same sense of dread and relief that the millions of innocent victims of the Khmer Rouge had awaited the blow of the club or the tightening of the noose that would end the pain and misery. *"At oy te…It will be over."*

Just as the blade began its descent, a wave of blue light suddenly cut through the air, intensifying as it traveled, until it was a force field of enormous strength. It washed across Ramonne with the life-giving coolness of a waterfall.

It froze the fall of the serpent king's axe in mid swing. It caused the zombies to release their hold on Ramonne and shrink back in awe.

It caused the Naga to turn his mighty head to the direction of the source of this blue force field. It caused Ramonne to gain the strength to lift himself off the stone and also turn in wonder and awe.

The source of the mighty power that had invaded the serpent king's tableaux of death and destruction…

A tiny five-year-old boy.

Black eyes wide with innocence and wonder, little Hon stood alone at the entrance to the upper platform of the temple. In the flickering light that was now a mixture of the red and the blue colliding in the center of the temple, the faces of King Jayavarman seemed to be smiling down on the boy.

Ramonne sighed. When he inhaled, it was like being reborn…again. He had been right. He'd recognized a force that night in Paris in the bedroom of a sleeping child that had been unlike anything he'd ever experienced. It was *magic.* Powerful magic. Pure magic. Ramonne had known at that moment that if this force was channeled through the art of necromancy, that he and his kind were capable of manipulating, that the boy's innocence could prove to be a match for any evil trance or spell that it would challenge.

The boy was the *vessel*, and he'd been delivered by his friend. Though he had yet to see him, he knew that Martin had brought the boy whom he considered his son. He had brought that which was nearest and dearest to him, to a place alive with death—to save his friend. The thought of this great sacrifice gave Ramonne the strength to slowly rise.

As he rose, he concentrated his returning energy on manipulating the boy's force. His powers began to return, and as he stood, his body began to return to its former glory.

The blue force now rose in power and intensity, washing across the courtyard as a tidal wave would. It blew the ghouls away, stacking their corpses like kindling around the perimeter.

Ramonne stood fully erect and fully restored. The wind blew his magnificent mane with its shock of pure white. His skin glowed like polished marble. In front of him the Naga remained frozen with the axe above his head. His appearance was of a statue...except that his red eyes moved. They darted about the room in an attempt to understand what was happening to him. They ratcheted upward as Ramonne reached and took the axe from the serpent king's claw hands.

Ramonne dropped the blade to his right side. With his left hand he reached out and touched the serpent's bare chest. He placed his palm flat against the cold flesh. The blue wind howled and its force increased tenfold as, suddenly, the first of dozens of wispy shapes emerged from within the naked chest of the demon. They floated for a moment and then descended rapidly into the night sky. As they did, the corpses of the ghouls dissolved into particles which were scattered by the wind.

As the souls of his victims were drawn out of the serpent king's body, it began to shrink and return to its mortal size. The snake head disappeared and the smooth-skulled countenance of Zhoupeng replaced it. As the demon's appearance changed, it began to move. Zhoupeng was regaining his strength. He was channeling his energy force into combating that which Ramonne now controlled.

Ramonne raised the blade above his own head. He locked eyes with the devil-spawn that had been so close to destroying him. The beast that had threatened mankind's existence. The creature that had transformed him into its unwilling accomplice.

Not fully recovered, Zhoupeng used his wiles rather than his strength in an attempt to ward off his fate. "*Delacroix*," he pleaded. "*I'm your father.*"

Ramonne hesitated and lowered the blade. Zhoupeng smiled. Ramonne smiled. "*See you in hell...father.*" And he swung the blade up and down in a mighty stroke that separated Zhoupeng's head cleanly from his torso. The head flew to the floor and rolled, while the body stood erect. Ramonne, bloody axe at his side, reached out and gently pushed the headless corpse. It fell backwards to the stone below.

———

Martin rushed to the boy.

He and Dr. Kaestle had arrived just as the serpent thing was taunting and baiting what appeared to be a bloodied corpse being torn apart by skeletons. It was only when Martin had gotten over the shock of the scene they had stumbled upon, that he recognized the horribly disfigured wretch as Ramonne. He had wanted to cry out, but Kaestle had stopped him and pulled him down behind two stone columns where they could observe without being seen.

Martin tried to keep the boy from seeing, but Hon squirmed free from his grasp. "Hon. It's not real. Just make believe. An illusion," he whispered. The boy's gaze was fixed on the scene. Martin could not tear him from it.

Then, as the serpent took up the axe to deal its death blow, Hon slipped out of Martin's grasp and started to walk to the center of the room. "No!" Martin started to go after him, but Kaestle pulled him down.

"Let him go. Have faith."

It was at that instant that the blue glow emanated from the boy and started across the room. Martin watched the rest of the end game play out in silent wonder.

Now that it was over, he rushed to the boy. As he got to him, Hon collapsed. Martin caught him in his arms. Kaestle was at his side. "Water," Martin blurted out. Kaestle looked at him, puzzled. He understood that the boy was exhausted, spent, and that water would be a very good idea. But where to get it? They had not brought any with them. Then he remembered the monks' shrine just below them and the stone urn of holy water that tourists used after offering money. He made his way as quickly as possible.

"Hold on, Hon. You'll be all right, son. Just hold on." Martin cradled the boy in his lap. The boy had closed his eyes as if to sleep. This scared Martin. "Stay awake, son. Stay awake." He saw that the professor had returned with a hammered tin cup. He put it to the boy's lips. The boy didn't move. He didn't open his mouth. He didn't open his eyes.

"Come on, son. Drink something." Martin tipped Hon's head back and the professor poured some liquid from the cup. It just ran down the boy's chin.

"No. No. Don't you die. No. No." Martin put the boy down and felt his chest. He put a hand to his nose. "He's not breathing...He's *not breathing*." He tilted the head back, pinched the nostrils, and gave the child artificial respiration.

This went on for ten minutes. With no sign of life.

———

Ramonne held the demon's head and stared into the eyes. Being hairless, it rested in the palm of his hand. Whatever life-force had possessed it was now gone, and the eyes were vacant.

Clouded over. No longer would their red orbs burn into human skulls, commanding and devouring their souls. No longer would they scour the countryside for victims; no longer would the beast exercise his reign of terror on the Khmer land and people.

Ramonne's instinct was to hurl the loathsome skull into the night sky. To rid his eyes of its painful appearance. But he knew that to guarantee the beast's total demise, the head and corpse must be incinerated together in the morning sunrise, on the hallowed temple grounds of the Bayon. Only when the ashes had been scattered to the four winds would he be truly rid of his scourge.

Ramonne closed the jaw. He had found the gaping mouth obscene—as if the beast had one more thing to say. "Enough." He placed the head on the stone floor and laid the axe between it and the corpse. The blade was made of silver and thus guaranteed that no necromantic force still in function could pull the two severed parts together. The body would remain cloven in two until its incineration on the morrow.

The moment he set the bloody blade down, he heard the cry.

*Martin.*

He knew immediately who it was.

It was an agonized plea against all that man holds holy. It was a challenge to God. It was the ultimate question. The question Ramonne himself had purged his demons with not many moments ago. The word was not enunciated, but the meaning was there in the long plaintive wail.

*Why?*

Ramonne crossed the courtyard and knelt next to his friend. The boy was at his feet. Martin was tearing his hair in sheer agony.

"Why? Why?" Now the words were very clear. There was no longer an emotional barrier between the language and the meaning.

"Why?" The vampire was staring at the boy. Martin talked

to his back. "He saved *your* life. You used him. Did you know this would happen?"

Ramonne looked at Martin, who immediately noticed his eyes. Instead of the yellow cat's eyes, they were blue. Clear, waterfall, glacier blue.

"No."

The single word seemed to absolve Ramonne of all guilt.

"He's *dead*," Martin cried. A guiltless vampire with blue eyes was not getting off that easy.

"Martin. You came for me. You came to save your friend. This is a debt I can never repay."

Martin turned, tears choking his eyes. "I came for you. You said bring *my son*. I did. I did not come to sacrifice *him* for you. Fuck you." Martin spat out the words.

Ramonne held his ground. Unmoved. Slowly he wiped the spittle from his face.

*This is getting tiring.*

He looked down at the boy. His face was frozen in a smile. A beautiful beam known only to cherubs and five-year-old boys.

"He's happy." Ramonne smiled.

"He's not happy, you cunt. He's *dead*," Martin retorted.

Ramonne continued to study the boy. His smile unnerved Martin even more.

"You fucking assured me you were my *saviour*. You told me to trust you. You would assure the safety of my family. This—"

He stared at the boy's body.

"This *is* my family. Is this how you repay me for my kindness? Is this how you honor my trust? My child is *dead!*"

Martin stood. He looked around. Kaestle, an old man dying of an undiagnosed disease in a foreign land, was his sole companion. The doctor looked away. He had no comment.

Ramonne did not change his countenance. He merely reached out and touched the boy's forehead. Slowly he withdrew his hand and smiled.

"You bastard," Martin hissed. "You relish my son's death?"

Ramonne turned his smile to Martin. "No, Martin. Not at all. I relish your faith in me that you would sacrifice your son for me. That you would enter into this land of certain death for me. That you are my one and only *true* friend."

He reached over and took the hammered tin cup of holy water and poured a small amount upon his hands. He passed them over the boy, anointing him from head to toe.

"Your child is not dead, Martin." He smiled down at the boy. "He merely sleeps. The sleep of the innocent." He placed his hand on Hon's forehead once more and suddenly the boy's eyes opened.

Martin collapsed to his knees and cradled Hon to him. The child's now open eyes drifted to Ramonne. He reached out a small hand and Ramonne took it between two fingers. He bent forward and kissed the little hand. The boy beamed.

**24**

Dawn.

Martin stood vigil high on the walls of the Bayon. The sun rose so rapidly that he hardly had time to arrange his grisly barbecue before the corpse started to incinerate. In the soft morning light, Angkor Wat, just to the south, could be seen welcoming the deluge of tourists that always greeted the coming of dawn: photographers, digital shutter-bugs, armed with every conceivable camera, lens, and tripod combination. Determined to capture their own image of the daily awakening of one of the great wonders of the world.

Little did they know that less than a kilometer north, at the second most popular temple, a purification ritual was being held that would change mankind's destiny.

This once sordid little footnote in Southeast Asia's history known as Cambodia would now have a chance. Its children would have a chance.

Martin was surprised at how quickly the body and its severed head burst into flames. He had almost been dozing off, having entrusted Hon to the doctor.

Ramonne was gone. Back to his estate. Kaestle said the future was unknown. But Martin was glad to know that Kaestle had agreed to share it with Ramonne. Not as a servant, but as another friend. Kaestle was convinced that he was now cured by the demise of Zhoupeng. Martin had to admit that he was certainly more sprightly as he sauntered down the steps.

*Good. Ramonne needs another friend. I'm too busy.*

The funeral pyre burned furiously, unleashing a thick cloud of black smoke into the morning sky. Martin feared that at any moment the police would scramble up the stairs of the temple with a fire extinguisher. The blaze would be extinguished and he'd be arrested.

But some inner voice assured him that wouldn't happen. After what he had been through in the long night, he was confident he had earned the karma to be left in peace to finish his act of purification. And there would be nothing left of the demon to retrieve, as there had been of Ramonne's ashes after Wat Arun. Martin would make sure of this.

"Scatter the ashes to the four corners," Ramonne had instructed him. "Guarantee his utter and complete destruction."

The blaze was dying and soon Martin would have completed his task.

———

Three weeks passed.

Martin's life was sweet again. Sweet as the ripe mango he held.

The open market offered all of the great variety of colorful and exotic produce that Southeast Asia is rightly famous for. Papayas, mangos, bananas, mangosteen, rambutan. All arranged in pyramids. Each one singularly declaring dominance over its particular hue of the rainbow.

Martin strolled with Areeya on one side and little Hon on the other. Julianne was with Justin. They had been inseparable since *that* night. Martin was glad. Otherwise, without the constant love of another, he had no idea how she would ever recover from the horror of both Antoine's murder and his betrayal of her trust and love. She had little Micki, and Justin held the tiny hand of Minnie. The inseparable twins had latched onto the new inseparable couple. Julianne's tenure with the restoration project was coming to an end. Another group of archeology students would be arriving soon. But she had already approached Martin with a request to fill Jane's vacancy at the school. Martin was delighted. And when Justin's tenure was up, he was welcome, as well. Pom could never get over Jane's loss and had finally returned to Thailand within a week of *that* night, and his battle with the imaginary snakes.

The statues had been returned to the temples and the remainder of Zhoupeng's foot soldiers had been captured in their mountain camp. They had been totally unaware of the various battles that had decimated both their leader and his followers, and the half-dozen men had been taken without a struggle as they were cooking breakfast. They were transported to Phnom Penh to await trial. Martin didn't hold out much hope that they would ever truly meet justice. These pathetic geriatrics were twenty years overdue for their trial. Trials that he doubted would ever come about.

But progress had been made and there seemed to be peace again in his little kingdom.

Areeya handed him a bag of mangos and papayas and he slipped it into the little rucksack he carried slung over one shoulder. He felt a tug and looked down.

"Mango," Hon pleaded.

Martin smiled. He'd never been able to refuse him anything. *This special child.*

He'd told Areeya of the boy's part in the bizarre passion play in the temple of the Bayon. He'd told her also of the child's apparent death and resurrection by Ramonne. She had hugged the boy to her so hard that he feared again for the boy's life. But all he was in danger of was drowning in the tears she shed over him. They agreed right then and there to adopt Hon. He really would be their son. He would never want for anything.

Areeya told Martin of Dr. Kaestle's complete recovery. The man who appeared at her door in the hour just before dawn with little Hon looked twenty years younger and in perfect health. He was overcome with joy and relief, and she practically had to pry his hand from the boy's, so attached was he to the "little miracle worker" as he referred to Hon.

Martin took out his pocket knife and handed it to Areeya. As with many other simple chores in that part of the world, the slicing of a mango was an art never exactly mastered by a Caucasian, and Areeya made swift work of peeling and dividing the ripe fruit.

All was well. The sun rose today and it would rise again tomorrow. His brood was safe. Siem Reap was safe.

Or was it? This was the one thorn left in Martin's side. A thorn. An appropriate anachronism for Ramonne, he thought.

Ramonne had saved them all.

*But at what price?*

How could Martin reconcile the deaths that surely would come?

Martin had paid close attention to the local press, and had a weekly breakfast at the Foreign Correspondents' Club in Siem Reap that included a briefing by the local police commissioner. There had been no reported deaths since *that* night.

Martin hoped that Ramonne had returned to Bangkok.

Martin *assumed* that Ramonne had returned to Bangkok. It would have been simple enough to find out. But he couldn't bring himself to visit Oiseaux, the country house the vampire had made his lair.

And so Martin carried on. No news was good news.

"Martin."

Areeya brought him out of his musings with a slice of fruit. Martin smiled and opened his mouth. Areeya popped the slice and let her finger linger just a moment. Martin touched it with his tongue and she blushed.

"Daddy."

The fruit was melting in his mouth as he heard little Hon say the word he had been praying to hear.

*Just a matter of time.* He looked down at the boy.

"Daddy," he said once again, and Martin reached to smooth his tousled hair.

But the boy's gaze was not directed at him. He was looking across the courtyard and his little finger was pointing.

Martin followed his gaze. "Impossible."

At the edge of the market square, a tall man with long hair studied an object in a vendor's cart. Slowly he turned and the unmistakable shock of white in the hair caught the morning sun. His bright blue eyes glowed and he smiled.

*No. It can't be.*

The man nodded at Martin, just as a group of Japanese tourists, cameras clicking, passed between them. When the tourists were gone, the man had vanished.

Quickly Martin crossed the courtyard. The sun was hot on his back as he stared into the vacant alley alongside the market stalls.

"Martin. What is it? You look like you've seen a ghost." Areeya was at his side and she took his hand.

Martin's face wore a look of shock and wonder. *In the daylight? How can that be?*

Justin and Julianne were unconcerned and unaware that anything was wrong. They leisurely surveyed the knickknacks and bric-a-brac displayed in the various stalls.

Martin continued to stare at the vacant alley, but there was nothing to see.

Slowly he turned back to his group.

"Martin. What is it?"

He looked at her. She held the boy. The boy also looked

down the alley. He took Hon from her and held him close. The boy's gaze remained on the alley.

"Nothing…Let's go."

They started to leave when an old woman approached Julianne.

She had a small paper-wrapped parcel in her gnarled hands. She gave a betel-stained smile and extended the package to Julianne.

Julianne stared at it, puzzled

"The *barang* told me to give this to you."

Surprised, Julianne was sure the woman was mistaken. "Me…? Who…what *barang*?"

The old woman shrugged and continued to hold the package in her outstretched bony hand.

Finally Julianne took it. "Thank you…I guess."

The woman kept her empty palm extended until Martin placed a few riel bills in it.

"Bless you." She returned to the shadows of her stall.

"What is it?" Areeya asked.

"I don't know."

Julianne unwrapped the brown wax paper. A thin silk cloth was folded around the object. She carefully removed it.

"Oh! How beautiful!" Areeya exclaimed.

It was a pocket watch. An ornate, carved silver case with a short gold chain attached. "Martin, look."

Martin held his breath. He had seen the watch before.

It was Ramonne's. It had been the only remaining possession from his mortal life. Martin had kept it for over a year and had personally given it back to Ramonne when the vampire had re-entered his life.

"Open it," Areeya excitedly exclaimed.

Julianne fumbled a moment and then managed to spring the latch that allowed the case to swing open. Inside was a sepia-toned portrait of a beautiful young woman.

"*Oh my God!*" Julianne gasped. "It's my great grandmother."

*Shhhhhhh. Shhhhhhh.*

The young man fired short blasts from the air hose. He wore a surgical mask and performed his delicate work with the finesse of a surgeon. He stood atop a metal extension ladder working the air hose with his right hand and a soft brush with his left. The brush caressed the delicate carvings of the lintel on the seventh-century brick temple at Lolei, almost miniature in scale when compared to the enormity of Angkor. In the center, an elephant's head looked as if it had been carved yesterday.

Martin stood at the base of the ladder and watched with admiration as the team of three young men performed their work. There were no construction cranes here, no thousand-pound blocks of stone to be hoisted back in place. Here the work of restoration was quiet, slow, and precise.

Opposite the brick towers, a large wooden building was set on stilts next to a modern Buddhist temple. Up the stairs Martin could see young boys gathered at the feet of a leather-skinned monk. They were chanting, and their drone seemed the perfect accompaniment to the pastoral scene.

Martin had stopped at the temple site to make a modest donation. Mission accomplished, he got back on his bicycle.

It had rained in the early afternoon and there were puddles in the red clay road that led to the highway. Martin slowly pedaled his bike up the slight incline. As he turned onto the highway, two tractors passed by pulling wagons piled twenty feet high with straw. He rode behind them for five or ten minutes. They completely obscured his vision ahead until they turned off the main road.

Without warning he found himself in front of the estate known as Oiseaux. Martin slowed as he studied the property. The brush that entangled it for years had been cleared. The house itself had been given a fresh coat of mustard-yellow paint and all the windows, doors, and fencing were an avocado green. The climate had already discolored and stained large sections of the walls.

Martin pulled to the side of the road and stopped. He got off the bike and removed the helmet. It was late afternoon and the day was just beginning to cool off. Still, sweat ran down his face. His shirt was soaked through from the exertion of the ride, but he didn't feel the heat or notice the humidity. He laid the bicycle up against an iron gate and took off his sunglasses.

The villa had been reborn. It could have been in Provence. But the building's resurrection was not what had drawn Martin.

Behind the house he could see a group of men moving about. On a distant rise, he wasn't sure, but he thought he saw Dr. Kaestle supervising the work. They were laying out stakes and running lines between them. An acre or more was already finished in a very tight, rigid pattern. Two other men were opening crates and removing what appeared to be plant cuttings.

*My God. They're planting a vineyard.*

Martin moved closer to the fence. His eyes searched the back yard.

But there was no sign of Ramonne.

Martin considered pushing the gate and entering the property. Thought long and hard about knocking on the freshly painted door. He imagined the vampire greeting him, inviting him in for a glass of wine. They'd swap old stories. Share their memories.

But instead he put his helmet back on.

*Those stories, those memories, are best forgotten.*

Besides, Ramonne was a vampire. What was this nonsense about him being out in the daylight? Martin chose to get back on his bike and continue his journey. Acknowledging his presence wasn't really necessary.

*He knows I'm here.*

They were inextricably linked.

*Clacka clacka clack*

The man looked up from his book as he heard the bicycle shift gears.

Seated in the shade of a huge banyan, book in his lap, wine glass at his side, he had been invisible to the man on the bicycle. He smiled as he watched the figure recede down the road.

A slight breeze ruffled his long hair. He brushed it out of his bright blue eyes, sipped his wine, and returned to his book.

*Fin.*

# AUTHOR'S NOTE

This is obviously a work of fiction. If only it were so simple to rid the people of Cambodia of the scourge of evil that has visited their poor land for so long.

Jim Newport,
March, 2006

# ABOUT THE AUTHOR

Jim Newport is a writer and Emmy-nominated production designer of both film and television. His film credits include *Bangkok Dangerous*, *Brokedown Palace*, *The Stepfather* and *Heart Like A Wheel*. In television he has set the "look" for many series by designing the pilot episodes of *The Lyon's Den*, *The Shield*, *The Education Of Max Bickford* and *China Beach*. His work on *The Piano Lesson* for the Hallmark Hall Of Fame was nominated for an Emmy in art direction. He was the production designer of season four of the worldwide hit TV series *Lost*. When not writing books or designing films, Newport performs as his alter-ego Jimmy Fame—a blues shouter, known to haunt the saloons and annual Blues Festival of his adopted home, Phuket, Thailand.

Please visit the author's website: www.vampireofsiam.com.

# THE VAMPIRE OF SIAM SERIES

*"These books are rich in cinematic imagery… and fascinating details of Thai history."*

— THAILAND TATLER

*The Vampire of Siam series is an epic tale that spans half the globe and a course of 150 years.*

In *The Vampire of Siam* (Book 1) a nineteenth-century explorer, Ramonne Delacroix, encounters an ancient Chinese demon in the temples of Angkor Wat. His subsequent nocturnal transformation leads him to the capital of Siam, where he witnesses the coronation of kings and the city's metamorphosis into the modern day sin-city of Bangkok.

Living the life of the lone hunter for the first 145 years of his incarnation as a night stalker, the vampire is reborn in *Ramonne* (Book 2) and eventually seeks to know the true extent of his powers. As he learns, he evolves. By the second book's end, the vampire's strength is enormous and he has control of the true magic he has been vested with.

In *The Reckoning* (Book 3) Ramonne, armed with newfound knowledge, seeks the source of his powers. He journeys back to Cambodia and the ancient temples to a fateful encounter with Zhoupeng—the mighty devil who "turned him" so many years before. Ramonne vows to put an end to Zhoupeng's reign of evil over the poor land.

Throughout the three books, Ramonne's fate is inextricably entwined with that of Martin Larue—wealthy American expat. Drawn to each other by mutual admiration and fascination, they eventually end up relying on each other to sort out the twisted path they find themselves thrust upon.

Together they face vampire-hunters, corrupt cops, opium dens, bordellos, blind fortune-tellers, jealous lovers, terrorists, suicide-bombers, smugglers, warlords and soul-sucking demons.

*The Siamese Connection* (Book 4) begins in 1948 Bangkok, shortly after the end of WWII and the Japanese occupation of Siam. The vampire, Ramonne Delacroix becomes involved in a quest for a mysterious artifact—The Oracle—hidden during the war by the Japanese. He joins forces with the famous American Expat Jim Thompson, (before he was the Silk King he was an OSS agent) and together they do battle with the nefarious Japanese Black Dragons.

The tale continues in the present day picking up where *The Reckoning* left off. Martin Larue and his pregnant wife Areeya cross paths again with the vampire and soon they too are involved in a deadly game of cat and mouse with the descendants of the Black Dragons, who are still in search of the mysterious Oracle.

A fast-paced blend of fact and fiction, *The Siamese Connection* finally solves the mysterious disappearance of Jim Thompson.

*"Newport artfully shapes the vampire legend into a Mekong cocktail of surprises."* Christopher G. Moore.

# CHASING JIMI

Chasing Jimi is a rock 'n' roll period piece. It spans one year - the summer of 1966 to the summer of 1967. From New York's Greenwich Village to swinging London to the stage of the Monterey Pop Festival. It follows the ascension of one Jimmy James, a struggling back-up guitar player, to the exalted throne of rock-god superstardom.

On the road through merry-old England with the re-named Jimi Hendrix we meet the madcap royalty of the British pop scene. Jimi forms an endearing friendship with Rolling Stones founding member Brian Jones, whose battles with numerous personal demons and plunge from the top mirror Jimi's rise and fascination with the drug culture.

As the Jimi Hendrix Experience gains recognition, Jimi's past associations throw their own stumbling blocks in his path. Contracts signed by him as a hungry studio session musician surface. Jimi's management team are able to put out most of these fires, but one particularly sleazy New York record producer refuses to be bought out, and even goes so far as to send a couple of Brooklyn wiseguys to London to bring back his artist.

Chasing Jimi is "The Sopranos" meets The Beatles. The author's intense admiration for Jimi Hendrix, his own magical experiences as a hippy in the great Summer of Love and a stint as a touring rock 'n' roll photographer in the 70s served as inspiration for Chasing Jimi.

Knowing the scrutiny he would be under for daring to write a fictional piece about Jimi, the author strived to be as accurate as possible in the timeframe of events. Liberties were taken, but they were taken in order to craft what hopefully is an amusing and entertaining tale that transports the reader back to a better time.

# TINSEL TOWN: ANOTHER ROTTEN
# DAY IN PARADISE

*"Tinsel Town is the best introduction-to-Hollywood novel I've ever read."*

— DAVID GILER, PRODUCER/WRITER *ALIEN*,
*UNDISPUTED*, *MYRA BRECKINRIDGE* AND
MANY MORE.

A Hollywood novel by an author who has been there - done that. Jim Newport is an Emmy-nominated production designer of both film and television. His experiences in the early years of his career served as the inspiration for Tinsel Town.

Memoirs from those in the film trade are nothing new. The bookshelves are crowded with star biographies—directors, writers and producers offering to show how difficult and arduous it is to either direct, write or produce a movie. But Tinsel Town is no simple straightforward autobiography. Like Chasing Jimi, it is a work of 'faction' - combining fact and fiction. Tinsel Town doesn't gloss over the cracks in the scenery —the grit, the stench, the plain old-fashioned blood and sweat that making movies was really about in the wild and woolly Easy Rider days of independent filmmaking. A non-stop party.

Art student Joey Morton arrives in Hollywood in 1968 and stumbles onto a sound stage. It was everything a young New Yorker could possibly hope to find—sex, drugs, gorgeous women, backstage passes, access to movie stars, rock 'n' roll… and more sex and drugs.

The author not only gives the reader a glimpse into what it

was like to enter this privileged profession in arguably its most exciting time (when movies played out in front of your own star-struck eyes, rather than against a green screen to be digitally composited later), but he also spins a tale, unravels a mystery, and takes the reader on an adventure.

*"Newport's novels succeed in their purpose ... they entertain."*

— THE NATION.

*"It moves like a runaway asteroid."* Tim Hallinan, bestselling author of the Poke Rafferty series (set in Bangkok).

— TIM HALLINAN, BESTSELLING AUTHOR OF
THE POKE RAFFERTY SERIES (SET IN
BANGKOK).